HOW THE ONE-ARMED SISTER SWEEPS HER HOUSE

HOW THE ONE-ARMED SISTER SWEEPS HER HOUSE

Cherie Jones

TINDER
PRESS

First published in 2021 by Tinder Press
An imprint of HEADLINE PUBLISHING GROUP

3

Cataloguing in Publication Data is available from the British Library

Hardback ISBN 978 1 4722 6877 8
Trade paperback ISBN 978 1 4722 6878 5

Typeset in 10.75/14.75pt Sabon by Jouve (UK), Milton Keynes

Printed and bound in Great Britain by Clays Ltd, Elcograf S.p.A.

Headline's policy is to use papers that are natural, renewable and recyclable
products and made from wood grown in well-managed forests and other
controlled sources. The logging and manufacturing processes are expected
to conform to the environmental regulations of the country of origin.

HEADLINE PUBLISHING GROUP
An Hachette UK Company
Carmelite House
50 Victoria Embankment
London EC4Y 0DZ

www.headline.co.uk
www.hachette.co.uk

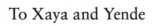

To Xaya and Yende

PROLOGUE

12 September 1979

Lala comes home and Wilma is waiting, having returned early from visiting Carson at the hospital. Wilma is still dressed in her going-out clothes, one of the outfits she prefers to be seen in by strangers – a steam-pleated lilac skirt that falls just below her knees, a pale aquamarine silk blouse tucked into the waist with a broad purple belt, and a navy cloche hat that once belonged to her mother. When Lala walks through the door, Wilma is standing on the stone floor of the kitchen, arms akimbo, eyes wide with relief.

'Where you was, Stella? Is almost eight thirty!'

Visiting hours end at six; it is one of the myriad indignities of hospitalisation at Baxter's General – having to bid visitors goodbye and get ready to go to sleep with the birds. But today, Carson has fallen into a type of coma way before bedtime, a deep sleep from which the doctors cannot rouse him. Wilma spends the first visiting hour sitting upright next to his bed, and it is only when she dozes and falls off the chair and lands with her knees still bent at a right angle that she is persuaded to go home and rest. There is not much that anyone can do, say the nurses, as dribble oozes out of the corner of Carson's mouth and slimes its way towards the sheets; the doctors are doing tests.

This coma, these tests are why Wilma is able to take the long walk from Baxter's General back to the Bridge Street bus stand at a stroll instead of a run and still manage to secure a place at the front of a long line of commuters. They are why her steam-pleated skirt has escaped the tell-tale crinkles of the push and shove and crush of the queue in its collective effort to catch the Route 12 going to Baxter's Beach, from which she usually alights around 8.30. This evening Wilma has managed to catch the 7 p.m. instead of the 8 and has therefore been spared the usual visiting-hours crowd from Baxter's General. This evening Wilma has returned home almost an hour early and found that Lala is not there in her bedroom, reading Malory Towers.

'Where you was, Stella? Answer me!'

'My name is Lala.'

Lala is, at first, not fazed by the fact that she is already in trouble or that lashes are likely, and her obstinacy makes Wilma's right eye twitch.

'Your name is whatever I say it is!' Wilma yells.

'I went for a walk, Wilma,' Lala stammers. 'It was dark in the house and I was frighten and I went for a walk.'

Wilma does not know whether to believe her. Lala's hair is intact, her dress is not unusually ruffled, she can look her right in the eyes – it is possible that she is telling the truth.

'I say I would come out and meet the bus, but I lose track of time . . .'

Wilma removes the cloche hat, which she kept on until Lala walked through the door, just in case her head had to brave the cold wind to try to find her. She sheds her Chinese slippers and sits down. Suddenly she is too tired to share a beating. She is too tired to go to bed. She is thinking about the prospect of Carson dying, at last, and leaving her alone, alone except for Lala. She looks at her granddaughter – the only child of her dead only daughter. This granddaughter has not, up to now, really caused her any trouble. She does her schoolwork so well that her teachers say she can be anything she wants. She says 'yes, ma'am' and 'no, ma'am' at the times and on the occasions that Wilma has taught her to. She stays well out of the sight and sound of her grandfather, Carson. What more, Wilma asks herself, can she ask for? The child is not a beauty, but perhaps, thinks Wilma, this will work in her favour. She considers that this is the person who will have to help her in her old age, and so she softens her voice until it is almost pleading.

'I ain't tell you that young girls like you must stay indoors?' she chides, mildly. 'I ain't tell you about the things that live in the Baxter's tunnels? You walking 'bout to find out about them yourself?' When Lala doesn't answer, she says, 'Let me tell you about a little girl like you that didn't listen to her mother.'

Wilma tells the story of the One-Armed Sister:
The village vicar and his wife had two little girls. Such beautiful children you never did see – skin yellow and pretty like peanut milk, hair curly and silky like *peau de soie*, eyes big and light brown with long, long lashes. But although they both beautiful, only one of them was gifted with good sense – the other one was own-way and like to give the mother mouth. So it just so happen that there was an entrance to the Baxter's tunnels right on the vicarage

lawn, at the bottom of the garden. Nobody sure what it doing there, but it there none the less. The vicar wife have half a mind to get the yard boy to seal it off with stones and cement but is only half a mind and she never actually send the boy into town to buy the bag of cement and the cement blocks and do the job. The vicar's wife tell her little girls about this tunnel, how they mustn't go into it, how it have monsters that live down in there, how any little girls go in there they never come back out. The tunnels is where bad men go when they die, says the mother, men that are too bad to rest easy in their graves down in those tunnels walking about night and day, looking for more badness, harvesting souls for the Devil.

The mother tell them, but the little girl with the good sense listen and the one that don't have any get more curious than ever. This sister question her mother, wonder what in the tunnel that so sweet she warning her away from it, because this good-for-nothing girl already developing a taste for things that her mother tell her not to have, this slack-from-she-born, force-ripe sister already thinking that some bad things real sweet and if something so sweet it can't be evil. This sister thinking to herself, it not that dark, it not that spooky, what is the use of a tunnel if you don't get to see where it lead? Is just this kind of tunnel that this sister decide she must explore, say Wilma, so she ups herself one evening when her mother was taking tea with the doctor wife. It was important matters they was talking, says Wilma, because the vicar's wife was a good mother, not one to leave her children alone for even a few seconds. But a few seconds is all the Devil need.

Pretty soon the vicar's wife hear screaming so sharp and piteous it shake the teapot on the table with the tea. The vicar's wife and the doctor's wife run out and see the good sister holding on to the other for dear life and something they can't quite see pulling the stupid one by her other arm back into that tunnel. Well the vicar's wife and the doctor's wife and the yard boy all grab on to the good sister and they pulling her and she pulling the bad sister away from the thing in the tunnel. And, says Wilma, maybe is only because her husband is the vicar and a man of prayer that they get the stupid sister out, but that monster in the tunnel take her arm from her. Sure as day, when they rescue that sister there is a bleeding stump where her arm used to be, that left arm end in a knot just above what used to be her elbow. She survive, of course, says Wilma, the wicked often do, but she have a stump to remind her what stupid get her. Sure enough, the mother get the yard boy to seal up that tunnel *quick quick* after that, but the arm already in there. Curiosity kill the cat, says Wilma, don't make yourself stupid like the one-armed sister.

There is something about the story that angers Lala, perhaps the fact that Wilma expects her, at thirteen years old, to believe it.

'And none of them went back to find the arm?' she wonders. 'Not even the yard boy?'

'Yard boy know his limitations,' says Wilma. 'Yard boy no match for a monster.'

She has mistaken Lala's silence as the proof of a scaring, just the kind to keep her out of the type of trouble that long walks at night can bring, so she is picking up her hat and her bag and her belt and getting ready to go to her sewing room, where more work is waiting.

'I bet if it was the other way around, if the good sister was the one in the tunnel, the other one would have gone after that arm and found it for her,' says Lala, 'I bet she would've.'

'The good sister not so stupid to go in there in the first place,' says Wilma, and her eyes are flashing and she is thinking that maybe she should just have mustered the energy and given Lala a warm dose of licks instead.

'Well I bet it not so bad having one arm,' says Lala. 'She can still do things like everybody else, she can still get a husband and some children and a house.'

'Stupid girl,' says Wilma. 'How she gonna sweep it?'

CHAPTER ONE

Lala
20 July 1984

About an hour after Adan leaves her at home alone, Lala stands barefoot in the dark doorway of his house, in a scratchy white nightgown she has stolen from Wilma, assuring herself, despite the obvious, that everything will be OK. The salty air was still when she opened the door, and sweat still beads her face when she slips her feet into Adan's old sneakers and grabs hold of the inner soles with her toes, worrying about her descent to the grey velvet blur of beach so far beneath her. She has been cautioned not to climb or descend the stairs on her own, in her condition, and Adan has been instructed to build a banister to steady her, but they have both ignored the good sense of the fishermen who sometimes help her up them with her groceries. The twenty-five cement steps to the ground remain just as treacherous as the day she first climbed them, eighteen months earlier, with a string bag stretched into the shape of everything she owned. They are perhaps more treacherous, she reasons, with a belly the size of a beach ball disrupting her balance, so she leans on the weather-beaten wood of the house on her left and shrinks away from the sheer drop to her right.

Holding onto the holes in the wooden side of the house, she eases herself down the first few steps, until the splintered wood falls away into nothingness on her left side and there is still the nothingness on her right and several steps remain to be negotiated before she reaches the sand. She pauses, stretches her arms out on either side of herself to maintain her balance and does not dare to wipe her face when she sweats from the effort, and the hurt and the heat. When her stomach starts to twist in on itself she whimpers for Wilma, who even now she cannot call 'Granny'. She forces herself not to hug her arms around her belly, she keeps them outstretched to maintain equilibrium and bites her bottom lip instead. She bites it until it bleeds.

Lala does not know where she will find Adan. All she knows is that he is somewhere on the beach, doing a job. Adan doesn't tell her much before he leaves for this type of work, least of all where he will be working. Still, when his sneakers carry her off the last step and onto the sand, she propels herself forward because she knows she needs to find him, she knows that something is wrong, that more than a month before she is due to have her baby, she should not be bleeding blurry poinsettia flowers everywhere she sits.

Ten minutes later, she finally reaches the sidewalk behind the big houses on Baxter's Beach and is barely limping along, despite bleeding that would warrant a run. The big houses, for the most part, have their backs to the road, with impenetrable wooden gates, unscalable walls and hedges higher than her grasp extends. While she works on the beach during the day, braiding and beading the silky hair of tourists, Lala sees the fronts of these houses, their patio railings low enough to be kissed by the water. Tonight, she thinks, the houses have firmly turned their backs on her, and she does not dare to rattle a gate and ask for help. There might be dogs, she reasons, or security guards with guns, and the sticky slick between her legs does not seem like a good enough reason to risk having to face them.

When the pain grows sharper and she cannot catch her breath and the sneakers are spotted in red and the flowers have made a carpet on the back of Wilma's white nightgown, Lala becomes brave and decides to ring the buzzer beside the ornate service gate in the guard wall of the house nearest to her. And once she has rung it once, she finds that she cannot stop and she presses it so desperately that it pulses more quickly than each gasping breath she takes. By this time, she is no longer sure that the dogs and the guns could be worse than the suffering she is enduring. By this time, she is no longer just looking for Adan, she is looking for help.

While she is pressing this buzzer, Lala hears a gun go off, and while she is still wondering whether it really was a gun or just the noise a malfunctioning buzzer makes – a *pop pop* instead of a trill – the gate beside her is wrenched open and there is Adan, right in front of her, calm as the day but for his throbbing scar and the menace on his face.

Lala does not believe in coincidences, and apparently neither does Adan. She does not quake with relief when she sees her husband close the service gate of the big house behind him. He does not ask what the fuck she is doing there. Instead, he turns her around and shoves her ahead of him, and then he sees the red on the back of her skirt and Lala hears him *hmmm* and believes he understands that the God she prays to has led her to just this house at just this time so that she can find her husband just when she needs him most.

Adan wrenches his bike from the back of a bush with his big hands, and Lala sees one of her stocking legs hanging like a limp tongue from his pocket, spattered in blood that is not her own. Understanding dawns on her face in the breath between contractions, and then fear. At that moment, Lala loses the ability to do anything but stand there, staring at him. It is Adan, she thinks, who puts her on the bar of the bike and reminds her to lift and point her legs so he can pedal without tripping over her feet. It is Adan who tells her to cover her ears when someone starts screaming from that same house. It is Adan who snaps that she should shut the fuck up when she starts to explain why she came despite everything he told her. Whatever she does, Adan says, pedalling so hard that his thighs *whomp-whomp* into her back as they ride away from the service gate, do not look back, do not look back. We have to get out of here, he says. Fast.

When they careen into the car park of Baxter's General twenty minutes later, Adan removes the stocking from his pocket, the gun from his waist and the black T-shirt he is wearing from his back so that his white vest and dark chest are exposed to the early-morning air. Lala does not remind him that by doing so he is risking worse illnesses than they can afford. Lala is quiet. Adan throws the stocking, the gun and the T-shirt into a peeling yellow skip at the east end of the car park, while she waits bleeding on the sidewalk. He is calm as he does this, so that he does not arouse suspicion, but there is hardly anyone about. He rearranges some discarded wood sitting in the skip so that it covers the gun and the stocking, as if it is the most natural thing in the world for him to be doing at two o'clock on a Friday morning. Lala is beginning to feel like she is fading, but she is not sure that what she feels is faintness. What she *is* sure of is that the scream she heard begin the moment Adan's bare feet left the pavement outside the service gate with the buzzer was the scream of someone mourning a loved one newly dead or dying. That scream fills her head so much that she cannot trust herself to speak after she shuts up, because she believes that if she opens her mouth, it is the only thing that will come out.

Three things are true about Baxter's General Hospital.

One is that there is never any toilet paper in the bathroom in the accident and emergency department. Instead there is a little sign next to the one wide mirror, pockmarked with rust, saying that paper is dispensed by the nurse on duty. You can miss that sign if you are not looking. If you are frantic. If your visit to the bathroom is a by-product of your emergency. If you are in a rush, it is only once you are seated in the stall, expelling what must be released, that you realise that you are without a means to clean yourself up, without the ability to call someone to help you. Which is why the stalls are full of the evidence of human accident – palm-prints of excrement on the cistern, blood spatter beneath reminders that *Fizzy wuz here* and *Rockie and Raina 4 eva* on the walls.

The second true thing about Baxter's General is that the nurses really do tell you to shut up, you were not screaming so loudly while your man was impregnating you, so why are you behaving so badly now that what he has left inside you is finding its way back out?

Three is that the nurses do not look you in the eye when they know they cannot help you, when you are pushing out a premature baby they know will soon be born dead. If it is you and two nurses, and if you scream that they must call a doctor, they assume you are unaware that doctors at Baxter's are scarce and that there are no doctors to waste on a baby that is already in the realm of the spirit.

Lala learns the first thing at four o'clock in the morning, when she and Adan have already been in the accident and emergency department for two hours and she feels the need to go. They are sitting side by side on two blue plastic chairs, his right hand clasping her left, his left hand rubbing the scar on his forehead, both of them bent over at the waist as if genuflecting before the big grey double doors behind which is someone who can save the baby.

Adan inhales sharply and looks around with the slow sideways stare of a snake every time the main doors slide open. He exhales only after he confirms it is another someone ailing, and not the police looking for him. He has already spelt out Lala's name to the nurse staring at a computer screen behind bulletproof glass. He has already returned to the glass, leaned into the series of holes in the shape of a flower until his tongue is almost flat against them, and reminded the nurse that his wife is bleeding. He has tested the limits of his patience so much that his anger can no longer contain itself and trembles through his shoes to tap on the green linoleum tiles of the floor. When Lala starts shaking and fainting in and out of a sort of sleep, this anger radiates outwards, and Adan jumps upright, sends the chair skating backwards and starts to boom swear words into the quiet of the room.

'Wunna understand that my fucking wife here bleeding till she ready to faint?'

The nurse behind the glass is fastening a little watch, made like a brooch, onto her starched white tunic. She takes her time doing so, despite the ominous rumble of Adan's distress. The nurse has suffered these types of outbursts before and has become immune to them.

Adan sprints into an adjoining room, wrangles a blanket off another nurse and returns to wrap it around his wife. He is still looking at the door, still thinking about the gun in the skip and what happened at the house and, finally, when they hear a siren wailing closer, he says that he must leave her there, go somewhere where he can lay low, just in case. And Lala doesn't remind him that it is possible that she could be about to lose his baby.

Lala thinks she asks him to help her to the toilet first, but she is sure he leaves her in the doorway. She searches every single stall but all the toilet tissue dispensers are empty and she hasn't seen the sign and she comes outside and Adan is gone and her head is spinning and she stumbles into the male bathrooms and searches them also because there is blood all over the back of Wilma's nightgown and she will be damned if there is now going to be shit all over it too. And right when she comes back outside to ask a nurse or a guard or another one of the sick and waiting whether they have a pack of tissues or baby wipes or a napkin from a forgotten sandwich, a voice calls her name over the PA system and the grey doors open and a nurse appears, a squat woman with an ill-fitting wig and a uniform too white to suggest a good bedside manner and the nurse says hurry up we don't have all night and Lala does not move because now she's wet herself and she's embarrassed and hurting worse than before and the nurse sucks her teeth because now it will have to be cleaned up and didn't she know she wanted to go, and then she notices Lala's belly is rounder than just fat and she notices the bloody prints the soles of Adan's sneakers have made on the green-grey floor and she shouts.

A stretcher comes, and Lala is lying down when she enters the doors and passes into a hallway with prone people groaning. She sees arms held at odd angles and gashes and wounds and shirts and towels being pressed to foreheads and mouths and bleeding places and she looks up to spare herself and there is a grid of roof tiles and square fluorescent lights tic-tac-toeing into the future and she wonders whether, after all she has already been through, she is going to die here. And the thought does not distress her. The stretcher stops and another nurse appears and when next she comes to, they are telling her to push but Lala does not want to push because she is afraid of what she will find.

Lala learns the second thing now, because when she opens her mouth to ask for water, the scream she has been hiding comes out instead. She wants to tell them, this is not my scream, this is a scream I picked up from a house on Baxter's Beach, because she is hoping that the nurses will understand that this scream will also require treatment, but they don't. The nurse with the bad Boney M. wig says shut up and asks her if this is how she was screaming when she was taking the man that got her into this mess. Her eyes tell Lala that she cannot, will not, allow Lala's screaming to get into her own head because it doesn't look good and these teenaged girls without a pot to piss in are in here every day at younger and younger ages.

So Lala closes her mouth and swallows the scream she caught on Baxter's Beach the way some people catch a cold and in her mind she begs the baby not to die as she pushes and feels the vessels in the whites of her eyes pop and flood her vision.

And Lala learns the third thing, because when she gets past the stinging and the tearing and the stretching and the slippage and is suddenly, breathlessly freed of a weight she has been carrying within her for the past eight months, she recognises that she does not hear the squall that in every television depiction she has ever watched signals the birth of the baby. So she says, 'Nurse, nurse?' because she wants the reassurance that everything is all right, that the baby is fine, but the nurse does not look at her, the nurse wrenches her wrist out of Lala's grasp and tells the other nurse to call the doctor and her hands are holding something that does not move. She is rushing the baby to the spot of light under a lit lamp on a table, putting a bulbous tube into its nostrils, rubbing and pressing and listening to the baby's chest. And Lala understands that it is not good and she does not want to look but she does and she wills the baby to live because she can see that the nurses have already given up and because, suddenly, she is angry that Adan is not there and after tonight she is sure that she can no longer love Adan and perhaps the baby is all the good in him and she wants it to live so she can love it instead.

Another nurse bursts into the room and a very young student doctor is behind her and it is the two of them who stand over her baby on the small side table and slap it and prod it and prick it with tubes and needles until Lala hears a weak little cry. And it is only after Lala starts to whimper her relief that the student says, 'Is she stitched up?' and the nurse who worked on saving Baby says, 'No,' and comes back to her and pats her arm and says it is OK, they are doing everything they can.

By the time they are done, Baby is still blue, but she is breathing, and she is taken from the small white table and shown briefly to her mother and then whisked away. The room is quiet while Lala is stitched up and stabbed with more needles and transfused with someone else's blood and she is cold and she is shaking and the nurse with the wig is wrapping Wilma's blood-soaked nightie in a ball and putting it into a bag and preparing the room for another delivery and Lala asks if they can call Wilma and tell her Stella had the baby and ask her to come, even though she knows that Wilma will not come. And the nurse, unimpressed by the fact that Lala calls her grandmother by her first name, but softened by Lala's apparent ability to beat the odds, says OK but the baby probably won't be able to have visitors for a while. And her tone says maybe the baby will never see visitors.

She leaves Lala in the cold quiet room on her back with her legs still splayed and no feeling at all at the intersection of her thighs and it is nothing like the bliss on the posters in the clinic or on the TV ads or the faces of the wealthy tourist women who walk with their newborns on Baxter's Beach. Instead, she realises that she has now brought another person into the dark, that birth is an injury and having the baby has scarred her, and when the nurse asks her if she wants to go with her to see her baby in ICU she shakes no and the nurse clucks *tsk tsk* and Lala thinks of Adan, who hasn't come back, and she wonders if he went back for the gun but she keeps her mouth closed because some of the scream is still in there.

CHAPTER TWO

Mrs Whalen
26 July 1984

For the first five days after the murder, Mira Whalen is mute. She cannot speak when the maid says good morning, she cannot tell the swarming policemen to move their booted feet off the white carpet in her bedroom, she cannot say anything when the police insist on showing her photographs of all the robbers they know who were out of jail at the time of Peter Whalen's murder. She can only moan refusals (*don't come, don't arrange for the body to be taken back to England just yet, don't cry*) when her mother calls with offers of assistance.

But her voice is not the only thing that leaves her. On each of the five nights since the murder, Mira Whalen has also lost her teeth.

Painless though it is, it fills her each time with an unexplainable terror as she dreams it, a terror that remains unabated on waking. It is often an ordinary dream, as dreams go (walking the dog, washing the dishes) save that, before she knows it, her two front teeth tumble from her mouth and into her hands. Every night.

In her dream, she is warned by a mental tearing-away devoid of physical sensation that nevertheless compels her hands upwards until they reach her lips. She parts them slowly and feels the proof plop into her palms. It is always baby teeth – bloodless and tiny – the kind you might leave for the tooth fairy. Her Morphean self stares at these miniatures, whiter and more multi-faceted than she remembers, and while she stares, the mental rending starts afresh, the central incisors in her palms are elevated and there is the slow parting of lips and the silent crash of more of the teeth she hasn't owned since she was a mere little girl.

What disturbs Mira Whalen most about these dreams is not the threatened loss of her ability to chew, but rather the fact that she often continues to stare at the teeth in her palm, even though she knows that more are to be lost. It does not matter to Mira that she is dreaming. Surely, she thinks on rising in the near-morning, surely her sleeping version should be smart enough to foresee what will happen next? To do something to prevent the loss of more teeth? While Mira Whalen ponders the stupidity of her somnolent self, her sensible side repeats the same actions each morning on waking. She walks the twenty steps from the makeshift bed on the carpet behind the closed bedroom door to the mirror above the bathroom sink. There she takes three deep breaths before forcing herself to face the glass, at which point she watches her reflection bite the back of her hand, hard enough to mark it, and then examine each curve in the smarting impression.

It is only after she has convinced herself that her real teeth are all grown up that she counts them, every morning after the murder. She counts aloud, as counting her teeth in her head gives her the sensation of still being asleep and the prospect of being a sleepwalker is the scariest thing of all, but today is the first day that her voice actually makes a sound. Her voice grates over her tongue and teeth, and emerges from her mouth a rasping thing that whispers even when she doesn't want it to. On each of the first five mornings after the murder, Mira Whalen considered it a blessing that she could not speak and wake the children even if she was so inclined. On this, the sixth morning, she chides herself for being so stupid as to still believe in blessings.

On the sixth morning after the murder of her husband, Mira Whalen looks at the lonely pink electric toothbrush in the medicine cabinet while she swallows three Panadols and one Celexa with a gulp of water she catches in two cupped palms under a hot tap. She does not realise that she's opened the tap marked 'Hot' but she does not burn her fingers, because she never needs more water than she can catch in the ten seconds before it begins to steam. She swallows all four tablets in one gulp and lifts her head from the spigot just as it reaches a temperature that could singe her skin if she isn't fast enough, and then she is faced with the mirror again. For the first time since the murder, Mira allows herself a look, a long look, at a witch with wild hair, wandering eyes and a wet, crusting bruise on a cheek now shaded with purple and blue. Then she turns away, partly because, outside of the teeth, the person in the mirror isn't someone she recognises and partly because she has better things to do than try to fix that woman's face. Things like calling the Baxter's Beach police station, for example, to determine whether they have yet caught the man who killed her husband. Things like calling the mortuary at Baxter's General to find out whether the forensic pathologist has flown in from Sweden so he can tell them what they already know and she can take the children and get the fuck out of here. Things like trying to reach Peter's ex-wife and the mother of his two children to tell her what has happened, because the first Mrs Whalen is an artist and has gone off on retreat in a mountain in India somewhere where she doesn't even have access to a fucking phone. Things she hasn't been able to bring herself to do in the first five days since she lost her husband.

On the sixth morning since the murder, after counting her teeth and her medicine, Mira Whalen counts the children. She reverses the twenty steps from the mirror to the soft stack of bedding on which Beth and Sam are still softly snoring. She sits on the carpet and watches them first, counting the rise and fall of breast and back. After two sets of ten counts of breath, she counts two sets of ten fingers, two sets of ten toes. And then she counts two sets of ten breaths again. It is only after this second set of ten breaths that she can close the curtains more firmly against daylight, go back to bed and drift into the future. In this future, she is leaving for Peter's retirement party, getting dressed for Beth's wedding, sitting in the audience at Sam's graduation until, inexplicably, she decides to walk a big white dog she has never owned in real life and the moments start to slow down the way moments do when something is about to go terribly wrong.

On this sixth morning, Mira Whalen hears clicks and

spits teeth and gasps awake to the sound of a young girl's screaming, Beth's terror a fuller, deeper version of her own.

The day before Peter died, they had been arguing: one of those pointless rants about nothing important that Mira will now never forget. He'd ask her to bring raisins on her way back from the beach, because he wanted to make her bread pudding, her favourite dessert in the whole wide world. Peter wasn't a good cook. As far as she was concerned he didn't need to be, and he certainly didn't need to cook for her – he could afford to eat anywhere he wanted every day for the rest of his life, and therefore, by extension, so could she. She hadn't understood why he'd insisted, this visit, on making her bread pudding, why he'd gotten so upset when she said she'd forgotten the raisins. He hadn't understood why she couldn't appreciate that the argument was about more than bread pudding and raisins.

In the end, when the argument had escalated past raisins and cooking, Peter had decided to spend the night in the spare room again, and this time he didn't bother to wait until the children were asleep before he took his things down the long lit hallway to one of the other bedrooms. She'd watched Sam's face fall and had said, 'Daddy's making room for you to sleep with me,' because a seven-year-old accepts such explanations. For Sam that had been enough, but his sister had rolled her eyes and slunk off to play her stereo much louder than she should have been allowed. Mira had rolled her own eyes. If she and Peter were never able to make the baby they so desperately wanted, she'd long decided, if the gods decided to be that unkind, she'd still count herself lucky to be the stepmom to these two, even when life with Beth was beginning to get a hell of a lot more challenging. Sam remained as sweet as ever.

She'd admired Peter that evening as he'd passed her with his arms full of bedding. She'd taken in the slightly sagging skin of his arms and chest, the laugh lines that never left his cheeks, the cotton-candy wisps of salty hair under his armpits. Inside, she'd acknowledged that he was a good man. The thing that had come to her mind then was 'But he is a good man', and she sometimes forgot now that if her thought had been a qualifier, then what must have come before it was that he was somehow *not*. That night she'd taken in the sight of him walking with a pillow with a blue-striped pillowcase under his arm, trying his best not to look at her. She'd thought him beautiful, but hadn't told him. A small, a stupid thing. A thing you do in full expectation of waking up the following morning on the other side of the argument, brushing his back on the way to breakfast, catching his eye when you both laugh at something one of the children says over pancakes. That night she'd gone to bed secure in her entitlement to another chance. At the time, three weeks into their summer vacation at their luxurious beachfront villa, the arguments had been new, and never about the thing they were *really* arguing about. She had hoped to finally be able to argue about the real thing this holiday. To get things out and off both their chests. She'd felt entitled, at least, to *that* argument.

But that argument had eluded her.

That night, she'd surrendered to sleep despite the bump and scrape of Peter's restlessness through the wall, drifting off fitfully. Later she'd been awakened by the barrel of a gun prodding her face. She'd got up groggy, and thought it was him, which still pained her – that the conclusion that it was *her husband* who'd broken into her bedroom to do her some evil was the first one she'd come to. Perhaps Peter would have been perfectly entitled to want to kill her for all the wrong she had done.

But it hadn't been him.

It had been a blue-black man with a grey-blue gun and a palm wide open, standing at the side of her bed demanding money. At the sound of her scream, Peter had come running. He'd opened his arms and offered his wallet to the robber and when the man was still not satisfied, he'd begged him to spare her. *Please*, he had said, *let my wife go.* And the robber had looked at him, focused in on the fact that he was pleading for a life other than his own, and laughed. A deep laugh he'd lost a moment later, when he brought the butt of the gun down on Peter's nose until it bled. The children had been sleeping, Sam having decided that he would stay in Beth's room for the night, and Mira Whalen had witnessed Peter's efforts to muffle his anguish when his nose broke, so that the children wouldn't hear him cry out, wouldn't wake and come running into the room with the robber and the gun.

'Don't look at me, pops! Don't. Look. At. Rass. Hole. Me!'

And then the buzzer had sounded, at two o'clock in the morning. Two o'clock in the fucking morning. She had almost wet herself with the shock of it, wondering what it could mean. In six years – *six years* – of holidays, the buzzer had never sounded at that hour. Visitors out for a drunken stroll after a night at the sleepy hotel disco, she'd thought, or local teenagers playing pranks on the tourists, or (*please God!*) the police responding to someone who had reported that they'd heard something. But she'd never got to find out who was buzzing.

The robber had paused. The buzzer had continued. She'd thought she'd seen a chance and she'd run and grabbed at the gun with one hand and with the other she'd clawed at the gauzy second skin the robber wore on his face. A small, a stupid thing. The robber had struck her hard on her cheek and Peter had run towards her and she'd wanted to kick him for being the fucking gallant one. Again. He was supposed to run outside, call the police, answer the door, tell the children to get out of the house. *Something.* Something other than run straight up to the robber and try to stop him from struggling with her.

Instead Peter had run right for the gun, pushed her out of harm's way, and she'd shouted for the children to run although they had likely not even been awake, and the gun had gone off, and the robber had yelled something which probably meant 'Stop!' and grabbed his stocking mask out of her hand and stuffed it in his pocket and then the gun had gone off again and out of the corner of her eye she'd seen Peter, falling, while the robber looked past him to fire at her. The gun had refused and finally the robber ran.

All it would've taken were small things: remembering to buy a box of raisins so they wouldn't have argued in the first place, for instance. Or walking the few steps into the spare room after he'd turned the light off, wearing a smile, and slipping into bed with him, so that the robber would have reached the master's bedroom and found no one there. Or, in the weeks before they'd landed on the island, all it would've taken was the buying of a big dog or an alarm system or a decision to go to America instead. Or, in the months before that, all it would have taken was her being good, so Peter would not have suggested a trip to Paradise to try to fix what she had broken. Any of these small things and Peter would still be here.

But instead he'd been shot, and had fallen and this is what bewitched her: that she hadn't even looked at him as he fell, that her eyes were still trained on the blue-black hand that held the gun. What bewitched her was that her acknowledgement, her apology, her regret had not been the last things her husband had seen of her before he died.

That they would never now have the chance to have the *real* argument.

A small, a stupid thing.

CHAPTER THREE

Lala
30 July 1984

Even now, with Baby sleeping open-mouthed between the both of you, when you are reassured of reality by the chirping of birds, the swish of the coconut leaves and the roar and retreat of the waves below, even now, you can look into the face of the man snoring on the other side of that small baby and wonder who he is. You can see those thin, spiteful lips, slackened into pleasantry by sleep, and forget how they feel when he kisses you. You can look into his wide, flat features, his closed, heavy-lidded eyes, and struggle to remember his name.

Baby stirs and stretches in slow motion and settles back into sleep.

You don't grudge him that, three days ago, you had to take a taxi all by yourself, from Baxter's General, to bring you and Baby home. You understand that he had to stay out of sight in case the police was looking for him so you don't grudge him that he come only once to visit you during the whole week the both of you confined in Baxter's General, watching the other mummies and babies get presents and flowers and visits from husbands and friends and church members. You don't complain that nobody else ain't come to see Baby, not even Wilma. You don't grudge him that the one time he come he stay only a few minutes, staring at Baby, stroking her little cheeks and cooing, before hearing a siren and saying he have to leave, that things still hot.

But you grudge him trying to stop you from braiding when he know it is the only thing that keep you sane. You born to braid like he born to breathe.

If you is woman enough to call your own taxi from the hospital and tell it where to go, you tell yourself now, if you can mince out of that taxi with your stitched-up parts still stinging and you can pay the taxi man and you can cross the sandy soil with two bags and five pounds of baby in a pink dress you buy her with money you make from the same braiding, if you can get up the same twenty-five steps you mince down that night you went to find him, with two bags and a new baby, ain't you woman enough to decide when you will take that baby and go back to doing heads?

How many of the women on the ward come home to nobody? is what you asked yourself when you open back Adan's front door with the blue PEPSI logo painted on it. He ain't miss you and the house miss you less – the dishes done stacked same as you left them that night you went looking for him, the bed still wear the same one of Wilma's rose-printed fitted sheets you wake up on, sweating like a suckling pig, the morning that Baby was born. The blood stay and dried on those sheets, it was there when you left the house and it still there when you got back home from the hospital. But *he* wasn't nowhere to be found for a whole three days. How he feel he can come and tell you what to do now?

28

This morning, only this morning, he knock and you answer and he crawl into the bed and fall into the same open-mouth sleep the Baby now sleeping. Is only this morning you can tell him you have to take Baby for a walk, the nurse say to walk Baby every morning. But you didn't tell him. He don't know you been walking with Baby two mornings already, because those two mornings he not there.

You is your own woman, you say when he lay down this morning, you can ease up the baby, quiet, and walk with her down the steps and you can fetch the pram from below the house and settle Baby in it and tuck your combs in the bottom, just in case. You can put one of Wilma's old hats on your head and set off down the beach, staying on the part of the sandy soil held together by the roots of the coconut trees, so that the wheels of the pram do not find themselves stuck. You can watch the early-morning swimmers take their tentative steps into water bathed in the lilac and orange hues of sunrise, and see their wonder at why the water feels so warm. You can watch the women, especially, lay back and float so that their silky strands of hair fan around their heads, and almost hear them sigh as their stresses dissolve in the caress of warm shallow water.

But you cannot stop him coming down the beach to find you when he get up and Baby is not there and neither are you.

A name, you think, is a pacifier. Like: if it is 6.30 in the morning and you are walking down Baxter's Beach pushing a pram and looking for a smooth rock on which you can rest a bag of bright beads and a plastic mayonnaise jar stuffed with combs of all sizes. If you are looking for a spot that will be shady enough to set down a small folding chair a customer can sit on, a spot that will provide enough room in the shade to protect a tiny new baby in an old-fashioned pram when the sun climbs the sky. If you are doing this and you pass Tall Pink Man walking his big, gruff white dog with pointed ears, and if the dog starts to growl at you, you might feel helpless, because now that you have a new baby you cannot run, not really. If the dog jumps and snarls and barks at you, and makes like it could eat you alive, were it not restrained by the warnings of its owner, you might not remember this thing about a name. But if you do remember, if you call its name, if you stop and say 'Betsy' the way Tall Pink Man does every morning when he throws a piece of sea-bleached stick metres down the sand for the big, gruff dog to go running, it will stop as if stunned. It will cock its head to one side and open its mouth in surprise and it will ask, 'I know you?' (Even a dog cannot be violent to someone it truly knows.) And if you laugh, if you say, 'Shut up, Betsy, of course you know me, you and me is friends,' it will sort of half sit behind the sweaty legs of Tall Pink Man and lower its head and make bewildered noises and Tall Pink Man will wonder what the hell is going on with his dog after he wonders how the fuck you know her name. The point is, the dog will no longer try to frighten you, simply because you can name it.

'This is my baby, Betsy,' you could say, and by this time Betsy would be so calm, so quiet, somebody might think you could introduce the two of them, Baby and Betsy. Somebody might think you could bring Baby closer to the dog and hold her out and show it how pretty she is, how warm and soft and beautiful.

But you don't. Because same time Adan come down the beach at a trot and give the dog one look, just one, and the dog lose interest in doing you anything at all. *Cha*, say Adan, he tell you not to even *think* about working in the hot sun with his baby, yet here you are – not even two weeks good and you got the combs in your hand already.

He not too sure about this walking thing, say Adan when he trot up to you and hold your hand and take the combs and the handle of the pram, he don't want to draw too much attention, things still hot, he think maybe is best you and Baby stay inside. You could take the baby out on the top step for a few minutes if you need to. Come back and lay down and rest yourself, say Adan, he is a man and he will take care of you, is not like you have to go and braid the hair for the money. He ain't that sort of man.

His face is wearing that brand of smile that worries you. It is a small smile – the corners of his lips barely turn upwards – but it worries you because above the smile the eyes are dead serious. And because you have seen that smile before.

Just walk the baby and come back home, Adan repeat, plenty of time to braid hair when Baby grow a bit.

And although you notice that he is looking around, checking to make sure that nobody is following him, that the police are not at that very moment closing in on him on the beach with their guns drawn, you also notice the pride that puffs him up when he says 'Baby'. It warms you, that pride, it almost makes you forget that that smile is a signal, or that you make this baby with a killer.

31

'Adan,' you might say then, 'Adan, I does get my peace from braiding people hair, you know? And it can't hurt to do a head real quick, with Baby sleeping. All she do is nap anyway. And we need the money.'

But you don't say that; you open your mouth to call his name, to say you are a grown woman and you can braid hair with the baby if you want to, but nothing come out. And he take that to mean you okay with him taking the handle of the old pram from you and steering it to smoother ground in the direction of the little house you just come from.

'Come,' say this giant man with the scar on his fore-head, 'come let we go and lie down with she. I tired. And you know I don't want nobody seeing me walking 'bout the beach just so.'

His face is beginning to cloud over, like rain, so you go with him because Baby just born and little for her age and you don't want him to frighten her with what he will do if you don't go.

When you are back in the house and lying on the bed, watching them sleep, this giant and his baby, you might marvel that even after two years of knowing him and one year of being his wife, the name of this flat-faced man in the bed, the one who sleep with his thigh over your hips when you lie on your side to be rid of him, the one with his arm over your shoulders while you squint at the fist he make even in his sleep, the name of this man still escape you at times, like when you are on the floor in his shadow, at the precise moment when the right holler of his name might stop him cold.

So maybe it is now, after you already allow yourself to

be led back to the house and back into the bed and after you are made to put Baby down between the two of you and to lay down yourself, fully dressed, and after you are reminded to keep your eyes open and on the door, just in case the police are coming, that you realise what you have brought her into. Maybe it is at this moment, with this man on the other side of Baby, that you understand that it is possible you make a very big mistake. Maybe it is time to accept that this man is not the laughing giant you meet riding a unicycle at a fair two summers ago. Maybe it is time you realise that this man don't make his living rolling this way and that under an arc of bright juggling balls, for coins people drop in a jar. Maybe there is a reason that this is a man whose name you sometimes can't remember, and it is not just that there were posters you shielded your eyes from on the way home, asking for information about a murder, with a description of a suspect you know. It is not just the newspaper you cannot stop to buy because it carries a front-page story of the robbery and the photo of a man who has died and you cannot be faced with the details of this death. It is all of these things and it is the little brown baby asleep beside you who should not be made to feel the fear you do.

Maybe when he stir and talk in his sleep you forget that you are grown and you are just quiet.

'Lala?' he is singing. 'Lala?'

You can reach out and touch the loose curve of his fingers, you can splay them open to see his palm, you can trace the lines that tell his future to see whether you and Baby are still there. You can turn his hand over and see the scars on the knuckles of his fingers, the long scratches that travel up his arm. But you cannot call his name, because you cannot remember it. You cannot call him by name and say, *please, not now.*

'No,' you are saying, because you are still sore. 'No.'

He tries your name on a different tune.

'No.'

But no does nothing.

You can bite your lower lip, and keep your eyes on the baby, you can say to yourself that what he is doing cannot be that terrible because it does not wake the baby, it does not make her cry even though she is being shaken hard in the sheets, not really. If it does not make a baby cry, but it makes you cry, then how much of a woman are you?

You can watch the door fly open and then shut, open and shut, open and shut. You can train your eyes on the Pepsi lettering in the brilliant blues of that brand and wonder where the door came from, which shop he robbed of its own front door. You can imagine that the door is slapping the side of the house in protest, that it does not fly open merely to make a wobbly window to the sea. You can imagine, with the appearance of a very big wave, that it will come in on you, that big blue sea. You can be afraid that, despite the logic of the intervening sand and a house on stilts, you could all be a few seconds away from drowning. But you cannot call his name, cannot make him stop because, like the wave that crests and falls and disappears somewhere beneath the wooden floorboards, he is out of reach. Somehow beyond you, woman or not.

CHAPTER FOUR

Mrs Whalen
31 July 1984

People try to be kind but it does not matter. Mira Whalen snatches the papers from the paper boy, snaps at Rosa when the toast is only slightly overdone, unleashes expletives on the gardener for mowing the lawn when she is trying to nap and hangs up the phone on insufferable long-distance condolence calls from Peter's business associates and friends and family in London who don't know what to say to her after they say *I'm so sorry.*

'What are you sorry for?' she asks one of Peter's sisters when she calls in teary-voiced commiseration. 'That it wasn't me instead?'

She finds herself unable to speak anything but the cold, hard truth or absolutely nothing at all.

'Mira,' her mother complains when she telephones and Mira is still silent on the other end of the line, several questions later, 'are you still there?'

Mira Whalen says they are. Dipping daily in warm blue water. Spending nights lolling in cane-bottomed chairs with polished bottoms that rock on mahogany patio floors that do not creak. Minding exotic tropical flowers and growing brightly coloured fruits that a servant makes into frothy drinks with unpronounceable names and serves with tiny pink paper umbrellas. They are *there*, says Mira Whalen, living a life of extreme leisure. Which, of course, they are *not*.

'Well, when are you going back to Wimbledon?' her mother pleads, annoyed.

'We are not going back,' says Mira. 'I wouldn't dream of it.'

Martha does not understand her daughter's sarcasm; Mira does not understand why she is being sarcastic to her mother.

'You can't stay there, it isn't healthy.'

'We are waiting on the pathologist, Mother,' Mira Whalen spits. 'They are flying one in to do the autopsy. I cannot stay here but I cannot leave Peter here alone, I . . .' She makes a little choking noise.

'What about a hotel?'

'I don't want a hotel.'

'I can come over there and help you, Mira. Last time I talked to him, Peter promised me a cheque. If I get it, I can be on the next plane, get you and the children on your way back to London. I could send the body . . . Peter . . . whenever they release him. I can help you with everything. You can get another place, Mira, a smaller one, just enough for you to live in while you recover, you don't need that villa, you could . . .'

Extremes of anything are bad, and the two extremes of possession – deprivation and deluge – are especially crippling to the soul. For that reason Mira Whalen's mother has always advocated having just enough. Enough to keep

36

you happy. Enough to eat. Enough to drink. No more or less. There is perhaps enough diversion in seeking to ascertain what enough is to last one a lifetime.

Mira Whalen can think of nothing worse than her mother's meddling help, the kind that she cannot help but reject, even if she knows it is not motivated by judgement. Mira Whalen does not want to go back to London without her husband, she does not want a small flat or 'just enough'. Mira Whalen wants Peter. She wants the life with him she had before – summers in Paradise with the lacy foam of breaking waves washing their toes as they walk hand in hand on beaches of powdery pink sand. She wants sticky-fingered Sunday picnics on the stretch of sand beyond the patio, with lobster claws bursting with flesh that Rosa has basted in butter and lemon, with Beth and Sam's sun-bronzed faces smiling back at her as if she belonged there, with them. Mira Whalen wants the regimen of the rest of the year in Wimbledon – the gym and the salon and the shopping and parties and dinners at their house hosting Peter's work colleagues and clients, followed by nights curled up in his bed until 3 a.m., talking and laughing and mimicking the people they have met. Mira Whalen wants what she cannot have.

'Don't come, we are fine, but I have to go now.'

'Wait, Mira, I think we should pray about this . . .'

She is probably still praying when Mira hangs up.

It is not a crime, thinks Mira Whalen, to want the best in life, and a bounty of it. It is not a crime to use what you have to get it, no matter what her mother says. This is what Mira Whalen is thinking when she jumps up in the middle of the night with her heart racing and her night-gown soaked in sweat despite the AC being on full blast. It is what she reminds herself when she is reading and the phone rings and she still fully expects it to be Peter calling to tell her his meeting is running late, and in fact it is her mother, begging her again to pack her things and come with her. It is what she replays in her mind while being shown pictures at the Baxter's police station after Sergeant Beckles, on recognising that, despite her cultured English and expensive clothes, Mira Whalen is really just a local who married a wealthy white tourist, masks his face without feeling and stops calling her 'madam' and does not notice that one of his pictures is missing from his binder.

'No,' she says, 'it is not him. No, it is not him, either.'

It is not a crime to want the best out of life, to use what you have to get what you want, Mira Whalen insists to herself, so why for fuck's sake is she still being punished for it?

CHAPTER FIVE

Lala
3 August 1984

The name is a game they play on good days when they are lying in bed, lost in their own laughter, and he is someone else entirely. On good days they are cocooned in cotton sheets covering tangled legs and torsos and he is either the man she'd hoped he would turn out to be, or the man whose potential for good is as yet unrealised, or the man tormented by her inability to love him completely. On bad days, the name is not a game. Lala cannot play this game when he is a thief, or a liar, or a man who turns into a demon when he makes a fist or covers his face with a stocking.

When they play this game, what Adan does is try to sing her. He tries every type of 'la-la' he can think of: soft percussive notes that stretch his throat and deeply resonant bass notes that vibrate when she touches him and barely audible sharps that hurt her ears. He has said to her that she will know them when she hears them – the real notes, the real name. Something in her will click, he says, and just like that she will know that he has happened upon her name. He is the only man who can find it, he says, he is able and up to the task. They play the game a little less often now that the baby is here, but she is warmed by the fact that he is still trying.

Today is a good day.

'La-la,' sings Adan. 'I think da's it.'

But Lala shakes her head. *No.*

It makes no sense lying, because he will know anyway.

'Laaa-la!'

No.

When he is tired, and she fears he is about to fall into a temper, she cocks her head at the next note that rolls off his tongue, she widens her eyes, she makes the bewildered glance of the big white dog on the beach, as if she will sit at attention and come bounding into the present if he says it again. And when Adan gets that rare smile of triumph, and tries to repeat it exactly, seeking confirmation, she holds his face between her hands instead. She kisses his forehead, traces the outline of the scar above his left eyebrow with the tip of her tongue, sucks on the thin skin of his eyelids so that he has to stop looking at her to see if he has, at last, got the name right. She loves him. And when she's finished loving him, he has forgotten that he has failed to crack it – that her name is still a mystery.

Adan starts to talk about the robbery. This robbery did not go to plan. It is the people's fault, he says. Everybody know you don't challenge someone who come into your house like that. He says that the white woman saw him when she pulled the stocking from his face in the struggle. He is thinking that her eyes made four with his, that this is worse than if she had just known his name or where he lived, because he could move if somebody only know his address, but if they know his face they can pick him out anywhere. He cannot let this woman live, he says, this white woman. Given a choice between her life and his free-dom, says Adan, looking at Baby, there is only one choice he can make.

She woulda been too scared to see you good, says Lala, remembering that stocking, that scream. She woulda be too shocked to remember your face.

But Adan is not convinced.

'One little puny white woman,' he says, 'one little bitch who felt she could do me something. That little bitch look me straight in the face when she pull off the stocking. I tell her not to look and she not only look, she take off the stock-ing to get a *better* look. One little puny white woman and her kiss-me-crutch old man. I woulda get her too,' he says, 'if the doorbell didn't ring.' And then he pauses to look at Lala.

Lala looks away.

As he continues to talk, she listens to him. She no longer listens to the words. Lala has long learned not to listen to Adan's words at moments such as this. She listens instead to the up-and-down of his voice covering the small space between them. It is possible, she is sure, that he can find the exact intonation of the two syllables of her name while saying something else entirely, and this is what she is lis-tening for. This, and nothing else, is why she does not tell him to get the fuck off of her, that he's an evil man, a liar and a louse and if he ever tries to hit her again, or to ravage her or to order her around, she will kill him with the other gun he has buried in an empty oil drum near one of the concrete pillars that saves their house from being swal-lowed by the sea, she will boil a pot of water spiked with oil and scald him while he is sleeping, she will wait until he is snoring beside her, and take a cleaver from the kitchen and make sure he gets one good chop in the head. In her dreams, one good chop, the kind that slices bone like butter, is all it would take.

She listens for the sounds, but she cannot escape the words.

Lala gathers from what Adan is saying that an old white man died that night she found him and that Adan knows that it is he that killed him.

She catches her breath and holds it.

Before Baby was born, when it had been a good day and Adan had smiled with her and sung to her, rubbed her legs and brought her strawberries for prices that made her dizzy, sometimes Lala was reminded that her memory is unreliable, that the things she heard, the things she had seen, the things she had felt were, possibly, not real. On such days she was not sure whether the awful things she remembered of Adan were indeed as awful as she remembered them to be. The time he found that bald patch in her hair, for instance, while kissing her head, and had asked her, sincerely, what had happened to cause her hair to fall out there. At times like those she was not certain that the man massaging her feet was capable of such damage, whether the injuries he had caused her were really caused by him.

This is why she is unsure, when she thinks about it now, whether Adan is really telling her how an old white man begged for his wife and not his own life, how he shook when he shot him, how the wife's eyes opened in shock when the man fell, until they seemed to take up her whole forehead. It is possible that Adan expresses regret at not collecting more, searching harder, making them take him to that part of the house with the safe that rich white people always have. It is possible that Adan's voice vibrates with anger, that it amplifies when he says he wishes he could have waited a little longer, made them give him everything they had. It is possible, thinks Lala, but it is not likely because, after all, this is the man who cups their baby in the crook of his arm, and rocks Baby so gently that she is wooed into the trusting abandon of open-mouthed sleep. This is the man who has reserved for himself the simple gift of naming her, who, not being able to find a name that does justice to the wonder of his first child, still calls her Baby over two weeks after her birth, a name that means she has none. This is not a man capable of irreversible harm, of murder.

'She can't get way,' says Adan. 'When I get her, she going wish she did dead the first time.'

His eyes are wild, his scar pulses with hot blood.

'She must be didn't see you,' pleads Lala, looking at Baby cooing on the bed.

'She see me,' says Adan. 'She pull off the stocking and she look right at me. She wouldn't look away. She see me and she have to dead.'

Robbery is one thing, but murder? Murder is something else altogether. Murder is one of those things you can listen to, thinks Lala, should you ever be so unfortunate as to be on the guilt-free side of a confession, or a statement of murderous intent, but it is not a thing to be repeated. Murder is a thing best forgotten, a thing best left a mystery.

CHAPTER SIX

Lala
16 August 1984

They are admiring Baby the night everything changes. They are quietly claiming things about her to the soundtrack of Adan's cooing – in deference to the mystery of her mother's name. Lala claims Baby's nose, the way the little legs turn gently inward at the knees before repelling each other, the elegant triple-jointed toes. Adan claims her long torso, the flat, broad bones beneath her face, the way her upper lip retreats when she smiles.

'Just like Penny,' says Adan. 'Penny daughter self.'

It is one of the things she protests that they have in common, in mental inventories liturgised at night, this habit of calling a mother by her first name. It is one of the reasons she cannot leave him. For both of them, this mother died before they reached the age of five. In these circumstances, it is not strange to refer to a dead mother the way you would a fondly remembered friend.

Adan has come to see them again, on one of his covert, night-time visits since Baby came home. They are seated on opposite sides of the bed, and the baby is in the middle, in a space cleared of rumpled bedsheets, smiling at her father. She does not smile that way at Lala. She never has, and it is only now beginning to be something Lala worries about.

Adan does not have to do much to make Baby smile – a twitch of his head so the light catches his bald pate and a clucking sound and Baby is already in hysterics. Lala is content to stay in the shadow of their joy. The warmth that ripples out from those giggles is like the sunny spot in which a dog seeks to lie down and curl inward.

Neither of them anticipates the knock on the door. They are so enraptured by the beauty of this new baby that they have forgotten that her father is a fugitive. Adan misses the first knock, coming as it does on the cusp of his clucking. Lala, on the other hand, hears the knock the first time and tries to ignore it, trying to hold on to her spot of sun. But when the door raps the second time and Adan jumps and puts his finger to his lips, easing his hand below the iron bed frame, where a machete lies waiting, she drags herself up, clutches Baby close, hears herself whistle, 'Who is it?'

But it is only Tone. And a woman. Looking for shelter from a sudden downpour.

She does not say 'come in'. Tone is the type of friend who does not need to be invited in or shown where to sit or offered a glass of the alcohol kept for company. Tone is not company, Tone is one of Adan's friends since boyhood, one of the ones who shadows him when he ventures out at night, watching his back to ensure that no one breaks it, the friend who soundlessly collects the spoils from Adan's jobs and returns to him with the money from their sale. Tone is one of Adan's inner circle, but he has never before sought to extend this privilege to people Lala does not know.

45

Recently, Tone has appeared not to take his status for granted and has started knocking when he reaches the top step, something that Adan has, wrongly, attributed to the expectation and then existence of Baby. Something Adan fully expects will stop soon, once Tone understands that a baby does not change things, that *we is still we*.

Tone pushes his way past Lala as soon as she opens the door. He is panting from having tried, and failed, to outrun the rain up the stairs and his face is contorted in a scowl because his brand new sneakers have been drenched. It is a beautiful face: almond-shaped eyes set deep in grizzled caramel-brown skin stretched tight over bones so delicate and pointed you could think that a scowl would break them. It doesn't.

'Is only Tone,' says Lala, and Adan emerges from the shroud of dresses and slacks and jackets Lala has hung from a piece of broomstick laid diagonally across the corner above the bed. He puts the machete gently down and beams.

Tone and Adan touch fists in their usual welcome.

'My man, I thought you supposed to be undercover,' Tone reprimands him, mildly. 'We went to the tunnels and you wasn't there. I thought we agree you was gonna stay in the tunnels . . .' He looks at Lala and falls silent.

'I come to see the baby,' Adan explains. 'I had was to come.'

Tone trots over to the kitchen sink, which stands shakily beneath a window through which the sky is grey and ominous and the rain is now pelting down, drumming on the galvanise above them so that they have to speak a little more loudly to be heard. Tone leans over the single basin

46

sink, barely held in place by the rotting wood that cradles it, and starts to squeeze the rain from his locks.

Lala watches the water dribble from Tone's matted hair and splash onto Baby's newly sterilised bottles. Perhaps this is the first thing that irritates her, that plants a seed of anger, this little intrusion. She and the baby have made their peace with the impossibility of breastfeeding by now, even though Adan still insists that she try Baby on her nipple first before each feed. It is partly her guilt at being unable to breastfeed that makes the ritual of sterilisation so sacred to her, that makes her so infuriated by Tone's indiscriminate squeezing of his hair. She does not know why breastfeeding does not come naturally to her, but Adan seems to be beginning to accept the bottles. Perhaps it is Lala's anguish each time Baby draws milk that makes the little one turn away from her mother's breast of her own accord, bewildered. Perhaps it is Lala's distress that causes Adan not to frown when she starts giving Baby the store-bought formula she has to scrounge coins to buy.

The rain drums on the rooftop and the glass panes above the sink tremble in the wind and let in the rain, but Tone does not close them. The woman is still standing at the top of the stairs, smiling in at them with the rain plopping down on her hair. It is the kind of hair Lala charges extra to braid, the kind whose soft, loose curls have to be gripped tightly and forced to behave.

'As man,' says Tone, 'this rain just start pelting down just so, I tell this girl let we come here by you until it blow over.'

His voice has lost the affectation it wears when he talks

to tourists. When he is hustling Americans or Europeans on the beach, he mirrors the foreign accents so central to theirs (*Hey baby, want someone to show you a good time, mayne?*). He offers them tightly rolled weed, or rides on a jet ski or the promise of the hard, rough sex of a slave put to stud in an accent they recognise and his smile lights up those delicate bones so that old tourist women cannot resist him. When he is talking to friends, to locals, however, his voice is undressed, unfussy and runs roughshod over the local dialect without thought.

Adan had retrieved Baby from Lala's arms after she announced that it was just Tone, and resumed his cooing, but he looks away from Baby when Tone says *this girl*. His eyes bore into Lala's back and then rise above her shoulder as he stands.

'Jacinthe!' he exclaims. 'Come inside, Jacinthe, don't stay outside and get wet so.'

When he says her name, Lala looks at her again, properly, this girl on the step. Before now she had dismissed her as one of Tone's girls, one of the ones who paid him, but such girls are never young, never brought to Adan's house and never attributed names. Not by Tone, and certainly not by Adan. A name, she knows, is often a revelation of things that are hidden. It is only after Adan says her name that Lala sees the way the woman refuses to allow her feet to cross the threshold of the door, even with the rain daggering her hair and back. It is only then that she understands this is not one of Tone's paying older women. This girl is something else entirely.

'I tell you come inside, Jacinthe.'

Jacinthe hesitates just for a moment before shedding her sandals and putting her foot on the welcome mat. She tries to pull the Pepsi door closed behind her, but it flies open again with the wind. She abandons her efforts, comes inside, sits down on the wrought-iron chair beside the bed and tucks the skirt of her neon Hunza dress beneath the spread of her upper thighs, as if she needs it holding her close in order to stay put. Adan looks at this woman's smooth beige thighs, Jacinthe smiles, and something in Lala's chest turns over.

Jacinthe is the colour of building sand, with a small-boned frame and a wary, restless manner that makes Lala think of the pigeons approaching jerkily on the little bridge in the garden of Baxter's General. When she can be coaxed to the very edge of the chair, closer to the side of the bed, Adan shows off his baby: lifts her and pulls back a bib to show a birthmark, displays her healed navel, lists the features he claims are gifted from his side of the family, seeks Jacinthe's agreement. Jacinthe nods. Says that Baby's smile is just like Penny, Penny self, and Adan grins in a way that Lala does not often see – with a sort of mirthful idiocy that does not acknowledge that this Penny lives only in a picture, that a picture is where she has only ever lived.

Lala searches her memory again for mention of Jacinthe, but comes up empty.

Perhaps her seed of anger grows.

When Jacinthe reaches out to take Baby from Adan, to join him in hugging and holding and cooing over how beautiful she is, Lala strides over and says she must feed Baby first, it is past time for her feeding. She lifts Baby from Adan's hands before he can respond, straightens Baby's pale yellow smocked dress and obscures her navel again. The baby, startled by the sudden loss of admiration and the sound and sight of her father's fawning, threatens a cry, but Lala pays no heed. Perhaps it is the tenderness with which Adan retrieves Baby from her arms before she can fetch the bottle and proffers her again to Jacinthe, perhaps it is the maternal madness that epilogues a recent birth. Perhaps it is that they are *both* a little house-mad from being locked inside, Adan in the tunnels and Lala inside with Baby, because they have to be careful, they cannot afford for Adan to be seen. Perhaps it is everything that came before it, or nothing in particular, but whatever it is that makes Lala not understand what she is starting, it is a costly omission.

When Lala snatches Baby from Adan's hands, before Jacinthe's grasp can reach her, everything deteriorates. Adan lowers his eyes from Jacinthe's but does not look at Lala. He looks at the ground as the sound is sucked out of the room.

'Gimme back Baby,' is what he says to Lala.

'I gotta feed she,' Lala protests.

Tone stops squeezing his locks, closes the window from the rain.

'It getting ready to clear up,' he says. 'We gone, hear, Adan? Gotta get this girl home before it come down properly.'

'Gimme back Baby,' Adan insists.

Jacinthe jumps up, relieved to have received the signal from Tone to go. She says to Adan that it is OK, she will come back to visit some other time, she will see Baby again then, let her have her feed, she look hungry in truth, is OK, Adan. Lala holds Baby closer, feels her stiffen and start to claw, refusing to be drawn into her mother's bosom.

Adan, insistent, tugs Baby back while sucking his teeth. A custard-coloured bootie falls onto the hard wood floor and does not bounce. Adan is holding on to a little naked foot. Baby wails again.

Adan is twisting the baby's legs away from Lala. Jacinthe is heading towards the door, Tone is approaching Lala and Adan as they start to move with the baby suspended between them. Lala reclaims both legs, Adan moves his big, big hands to Baby's torso and tries to lift her out of Lala's arms. Jacinthe has reached the door, is putting on her shoes. Tone stands behind her, takes up much of the space in the doorway, keeps the light out, blocks the sight of Adan and Lala struggling over Baby.

Thunder grumbles and barks. Baby jumps and both parents realise, at once, that this rite of possession is scaring her. Neither wishes to scare her. Perhaps this is why Lala lets go of the little legs at the precise moment that Adan lets go of the torso and Baby plummets to the floor in a flailing plumage of pale yellow and chocolate and lands with a soft thump and is silent. The rain pours down. Tone's eyes widen but his voice remains calm, for Jacinthe, who is behind him putting on her shoes and has not seen the baby fall.

'We going now,' says Tone, watching Adan stoop to pick up the baby. 'Come, Jacinthe.'

He looks at Lala and his eyes are wide and fearful but he steps outside, closes the door behind him so sharply that it rattles, ushers Jacinthe down the stairs in front of him so that she does not get the chance to look back inside, to see the baby being snatched from the floor. The thunder roars and Adan roars with it. Lala is crying. They carry Baby together, Adan's large hands cradling her head, Lala's fingers laced under her back. They place her on the bed, start running their eyes and hands over her, checking for anything broken. Baby is in that state of pure astonishment, the catch of breath in the build-up to shrieking her terror.

'You see now?' yells Adan. 'What the fuck you had to do that for?' And all the while his hands keep running over the miniatures of his own head, his own back, his own hands.

'Oh God,' Lala is crying. 'Oh God!'

When Baby finally cries, it is so deep and loud and long that it eclipses even Lala's sobs, makes the claps of thunder outside seem like the buzzing of insects. Adan sucks his teeth, looks around wild-eyed, feels again the same bones his hands have already examined. Nothing appears broken and he passes Baby to Lala, where Baby submits to her breast. A few minutes later, when her wailing has softened to a snotty whimper, she is patted on Adan's shoulder. Lala's breast flops out of her shirt while she continues to fawn over Baby.

'You think we should take she to Baxter's General?' she asks.

Adan sucks his teeth. He does not answer. He confirms again with his fingers that there are no large lumps on

Baby's head or back, no gross angles of arm or leg to signal that something is seriously wrong. He lays Baby gently down on the bed again, sits gingerly beside her, watches her nestle into sleep. Lala stands by his side, watching Baby, watching him.

'Baby,' he is cooing, 'my girl, my sweet, sweet girl.'

Lala is poised above him, breast still bare, when he suddenly turns away from Baby and towards her. He bites her breast so quickly, so savagely that at first she does not understand what has happened, but she sees his head on her chest, poised before the burning in her breast in the manner of a suckling baby.

For one breath she is silent, and then Lala is screaming, '*Murder! Murder!*' in the way of the women in Wilma's stories, as if the mere announcement of her imminent slaughter will save her. Adan's big right hand finds her throat; she goes reeling into the chair that Jacinthe sat on, slapping her hand to her own mouth so she will not wake the baby with her surprise.

Adan is about to yank her from the chair when Tone runs back up the stairs and through the front door. Tone is good at reassuring women, Lala knows, but she also knows that he has returned to reassure himself. When he comes through the door, she turns away from him, rubs the water from her eyes, tucks the mangled breast away and buttons her dress above it.

Tone feels the air crackling with something he cannot prove with his eyes. *See the baby asleep on the sheets? See Lala start to make their bed around her?* For a moment he considers that this is strange, her thinking to straighten the bed when the baby could be hurt, but the thought escapes him as Adan starts to relay the story of the fall, a story in which Lala is the villain who refused to hand over Baby until the very moment that Adan decided to let her stay, and therefore caused the fall. Tone does not comment on this story, he does not counter it with what he has seen or what he suspects. He does not challenge Adan, even though he knows that Adan's version is the one that will stick. Instead, he and Adan begin to whisper about the baby and how close she came to disaster.

Tone talks to Adan about lucky children he's known, children who survived falls from great heights, serious diseases and gory accidents, unscathed. It is going to be OK, Tone says with his stories, Baby will survive like these children. Lala listens, but she does not believe, she does not look at either man. She wants to ask Adan, again, if they should take Baby to hospital, but she does not want to inflame him further, does not want to have to test her throat and talk in Tone's presence; it stings so much she thinks she would be incapable of speech even if she did. Instead, she takes one of the sterilised bottles from the sink, washes it again briskly, just to be safe, puts a small pan of hot water on to boil and watches it, mesmerised, until it is just beginning to bubble. She retrieves the store-bought formula standing open by the sink and levels a scoop of vitamin-enriched white powder that quivers in her grasp, pours the hot water into the bottle, then the powder.

Tone does not stay long. He says he does not want

the baby to wake up on account of his presence, his unintentional noisiness, so he says his goodbyes again and says that he is going back to the beach, where he has promised to meet a friend. Lala's hands stop quivering when he says 'friend' and clench instead. 'Friend' is a word Tone uses to mean a middle-aged woman in need of a good time. A 'friend' is a woman who will pay him.

Adan is trying to convince him that it is OK to stay. Baby good good now, says Adan, she gone sleep. Stay and talk because he not going on any jobs tonight. He still laying low, he explains, and a fella from St Christopher coming to see him about a little job he think maybe Tone could help him with. Tone shakes his head, no. He is not looking at Adan, he is looking at a deepening purple mark near Lala's neck, a vivid red spot on the front of her flowery dress. Lala turns away, covers the bottle, shakes it fast, too fast. When she releases the teat, newly made formula foams out onto her hand and she howls, because it is hot, because she is hurt.

Adan shouts something that Lala cannot hear, something that makes Tone's fingers find the shark's tooth hanging just beneath his collarbones and hold it tightly.

Tone asks her something, checking to see if she is OK, so she nods and does not look at him and does not respond or look at Adan looking at him asking her. Instead, she puts the bottle in a container of cool water before setting about cleaning up dots of spilt milk from the floor.

'A man want to bring in a little food,' Adan explains to Tone. 'High-grade thing. That way you tell me about, through the tunnels, that is a boss way, Tone. The man serious, we could make something. He coming here just now. Ever since I make this plan with this man to meet tonight and talk.'

Adan doesn't understand why Tone still wants to leave, why he doesn't see that this offer of inclusion is a promotion of sorts, an elevation from being trusted with a half-pound of weed to sell to his clients on the beach at a premium, and having to return the cost of the consignment to Adan when he is done. Lala doesn't understand why Tone doesn't hurry up and leave. She does not like the two of them in the little house at the same time, but she guesses that Tone knows that by staying he will spare her, that he has already figured out what it is she needs.

'As man, I going, check you tomorrow,' says Tone, bouncing a loosely made fist against Adan's. 'Take good care of Baby. We going talk 'bout it tomorrow, seen?'

'She all right now,' Adan assures him dismissively. 'The man is a serious man, Tone. We could make something good.'

'Seen, seen,' says Tone. 'I going check you about that tomorrow, though.'

'Tone . . .'

But Tone is out the door and Adan's forehead furrows at the doorway for too long after his right-hand man has exited it.

Baby is so soundly asleep that she cannot be coaxed into taking the before-bed feeding, which Lala decides to save, in anticipation of Baby waking, hungry, around 2 the next morning, as usual.

But the next morning Baby does not wake up.

CHAPTER SEVEN

Martha
12 November 1948

Martha Mason is not a bright girl, but there are a few things she knows.

First and foremost, Martha Mason knows her place. She knows that she is a descendant of the scorned redlegs of St John, the poor whites whom both the black descendants of slaves and the white descendants of slave masters look down upon, and as such, that she is the equal of neither. Secondly, Martha Mason knows that she is penniless. Her father, Gilbert, has just been fired from the Central Foundry for throwing down a lit match he used to light a cigarette he shouldn't have been smoking on the job. Gilbert is a good technician, but this one foible has led to a fire that burns a hole in the centre of town and he is let go. He is lucky that all he has lost is his job, but it does not feel like luck to his family, for whom his pay is the only source of sustenance. For two weeks the family of seven has been rationing one meal a day, and as of yesterday, Martha has assumed the age of majority without the proverbial pot to piss in.

Martha Mason does not fool herself – she also knows that she has no head for numbers, no heart for nursing and no hands for housework, so she knows that she must find and hold on to whatever employment the gods might allow to fall upon her.

This is why Martha Mason is blinded by tears as she walks the wrong way down the gently curving driveway of Baxter's Plantation at seven in the morning, a driveway fringed by cabbage palms that legends say still hang heavy with the souls of the slaves who were drenched in cane juice and tied there to be tortured by the stings of red ants. Martha is crying because, despite all she knows, she has still managed to lose the gift of a job that is only three days old.

Martha is barefoot, and dust clings to her toes as she wonders what she will say to the auntie who begged to get her the job as a maid in the Martineau household at Baxter's Plantation, with the assurance that Martha was very good at housework indeed.

It is because of this crying that Martha almost misses hearing a spanking-new Morris Minor rolling to a stop beside her and James Martineau bidding her stop crying *this instant*. She is pretty as pretty can be, says James Martineau, but if no one has told her that she is an especially ugly crier he doesn't mind allowing her to know. Martha accepts the offer of a gentleman's monogrammed handkerchief from a hand the colour of fresh-cut mahogany and blows her nose without grace before she takes in the two kindly brown eyes staring at her from beneath lush black eyelashes.

Martha Mason may not be bright, but she is not above begging, either. By the following morning, she is at work as the secretary in James Martineau's office on Bay Street, typing his letters, making his coffee, managing his meetings, not unaware of the pleasure he derives from telling unexpected visitors to make their appointments to see him with her.

'See that white lady there?' he is wont to say, snapping his suspenders against the starched white of his long-sleeved shirt, a slight slick of sweat making his forehead shimmer. 'She works for me. You got to speak to her first before you can speak to me, you understand?'

It didn't take long for one thing to lead to the other is how Martha will describe the ensuing courtship to their daughter, Mira, many years later. It didn't take long for Mira to come along. Martha will explain, matter-of-factly, that Mira is named after a married Portuguese woman her father remembered from a brief affair he had in Brazil.

James Martineau puts his mistress and his Mira into a tiny stone house in Britton's Hill and hardly visits them there at all. This is not an issue for Martha, who understands that she is not a woman befitting of a Martineau. In the year in which the first black man has been elected to the island's parliament, an established black businessman like James Martineau does not then go and align himself with someone beneath his own precarious station.

Martha understands this, but she struggles to explain it to Mira.

James Martineau has his daughter cared for during the day by an old black woman selected by his mother, and baby Mira is brought to his office at three o'clock each afternoon, where she is taught to sit quietly near to Martha's desk and play with her crayons while Martha types and files and administers. Badly. Martha Mason is never promoted, but she does not aspire to promotion; she aspires to a roof over her head, clean clothes for her daughter, sufficient flour and oil from her pay cheque to make a month's worth of bakes for breakfast. She aspires to *enough*. Each month James Martineau slips her a white envelope with Mira's name on it, and it is from this envelope that Martha takes money for Mira's smocked dresses and frilly socks.

James Martineau, one of the few wealthy black men in Paradise, is tall and reedy, with a high, intelligent forehead and the ability to engage and dismiss at will. While he paces the floor, dictating one thing or the other to Martha, he sometimes stops and catches his daughter looking up at him open-mouthed, and on these occasions he reaches over and rubs circles across the middle of her forehead, taps her nose with his thumb and returns to his pacing.

When Mira is four, James Martineau marries a certain Ms Musson, the blonde daughter of a wealthy white merchant. In another four years, Ms Musson has borne him three *café au lait* daughters and these little girls also come to the office in Bay Street, all dressed up in velvet and lace that costs more than the sum of money in Mira's envelope. None of this is a problem for Martha, but how to explain it to Mira, whose forehead aches with longing when James Martineau fusses over and pets and kisses these three little girls? How to help Mira to understand her mother's hiss when she draws too close to James Martineau on these occasions, hoping for the reassurance of his thumb on her forehead? When Mira and one of the Martineau girls get into a fight over the seat placed closest to their father, James Martineau orders that Mira should no longer be brought to the office after school. To console her daughter, Martha offers her a trip to town and an ice cream, which she pays for with the money in Mira's envelope.

Martha Mason is not bright; she cannot see how this envelope will impact her daughter in future.

CHAPTER EIGHT

Mrs Whalen
16 August 1984

For the most part, Mira Whalen stays in her room with the curtains drawn, the light firmly shut out. When she ventures outside of her room, when she can be coaxed by Rosa or Sam to eat something, she sees the antique mahogany planter chairs with the curved arms, the Persian rug, the tables of carved limestone topped by heavy green-rimmed glass, and she remembers that this is what she has wanted for as long as she can remember – this spouse, this house, this *life*.

There are two versions of how Mira Martineau met Peter Whalen. In the first one, British hedge fund manager meets island girl and they fall head over heels in love, a love that leads to marriage and a joint life in London, where Peter is based. This is the story Mira had planned to tell their children and grandchildren; it is the carefully rehearsed version she relates at lunches and teas with Peter's friends in Wimbledon over Earl Grey and petit fours. In this version, the island is Paradise. It is hot, beautiful and drenched in beaches so blue you'd swear that blue is the colour of water.

But there is another version, which Mira never relays,

and she suspects that her mother prefers it. In the hidden version, Mira Whalen is a whore, the kind who chooses to be a whore, the kind whom people don't dare say is whorish, whose crowning achievement is becoming a wealthy man's wife. These whores are widely considered to be better than their counterparts who work behind the Holborn Hotel, simply because they are presented as having other options and therefore whoring is given the guise of something else. Usually, this something else is love.

Martha used to scream this version at Mira when she discovered that her daughter was seating herself at the bar at Sam Lord's Castle each week night and weekend, nursing a single martini until any one of the many businessmen who stayed there could be persuaded to buy her another one. By this time Mira sold perfume in the lone department store in town and painted her face with the samples from the make-up counters and flicked her hair and dreamt of being one of the women in the magazines she stole from the out-of-date stack in the book section. And she sat at the hotel bar with a few other like-minded girls and hunted.

One Wednesday evening, after Mira Martineau has spent three hours at the bar of Sam Lord's Castle with Peter Whalen, chain-smoking slender cigarettes with her bright pink lips in a tight white dress with padded shoulders that almost reach the end of her long chandelier earrings, laughing louder than his jokes deserve, he takes her to his room. It cannot be called a date *exactly* but Mira does not believe in waiting to go to bed with someone she wants to love her.

In the first version of their story, this is the night that

Peter sweeps Mira off her feet. In the second version, it is the night when he first receives what she can give in return for two diamond bracelets, a ruby ring and enough spending money in the month after she meets him to take a taxi to work each day at the department store and not even think about it. In fact, the waiting taxi outside the little stone house in Britton's Hill is what starts Martha's scoldings.

Mira does not mind.

For several months afterwards, Mira surrenders to Peter's kisses, returns his little muttered endearments, ignores the cloud of alcohol in which they are usually cloaked, and allows him to think that *she* is the one who has been caught. And soon after that there is a quiet conversation in his hotel room, with Peter trying gently to explain to the screaming voice on the other end of the line that he is sorry, so very, very sorry, but he has found the love of his life and will be seeking a divorce.

You simply cannot know that what you have is not the love of your life, Peter explains to the first Mrs Whalen, until you find the one you were made for and realise that everything that's gone before is prologue.

It suits the sentiment Mira Whalen suffers looking at her empty house – that everything now is epilogue.

This last time the Whalens visited Baxter's Beach it was because of the affair, to work on the love they thought they'd lost. Peter had bought the villa a decade before he'd met Mira, and resolved to retire there. His first wife had seen it and fallen in love and they'd travelled to the island as often as they could, renting out the villa for the nine months each year that they weren't there. It was on an unexpected business trip when Peter was staying at a local hotel that he'd met Mira. Mira had only visited the villa after they were married. They'd returned with the children for almost three months each summer since then, more often if their schedules allowed.

Maybe Peter had thought he could change things by bringing Mira back to the place where they'd met and the comforts of what a life with him had brought her, including being able to live the best of the island life in the land of her birth. Maybe he'd thought that a visit to the place they'd met, with all its memories of how they'd fallen in love, would remind her why she'd been so wrong to have an affair, why risking it all was so stupid.

Who can tell now? Peter is dead.

This summer, they'd landed at the airport and Peter had stumbled as he dragged their bags off the creaking carousel in the arrivals area. She remembered how the hopeful smiles of the redcaps had fallen into cold indifference at the realisation that this rich white tourist would rather lift his family's many cases himself than pay them a few dollars he could probably afford to wipe his ass with if he wanted to. She'd suspected then that lifting their bags was one of those things that Peter had done to help them all to believe that they were just an average family on a regular vacation. She'd watched him start to sweat in the car park with those bags. She'd watched how his skin reddened as if injured, how in the sunlit glare of the country where she was born his clothes started to stick to him, how his skin flushed as if infuriated and how hers started to deepen as if awakening from a sleep or sickness, as if nature was somehow colouring her in.

Beth and Sam had been happy that day. They'd talked excitedly about the beach, whether a swing the gardener had looped over a branch on the tamarind tree last summer would still be there, whether summertime friends would be around this year, whether Rosa had made them mauby or fishcakes or conkies wrapped in banana leaves to welcome them. In the car they could hardly keep still and she'd found herself wondering what the driver thought of them, whether he thought them exuberant or impolite. He'd sat and focused on the road and she'd watched him in the rear-view and wondered why he had allowed his broad shoulders to be tamed by a suit particularly ill-suited to hot weather.

'At last the sunshine brings a smile,' Peter had said, and she had nodded to acknowledge that he was trying and to show him that she appreciated that, at least. But for the rest of the ride there was no sound other than the chattering of the children and once, when she looked up, the driver was staring at her from the rear-view mirror as if he was wondering whether she was always this quiet, and she had stopped herself from engaging in chit-chat with him.

These are the memories that Mira Whalen's mind alternately clutches at and pushes away during the day, when she is not trying to remember if she has brushed her teeth that morning, and whether all her molars were still there and the right size when she woke up.

CHAPTER NINE

Mrs Whalen
17 August 1984

Sam's ghost confronts her at 2.20 a.m.

His face is bright and bug-eyed in the blue-tinged incandescence of a fluorescent bedside lamp now burning all night, every night since the murder. Once upon a time she'd thought she could never sleep with the lights on.

It's his arm this time.

'It's been bleeding all night,' he says.

She dresses his pale, smooth skin. There is no blood. With dull scissors she cuts pieces of gauze from the roll beside the bed. Places them in layers on the spot he is pointing out. Sticks on bits of masking tape. Her eyes sting. It is the facetiousness of fate that he has woken her on one of the few occasions that she was actually sleeping.

'You forgot the medicine,' Sam whines.

'Sorry, honey.'

She takes it all back off and does everything over again after rubbing the spot with the entrails of an empty tube of Neosporin. His big, bright eyes peer at the new patch. Since the murder, he has imaginary sores almost everywhere. And every time Rosa manages to convince him that one is better, he finds another gaping wound in the middle of the night and wakes Mira to dress it for him. The gauze is almost all gone.

While she works, he chatters.

He expects that Dad will be okay, he says, peering at the new dressing; he wasn't afraid of dying. He wasn't afraid of pretty much anything.

'Of course, honey,' Mira Whalen offers. 'Dad was very brave, and very smart and he is somewhere watching over us.'

'You mean like heaven?'

Mira nods.

'Dad doesn't believe in heaven,' says Sam. 'He says there is nowhere that people go and watch over us after they die.'

'Dad could be wrong,' says Mira, gently.

'Mom says there's no heaven either.'

Mira thinks of the first Mrs Whalen meditating in an ashram somewhere and decides to say nothing. Somehow it still seems like a slight when she discovers things that Peter and the first Mrs Whalen have in common – memories she does not share, ideals she does not subscribe to, the glib dismissal of a heaven she firmly believes in.

'Dad will be fine,' says Sam.

He seats himself beside Mira in the chair, but he fidgets, he cannot get comfortable and eventually he returns to the floor and stares at her.

'Will you be fine, too?'

Mira Whalen nods, because she cannot bring herself to lie through teeth she hasn't counted yet.

Sam slips back into sleep on the tumble of bedding on the floor, stretched out beside his sister. Mira rearranges her limbs in the chair beside the bed. She cradles a cricket bat she has promised herself she will wield if the robber comes back, watches the empty bed complete with three flecks of her husband's blood rusting in a corner of white Egyptian cotton. She runs her hands over these spots that Rosa's eyes have obviously missed. She smells her finger, starts to talk to him, moving her lips as she whispers apologies. She tells him that she and the children have rehearsed how they will flee if the robber comes back again, that they now have code words to signal to each other that something is wrong. Peter does not answer. As she rubs the flecks they grow bigger before her eyes until it seems like the blood is on her hands and the bed looks the way it did the night Peter died, when she dragged him there from the floor because she did not know what else to do. Before Rosa came, before the police came. Suddenly she is heaving, her chest is tight and she thinks she hears the robber disable the new padlock Rosa has had fitted on the service gate. In her mind she hears him lift the latch and start up the driveway on large, padded feet.

The children know the drill. As soon as she shakes Beth, she jumps up and reaches for her shoes, Sam grabs his shirt and a flashlight and Mira her purse and the bat. They run as rehearsed down the front stairs (because robbers rarely enter through front doors) and on to the beach, then the boardwalk. They run holding hands, silently, and every so often she and Beth have to bear Sam's weight when he cannot keep up. While she runs, she calculates the odds of the robber realising that they have escaped and coming after them, trying to tackle them before they can get to help.

She does not stop to call the police. In the four weeks since Peter's murder, Mira Whalen has come to the conclusion that the investigation into his murder is beyond the capability of the local police, simply because they have not yet found his killer. For this reason, she did not factor them into the escape plan that she is now executing. Gathering the children and running at the first sign of an intruder gives them the best chance to avoid a fate like Peter's, decided Mira, because to run would be better than to wait for the Baxter's police.

When they burst through the doors of the twenty-four-hour convenience store, the quiet order of the shelves of bright boxes and transparent bags stops them cold. A sleepy guard stares at them – a wild-haired white woman in pyjamas and two pale, emaciated children with wide, frightened eyes – and decides this is unusual enough to ask what is wrong. He pulls them inside, locks the doors, speaks into a walkie-talkie until a manager comes running from the back office, a middle-aged man who has had this happen to him before. Mira Whalen shifts from one foot to the other as she waits, peeping through the glass doors of the convenience store every few words to ensure that they have not been followed. The manager takes her in – she is a tall, thin woman whose shoulders and hip bones jut awkwardly through her clothing. Her lank, unwashed bob falls in greasy clumps just past her ears. Her huge hazel eyes are sunken and ringed with shadows. She is shaking.

'Is all right, Markley,' says the manager. 'Open back the door.'

'But sir . . .'

Markley stares at Mira Whalen and then at his manager's almost imperceptible nod. He unlocks the door and the manager shows Mira Whalen and the children to a tiny office just off the alcohol aisle. The office smells of coffee and a half-eaten bowl of pudding and souse sitting on a drawer-less wooden desk. He moves the bowl aside, gestures for them to sit down and dials the number for the security company from the card Mira Whalen keeps in her pyjama pocket. Then he calls Rosa, who has made Mira promise to ask a person she can trust to call her if anything goes wrong, no matter the time of night or day.

Mira huddles with the children in the manager's office while the security detail confirms to the manager that nothing is amiss at her house – the lock on the service gate is in place, the house is free of trespassers intent on doing harm, there are no signs of intrusion; the only door open is the one Mira Whalen used to make her exit on to the beach. Markley is new and particularly unsuited to security work, so he is still being gallant – he pops his head around the corner of the office and offers to accompany Mira and the children back home himself, and seems surprised by the manager's barely restrained '*Chhttt! Chhttt!*' that dismisses the idea before it is even fully expressed. The manager is not new and has lost the warm civility he wore the last three times Mira and the children burst into his store in the middle of the night.

'Nobody ain't in you house, ma'am,' he says when he hangs up the phone. 'OK? Not a fella in you house.'

'But I . . . There was a . . . I heard him, I . . .' Mira is looking around beseechingly, as if there are others within earshot who can be convinced to believe her.

'There ain't nobody there,' the manager concludes firmly. 'I understand how you feel, ma'am, but there ain't nobody there.'

When Mira Whalen still stares at the manager, stupefied, even after he has explained that there is nothing at all to worry about, the manager calls Rosa again and they wait until Rosa comes through the glass door and talks softly to her boss, like she is speaking to Mrs Whalen from a very great height indeed. When they have finished, Rosa asks Mira Whalen if she took her medication before going to bed and Mira Whalen says she cannot remember and Rosa offers to take the children home with her to get some sleep, and before Mira can refuse, Beth says yes, please, she wants to go with Rosa, and she curls into Rosa's heavy-handed hug and starts to sob. Mira Whalen struggles with the choice but she decides that, ultimately, Beth will probably be better off with Rosa, whose little wooden house she has seen. No robber will want to rob that house, thinks Mira Whalen, the children will be safe there. She imagines Rosa sleeping with them on the big iron bed her husband will be booted from. She imagines Rosa tucking them into the crooks of embraces pillowed by soft, jiggling fat. She says yes, the children can sleep there.

Rosa's husband is waiting outside in a bright blue Datsun with a sheet of sheer plastic bag for a back windscreen, neatly secured with tape all around the edges in a manner that suggests a situation of relative permanence. He is listening to a cricket match being played in Australia, but he gives his wife all of his attention as she explains that the Whalen children will be spending the night with them. When she finishes, Rosa does not wait for any indication of her husband's agreement and he does not seem to think one is necessary. Rosa's soft arms, exposed to the elements above a skirt pulled up over her breasts into a sort of dress, ushers Beth and Sam into the back of the bright blue Datsun. The husband smiles one of the all-teeth smiles of the locals in the tourist brochures, and nods at Mira's hesitant expression and assures her that it is perfectly OK for the children to spend the rest of the night with his family, no problem. Mrs Whalen can come too, he says, if she wants to. Mira shakes her head and says no and her voice trails off because she cannot find a reason why not and somehow it feels like a reason is necessary, and he smiles again, as if he is saying that this too is OK. And something about his openness to everything is so unnerving that she turns away and she hardly feels Rosa's gentle pats on her back, hardly hears her assuring the security guard that her madam is just a little tired, but no, she does not need a taxi, she will make her way home by herself. And Mira confirms she will, as soon as she has done her shopping. The children are driven away and Beth does not look at her through the plastic windows of the blue Datsun.

Mira Whalen walks back inside and suddenly she is alone in the quiet of the store because Markley has gone to see after a drunken tourist couple who are stumbling towards more local rum. She starts to wander the aisles. The twenty-four-hour convenience store is a recent addition to the beachfront. Several years ago, Mira and two other make-up attendants from the department store used to patronise the club upstairs because it was always full of tourists and the younger inhabitants of the luxury villas that faced on to the better end of Baxter's Beach. In those days the convenience store was a Chinese restaurant with red paper lanterns and *Guang Dong* in gold lettering above a mural of a dark-haired lady in a square dress. Not too long after she'd married Peter and become an inhabitant of one of those luxury villas herself, the restaurant had closed, and not too long after that, a convenience store had opened instead. The *Guang Dong* sign had gone, but the geisha had remained, unperturbed by the new *Fast Mart Convenience* sign, in the shadow of which she stares at its shoppers with the same coy grace with which she had welcomed the patrons of the restaurant.

When Peter was alive, in the times when they first came for three months a year to Baxter's Beach, there was no all-night convenience store. In those days they used to laugh if they had forgotten to ask Rosa to add citronella candles to the list of groceries she bought in the supermarket each day, because they knew they would be mauled by mosquitoes after turning in. They used to sigh and say, this is how it is on a small island. And although it was inconvenient not to have options for late-night shopping, it reminded them of why they thought this was a good place to call a getaway in conversations with friends. It was a good place to unwind from the stresses of London life. It was a good place to try for a baby.

Now vulgar neon lights advertise the store's twenty-four-hour status and at night the beachfront is perpetually ablaze with coloured lights in which the whores stand haloed. And you can buy citronella candles, cigarettes and *The Economist* at 3 a.m. What they had sought refuge from had found them.

Jack appears when she starts her third lap of aisle 5. He has probably been sent by the manager and he doesn't talk to her at first. Not really. A flash of recognition as part of his peripheral vision and a sort of sigh in welcome. He's crooked: half of his back sits lower on his spine than the other half and the half that sits lower drags, like part of him is a sleeping friend he has to carry along. He wears the yellow T-shirt uniform they all do, but under his he wears a much-pressed long-sleeved white polyester shirt with a loud tie knotted right up to his throat, and on his feet, large black shoes with rounded toes he never polishes. And he wears a ridiculous smiling button that shouts his name in a cartoon cloud.

'Hi, Jack,' she says, with the enthusiasm she'd use to greet a five-year-old, already aware that if she doesn't, he will worry and ask her what's wrong.

'Hi,' he says, and he licks the accumulated spit in the sagging corner of his smile. He is moving things around on the shelves. Randomly. Like he doesn't really want to. Like he doesn't have much to do. Like someone has asked him to go check on the crazy white lady doing laps in aisle 5.

'Do you go to work?' he says. It doesn't sound like a question.

'No,' she says. It doesn't sound like an answer.

'Work isn't nice if you don't sleep first.' He smiles. 'So how do you make money?'

'I'm already rich,' she says, walking away.

75

'What you looking for?' he asks, following, because he already knows. He has not looked straight at her once, like he is afraid to. Like someone he trusts has given him the rule about not talking to strangers. The same person who might have told him about looking both ways before he crosses the street. About not looking directly at the sun, lest it blind him. She wonders if they told him to lock his doors at night. Whether he knows you need that rule in Paradise.

'Raisins,' she says, and there is only the slightest catch in her throat.

'Aisle 8.' He is pleased that he remembers. 'Want me to go get them?'

'Yeah, one box.'

He comes back, licking spit and breathless. He ran the whole way. The proffered box is red with a milkmaid logo. It costs more than it should and she doesn't want to eat raisins, but she will buy them anyway. Because this is the last thing that Peter had asked her for, this tiny fucking box of raisins. This tiny box will join the others in the cupboard, similarly bagged in the smallest of the store's puke-coloured plastic bags. Maddeningly, Jack will only hand the bag to her after he has folded it over enough times that the box will not tumble out if she trips and falls. The bagged raisins mean that she has concluded her business there, that she has no excuse to stay.

The door rings as she goes.

Outside, the dark blurs the edges of her vision and she stands for a while in the stare of the blue-garbed geisha painted on the lit exterior wall of the store, unwilling to venture into that dark again, to brave the possibility that the robber is there, waiting for her.

The relative absence of sound tells her that something is wrong. The beach appears muted when the doors of the convenience store close behind her – there are about two dozen more people there than would be usual for this time of the morning, without the usual shock of sound that accompanies an egress on to a beach this busy. It isn't often that approximately twenty people populate the sand without a word, far less twenty with their arms linked, shoulders hunched against the wee-hours wind, walking in a row perpendicular to the shoreline. The row is made up of the 3 a.m. beach population – a couple of kindly prostitutes, the odd insomniac, a group of slightly drunk young tourists on their way back to the hotel from the disco, a few fishermen. The row stretches from the point at which the boardwalk disappears into soft, fine sand, past the dissolving sandcastles on the periphery of the beach, right into the silvery water. A few people in the linked line hold flashlights, saying nothing, combing the beach and flicking two-inch circles of light on parts where the sand dips unexpectedly or catches the feet of the fishermen and the whores in the line.

A short rust-haired Rasta runs slightly ahead, up and down the line in response to each gasp or muffled query.

'What's happened?' she asks him. She is thinking perhaps the security company was wrong, that there was indeed a robber, that he made his way down the beach behind her, that he has tried to rob somebody else and run away, that these people are now searching for him or what he has stolen. She swallows her panic and holds onto the Rasta's forearm, feels the fine dusting of salt on his leathery skin, notices that he is in beach shorts at three o'clock in the morning.

'Somebody kidnap de people baby,' he says. He takes in her smooth fair skin, her dirty silken robe half concealing pyjamas now too big for her. He looks at her harder.

'A baby?' She is stupefied. 'Who would kidnap a baby?

The line sweeps forward a few shuffling inches. The Rasta wrenches out of her grasp and is running in response to a small exclamation. Another false alarm. She must move out of the way, someone grumbles, or move with the line. She chooses the line. They are moving towards the rougher part of the beachscape, where clusters of boulders loom large and shadowless, marking the beginning of the luxury homes on Baxter's Beach, which cannot be safely accessed from this side, not at this time of morning.

'Move ya toes in the sand like this,' the Rasta demonstrates, 'in case there is a clue.'

'But if you disturb the clues, they are less helpful to the police,' chimes in one half of a middle-aged English couple. The man is bald and short with the florid face and round torso of a heavy drinker. His wife is taller than he is and grasps his arm tightly. They are both wearing the bright blue tropical printed clothing sold by the vendors on the beach – the man in a short-sleeved shirt printed with rum punches and the woman in a gaudy dress dotted with palm trees and dancing steel pans.

'Better not to mess things up,' she agrees. 'They can find more out if you leave things.'

'We ain't want no police,' a woman grumbles. 'Tourists always wanna call de police.'

A whore just joining the line clicks her teeth and strokes her hair back into a ponytail, as if the task at hand requires its restraint, her arms struggling under the weight of several gold bangles.

'Who bring she out here?' asks the whore, looking at the wife. The whore is wearing a gold Spandex catsuit that hugs her like a second skin, and the long leather strings that fastened her stilettos to her feet, gladiator style, now interlock to secure them like a scarf around her neck.

'Somebody kidnap my friend baby,' the Rasta explains to Mira. 'Somebody say they see a man with a baby crying out here on the beach this morning.'

'Are you sure? It could have been a man trying to get his baby back to sleep,' says the wife. 'My husband did it all the time, as a matter of fact, when Penelope was a baby.'

The whore borrows a flashlight and spots it on the wife, takes her in.

'Tell she to shut up, Tone,' she says.

'Look,' says the Rasta to the wife, 'we just got to focus on finding the baby, OK? We not too interested in police. If you helping, help, but don't be talking about the police all the time so, OK?'

The English couple are agog. The wife starts to pull her husband away – she wants no part of such a lawless approach to a search and rescue, even if they are trying to find a baby – but nobody else in the line seems particularly concerned about protecting clues for the police. She nods, shuts up and shuffles, releasing her husband's arm just long enough to link one of hers with Mira's.

The baby is found a little further up the beach, just before the luxury villas begin, stretched prone in the sand beside an empty, oarless canoe. A whisper crackles down the line and the Rasta runs forward, and then he is running back the way the line has come, with a little body covered in pastel cotton fluff in his arms. He is turning the baby over in his hands, shaking her gently, checking to see if she is still alive. When he passes her to a thick, dark-skinned woman, the woman's wails pierce the still of the morning. The links to the human chain disintegrate, the whores run behind the Rasta, others appear shocked and stand in the same spot where they were when the baby was found, moving their feet in the same way they were when they were still searching. Mira Whalen shudders as the wind whips. She is thinking of Beth and Sam and whether they are really safe with Rosa after all. She decides to call Rosa, tell her to bring them back home. She drops the arms of the people on either side of her and hurries away.

CHAPTER TEN

Lala

17 August 1984

Baby looks peaceful when they hand her to her mother.

She looks like she is just asleep, like she will wake up with the right whisper of her name, the right rub of her cheek, the right kiss on her forehead – but her cheeks are swollen, cold and clammy, her chest does not move up and down and she does not respond to Lala's fervent kisses on her forehead.

Lala takes her baby from Tone's outstretched arms and is shocked to find her floppy, like the best kind of doll, one of the ones whose limbs do not resist embraces, whose arms can be made to hug you back. Baby is neither stiff nor unyielding, not the way she'd imagined she would be. She is the same soft she was two hours before, when Lala had woken up to feed her and realised that she was not moving. Lala wraps Baby more securely in the blanket that shrouds her and hugs her close and pushes through the silent throng and goes to sit with Baby in a little wooden boat made black by the battering of salt and water and wind. She sits herself down on the rain-soaked wood and rocks her dead baby and pats her gently and looks at her and looks at the sea.

*

Wilma did not come when Baby was born, when the nurse had called to tell her that Lala had just delivered her great-granddaughter. She had not provided an hour or two's respite when Baby had squalled incessantly those first few days and Lala was exhausted, she was not a source of guidance on how to help Baby latch on to Lala's breast when Baby kept turning her head from her mother's milk. Wilma had not passed on to Lala the women's wisdom that she herself had been gifted – what bush to burn to keep duppies away from the new soul, which psalm to open above baby's head in her cradle to ensure that the Devil did not take her, what plant to bruise and soak in water she could sit in to soothe her stitched-together parts.

Wilma had not come then, but Wilma comes now, when she hears that her great-granddaughter is dead. Word travels fast in a small village and she is sliding her small feet into a pair of Chinese slippers within half an hour of hearing that Baby has been found. She comes and the crowd outside parts to the vision of Lala sitting still in that little black boat, staring at the sunrise, holding her dead baby, with the sea crashing and foaming in grief in the background. Wilma sits next to Lala, she puts her arms around her, she sobs, she puts her palm on Baby's forehead to see whether there might still be warmth there, whether perhaps this is all a big mistake.

'I sorry, Stella,' she says to Lala. 'I real sorry.'

This dead baby is still her great-granddaughter after all, she explains to two policemen later, even if she and Lala have not spoken properly since she married Adan, even if the girl would have avoided all this trouble if she hadn't gotten involved with that louse of a man in the first place. The death of this baby has something to do with him, she is sure of it. It is still her own-way granddaughter sitting there in the boat stiff as the tiny baby she is holding. She lost her own child in a way, says Wilma, she lost Lala's mother and raised Lala herself from the time she was a little one, so she also knows how terrible it is to lose your offspring. It is nothing she would wish on her worst enemy.

When Lala's torso does not yield to Wilma's embrace, Wilma sits shoulder to shoulder with her instead and in this way offers her granddaughter comfort. But Lala does not take this shoulder, she does not cry on it, she does not tell Wilma things she might think she should say, she does not tell Wilma anything at all. And when the morning sun is hot in the sky and the blouse of Wilma's dress is soaked with sweat and the policemen have taken the last of their pictures and measurements and the van from the funeral home honks from the beach, Lala surrenders Baby to two gloved men, gets out of the boat and leaves Wilma sitting there, alone.

CHAPTER ELEVEN

Wilma
17 August 1984

When Wilma Wilkinson is asked by the police, right there on Baxter's Beach, to tell them what she knows about her granddaughter, Lala, she decides to tell the story of conquerors. She does not tell the story about how her granddaughter ran off with a giant who beats her. She tells the police instead that Lala is from a line of land-owning women who do not need a man to survive. All she has, says Wilma, will be Lala's when she dies. It is import-ant for them to know, she says, that any tragedy that befalls Lala is one of her own making. Lala is not a woman without an inheritance.

The sun has by this time climbed to its zenith, and the beach is teeming with the squeals and laughter and towels and buckets and spades and books and jewel-coloured swimsuits of bathers oblivious to Baby's death. A few policemen still linger near the rocks where Baby was found, but other than that there is no sign that there has been a tragedy. The wind brings the buzz of faraway jet skis closer to the blue picnic bench where the police are talking to Wilma. They are tempted to take Wilma's words as the meaningless ramblings of a woman in distress so

84

they are not writing everything she says in their notebooks, which are nevertheless open and poised in readiness. They believe Wilma to be a woman overtaken by the heat beating her from the sky, the glare of unrelenting sunlight, the grief of the loss of an innocent little baby; it would be unmannerly to ask such a woman to understand that every word she says in this moment of grief will be recorded. It would be ruder still to actually record her.

Sergeant Beckles watches his men drag the canoe further inland so they can search it for clues. He has been called from his bed before dawn to investigate the discovery of a dead baby on the beach and he is therefore dressed in yesterday's slightly wrinkled slacks and jersey. He did not have the time to put on his jewellery before he jumped into his car and made his way here, and the lighter skin around his fingers where his rings usually are is visible as he rubs the sleep from his eyes with his knuckles. He watches the Rasta wait his turn to be questioned. He remembers how this Rasta had held the mother of the dead baby after she had finally surrendered the little body to the funeral home attendants. There was something about the way he held her that made him think of Sheba, who, he notices with dismay, is not on the beach.

Something does not sit right with him. There is an uneasiness in the lower part of his gut that tells him something is wrong, that there is more to this mystery than might meet the eye. It is this same gut instinct that he had planned to apply to the investigation of the murder of Peter Whalen, whose slightly faded good looks still stare at him from the cover of the daily newspaper, but he hasn't been

85

given the chance. The Whalen murder investigation has been unceremoniously removed from his responsibility and allocated to the new Criminal Investigations Department, to be solved with the assistance of Scotland Yard. It was no reflection on his capabilities, the assistant inspector assured him when he broke the news, but he had his orders. Peter Whalen had been a rich, well-connected British citizen. The newspapers mentioned the murder almost daily and everyone from the British High Commissioner to the remaining wealthy expats on Baxter's Beach and elsewhere was demanding it be solved, and quickly. After three weeks without much progress Beckles had been pulled from the investigation.

It still burned.

'Napoleon!' he orders now. 'I want statements from everybody – the mother, the Rasta and the granny, anybody who see anything.'

Sergeant Beckles had intended to speak to the dead child's mother himself, but after the funeral attendants took the body away, after she had been held by this Rasta, the baby's mother had fainted. He has ordered her off to be seen by a doctor for her distress. He watches the grandmother of the baby again.

'Yes, sir, Sergeant,' obliges Napoleon, and runs back to Wilma, still seated on the blue bench answering questions, tells her they will need a statement. He gives her the option of giving her statement now or back at the station.

Wilma chooses the station, and when they are settled inside it, Sergeant Beckles tells her to start again, don't mind if she already said something on the beach, say it again, they are interested in everything she has to say, not just what she saw when she got to the beach. They are interested, for instance, in why her granddaughter, a mere girl of eighteen, does not live with her, then, in this house she will inherit, but instead on the beach in a house such as that, with a man such as Adan, whom she calls a louse. Sergeant Beckles does not make the connection just then, that this Adan is the same one he himself had arrested several years before, on suspicion of involvement in a violent break-in. He does not realise that the Adan in Wilma's story is the man he was forced to set free when a jury accepted that a confession had been beaten out of him. He does not understand that this Adan has been channelling his energies into less confrontational thievery since then, and into the smuggling and sale of marijuana. No, for the moment Sergeant Beckles is focusing on Wilma's story about her granddaughter, the mother of the dead baby. It is for this reason that he is coaxing out of her anything and everything that might help them to better understand what happened to Baby and how its mother came to leave her grandmother's house to live with a man on the beach.

It is this coaxing that leads Wilma to share the story of the time her husband Carson molested her daughter Esme. By this time Carson is dead and it doesn't matter what Wilma says about him because those facts are not the focus of her story. In order, Wilma thinks, to explain how Lala came to leave her, she must first explain how she came to stay.

In a nest of dusty papers stirred by the rusty blades of a creaking ceiling fan, Wilma sits on the nearest tall chair (this is not a story she particularly likes to tell at all, far less seated below the person she is allowing into her weaknesses). And when a constable has provided another chair on which to place her bag and opened a window so that the stuffiness will not make her sneeze, she starts her story.

She explains how her own mother had tricked her into marrying Carson with the promise of land. Not just any land, Wilma explains to the policemen, but a patch of nearly an acre set on the side of a hill spiked with banana trees. Wilma was fourteen at the time, she says, and she had not understood the barter. To her it sounded like she would win twice. A husband would protect you like a father, Wilma's mother had explained, and she would get a big parcel of land which would make her very rich indeed, never mind that Carson was by then a man of thirty-four. Wilma would tell you that her mother had never said, to the day she died, what *she* had gotten out of the deal.

Wilma explains that she was one of a brood of nine siblings, three of whom had died before the age of eighteen. She remembers, prior to her marriage, sharing with the remaining five a soft drink in a Codd bottle stolen from a market stall and, as she licked the surface of the ball stoppering its mouth to give herself a taste of the dribble they had left behind, vowing to make something of herself so she could buy one of these drinks every single day if she wanted to. Wilma says that she married Carson, whom she had only met once, on a Thursday morning in the parish church and that she had made her own dress. She says that the thought of whether or not she loved Carson never even entered her mind when her mother suggested the marriage. It is this nonsense about love that causes all the federation, says Wilma. She had never had the time for such things, then or now. And then she has to be reminded, gently, that she is telling the story of how she came to have Lala.

1 October 1965

Wilma Wilkinson was a woman of order. So there was nothing unusual about her calmly cleaning her workroom while her daughter waited stoically on a three-legged stool, bits of blood and sick marbling the collar of her dress. Esme made periodic sharp and shuddery intakes of breath above the scrape and slap of Wilma's reorganisation, a signal Wilma appreciated, in the scheme of things. It meant that Esme remained alive.

A clean house is a clear head was what Wilma always said, and there was no doubt in her mind on seeing the state of Esme that this situation would require a clear head, so she had started studiously removing clutter the moment her daughter had been able to stammer out what was wrong with her, having burst through the door of Wilma's sewing room, and had continued while Esme sat and worried that at any minute Carson might come into the room behind her.

A Sunday school teacher had once told Wilma that the best way to deal with any bad situation, even a *really* bad one, was to make a mental list of things to thank God for. So while she tidied, she did: she thanked God that her only child was still alive, she thanked Him for the fact that He had seen fit to bless her with offspring, irrespective of the circumstances of Esme's conception, she thanked Him for the fact that this same child had made it back into the realm of her mother's protection, even if it was after the deed had already been done.

Wilma packed away the newly cut pattern for an empire-waist dress, rolling the brown-paper templates for bell sleeves and a gathered skirt carefully. For some cuts the brown paper was still attached to the fabric below it by common pins, and she did not want to lose any. Common pins were notoriously easy to lose and nearly impossible to find again. She stacked and re-stacked a rainbow array of folded fabric, fat little squares awaiting her refashioning into the garb of graduations and weddings and church services to come. She had stored each piece according to its colour and not its owner or the date each outfit was due or even according to the style of the magic she was to make with the contents. She found the stacks of fabric disconcerting if she did not fold and store them by colour, grouped into the many shades of every hue of the rainbow.

Before Esme rushed in, Wilma had been thinking about chicken.

Specifically, the two whose necks she would break the very same day, whose bones she would savour between her teeth by evening. She had been watching them clucking outside of her window before Esme threw herself against the door of her sewing room and splintered the wood around the handle. Wilma had been musing that the chickens ate corn and dug for worms like any other day, oblivious to the fact that it would be their last. So engrossed was she in this thought about the chickens that she had not heard when the back door closed, had not caught the frantic thunder of her daughter's sprint across the wooden floor outside the sewing-room door before she burst in, had known nothing until the door slammed against the partition, almost causing her dress form to collapse in the process. She must have started cutting Molly Marshall's dress for Christmas with an unusual diligence, she had thought, that must have been why she hadn't heard anything, that must have been why she hadn't felt anything move in her spirit while Esme was being raped. Esme was her daughter, after all, Wilma had thought, she was supposed to have a sixth sense that warned her if anyone was doing her harm. Sixth senses should not depend on whether you wanted this daughter or not. Sixth senses were a matter of kin and not of liking.

Molly Marshall's dress was an unusual pattern for her, something Wilma had had to think hard about to ensure she got the fit just right. Wilma had not much liked Molly Marshall; she was one of those women prone to fainting, claiming to be overcome by everything from the smell of sheep shit to the news of the collapse of the West Indies Federation. Wilma did not trust such women; they tended to attract calamity that impacted everyone around them. That morning of the rape, says Wilma, was the morning she decided that she would never make a dress for Molly Marshall ever again.

Wilma Wilkinson swears to this day that Esme did not scream or say a word when Carson attacked her. She had the ears of a dog then, protests Wilma, she had honed her hearing listening to pins drop – she would have heard the girl if she'd made any noise at all. Wilma says that that morning the first she knew of the disaster was when she heard the sewing room door splay open a few seconds before her daughter appeared beside her cutting table like an apparition, clothes torn off her, face and arms scratched, a huge knot on her forehead, another she would find later at the back of her head, like an egg in a nest of flying frizzy hair.

Carson was no bodybuilder, but he was a big man, a giant who carried his weight in his waist, a full forty-five inches around according to the pencil marks on one of the little flashcards in Wilma's sewing box. His waist, Wilma knew, was the barometer of her husband's strength, the key to his power, and as it was, it was more than enough to keep a slight teenager pinned beneath him. Make no mistake, says Wilma, she did not doubt Esme about what had happened, not for a minute. She had failed, she knew, to keep Carson contained. Locking the child in the little outhouse each night had not been enough.

Only when the worktop was clear of sewing detritus did Wilma turn to tend to Esme. In the background, above the clucking of the chickens, she heard Carson bathing, brushing his teeth, combing his hair, opening the tin of Germolene she kept in the little cupboard above the bathroom sink and applying it to scratches the length of his face.

She couldn't go into their bedroom and wrench the little tube of plaster-pink antiseptic cream from him to attend Esme's bruises, not when he had tainted it with his. So instead she fetched a little bottle of rubbing alcohol from a shelf in her sewing room, the same one she used to soak a wad of cotton and hold to her thumb when she was pricked by a pin or a needle as she worked. 'This will sting,' observed Wilma, and it did. She spent a few seconds applying it to Esme's bruises, after smoothing the soft wool of her daughter's hair out of her eyes and back into some semblance of order, after guiding her out of her shredded skirt. She watched her wince when she applied the alcohol and she hated Carson for using the cream.

She replaced the alcohol on the shelf, then slicked her hands with castor oil, lifted them to Esme's hair and started to massage her head, taking special care not to touch her forehead, searching softly for the sore lump at the back of her scalp. She found it, something to be worked around in future when she tried to settle on her pillow at night, something to be approached sideways with a warm cloth when she bathed, something to be ignored in conversation.

'It don't matter,' said Wilma, when the tenderness of the massage made her daughter cry. 'The hurt mean it healing.'

Wilma had believed then that her Esme was too tired to respond, too deflated by what had befallen her to confirm that the hurt was a sign of hope, of recovery and therefore a grace to be thankful for. It was a tiredness Wilma also gave thanks for because it meant that her one child would not ask her why did she have to leave her in a little wooden outhouse in the backyard at night that still stank of the shit of generations of Carson's family. It was a tiredness that meant Esme could not detail how her own father had shoved her down in the yard in broad daylight, how he had damaged her. It was a tiredness that overcame Esme's tendency to talk, to speak up, to ask questions that Wilma did not wish to answer.

The sewing room was quiet. The chickens clucked joyfully, as if suddenly aware that their lives had been spared. A number of safety pins, attached end to end, trailed from the collar of Wilma's simple cotton dress and danced as she rubbed oil into Esme's hair, limbs, face and back. Above her work table was a wedding picture: Wilma in the arched doorway of St. Saviour's Anglican church, standing dwarfed next to Carson in a patterned dress and matching hat, the intricacy of the design swallowed by her new husband's shadow. She had often wondered whether Esme had thought then that her mother looked like a little girl, whether the angle of her right arm as she cradled a homemade bunch of flowers had reminded Esme of the wishbone of a chicken, whether Esme thought too, as Wilma did, that in the wedding picture she had looked happy, like she thought she had won something.

Wilma saw Esme looking at the photo as she kneaded, wanted to explain to her that she was the same age as Esme when the grainy picture had been taken, hoped that Esme would understand that this, *this* was exactly what she had been trying to protect her from when she started making a bed for her in the outbuilding, felt and swallowed the need to explain to Esme what it had taken she herself so long to understand about Carson. But Wilma had not told that story then – Wilma had been too busy steeling her spine.

'Mammy,' Esme had started to whimper, holding on to her mother's hand when it found the bleeding knot at the back of her head. 'Mammy . . . Mammy . . .'

At that moment, explains Wilma, she recalled her own daughter's apparent need to wade in the deep waters of emotions she had no time for. At that moment, says Wilma, she was taken back to the minute the midwife had placed a squalling baby into her bony arms and asked her to name her baby girl. It might have been the delirium of birthing that had made her fourteen-year-old-self smile, thought Wilma, and whisper, 'It's me!' because in this new baby she had seen her own face, had sensed a brighter, better version of herself and the hope of the realisation of all the things she hadn't known she wanted to be.

It might have been the business of clearing away the evidence of birthing that had caused the midwife to hear 'Esme' when she asked Wilma to name her child. The midwife paused to say how beautiful a name it was, how fitting for this beautiful new baby. It might have been Wilma's need to believe that the child was indeed beautiful that had caused her to keep the name, to labour over its spelling as she recited it to the priest in the parish church a few weeks later while he blessed the baby with holy water. But with Esme whimpering before her now, Wilma suddenly understood how foolish she had been to label her daughter's life with a virtue so fickle as beauty.

'All that fussing don't make no sense,' she warned her. 'What's done is done.'

'Mammy, Mammy, Mammy . . .'

Wilma went wooden when Esme held onto her. The

voice that had refused to warn her when Esme was being raped remained silent as she looked back out through the window, past the chickens, to where the banana trees met the road and the bus stop where the Rocklyn bus trundled past with its cargo of labourers and hawkers and mauby sellers made drowsy by the breeze billowing through the open sides. She was already thinking about which story she would tell of what happened to Esme if it ever got out.

'Listen to me, Es,' said Wilma, 'listen good. Don't tell nobody 'bout this, you hear?'

The house held its breath – the chickens stopped their clucking, the tap in the bathroom turned off and the breeze barely blew through the open window. Wilma, and the world, waited for Esme's answer.

'You hear?'

Esme could not speak, so she nodded, because it seemed to be what Wilma wanted her to do.

'I have a new skirt,' said Wilma, 'just finished this morning. For you.'

Wilma could have guessed that Esme did not want her to leave to get the skirt. She should have known that if she left, the feel of hands in her hair would stop, and Esme did not want it to stop. She should have understood that if she left her daughter there to fetch a skirt that barely fitted her, she would be out of her sight and Esme would be more aware than ever of the awful singing that had recommenced from the bathroom. She should have figured that Esme wanted to sit and have her scalp kneaded better by her mother, her hair coaxed into behaviour so that a wild wind landing on her scalp would find it unwilling. But she didn't acquiesce when her daughter held on to her hands, and willed her to stay.

'Stop now,' she said, shaking off Esme's grasp. 'I am going to take you by your Auntie Earlie.'

Wilma could not have understood then that her refusal to stay, at this moment, was what cracked a little fissure of hurt wide open in Esme's mind. She did not guess that this, and not the nights in the outhouse, would be what her daughter would hold against her in future.

'And even when he rape me,' Esme would accuse her in later years, 'you di'nt stay and comfort me, you di'nt stay!'

Wilma went to get the skirt and came back with something with a waist she could not fasten. It would have to do, she said, balling an extra skirt and two blouses into a bag. Carson started singing a hymn from the shower. Wilma straightened the corner of her sewing table so it hit the right spot on the tile, took off her sewing apron and slipped on her outdoor shoes.

It was at that moment that Esme realised, against the soundtrack of Carson's singing, that *he* was the one who would stay.

Almost ten months later, Auntie Earlie sent Esme back home with Lala.

17 August 1984

Wilma's eyes mist over in the hush of the police station, where the policemen have been engrossed in her chronicle and Sergeant Beckles himself has ambled over to perch on the corner of a rusting metal desk, crossing his hands at the wrists and setting them on his knee to listen to a little woman, aged more by life than by years, tell her story.

She assumes it is a curse, says Wilma, this way the Wilkinson women have with men, this ability to so bewitch a man that he becomes besotted. A grown man cannot help himself, she explains, in the presence of a young Wilkinson girl. This is the way it has been for generations. It is not the man's fault, says Wilma, there is nothing he can do about it. It was this way with her mother before her, her daughter and granddaughter after her. It was this way with her. If she had to trace her lineage back, beyond the ancestors the Black Power people find, she imagines that she would find Delilah, the woman who was the downfall of Samson. Some Sundays, says Wilma, she feels for Delilah just a little bit. It must not be easy to be pursued by a man like Samson. Selling him for silver was probably the only way for Delilah to get rid of him once he set eyes on her. Equally, it must not have been easy for Samson to find himself in helpless pursuit. Most Sundays, says Wilma, she prays for the Samsons of the world.

Wilma doesn't catch the looks the constables are passing; she can't see through the tears that cloud her vision or hear anything but the story she is telling them. Esme had that curse, says Wilma, and, though God knows she tried, Lala came along with it too. There ain't nothing about the girl that'll make you call her a looker, says Wilma, but the men on the street used to watch her like she was the last drop of water in the land of thirsty. A man killed her mother, and Esme died and left that girl and Wilma took her and raised her like her own, raised her to keep her eyes down and her dress long and her breasts covered and men *still* looked. Lala started sneaking out to meet this Adan when she was only fifteen years old, Wilma tells the policemen. What is a good grandmother to do? When she set eyes on this Adan she knew he was bad news, but Lala had that Wilkinson way and the man couldn't leave her alone. She knew that there would come a day when Adan would wish he had never met Lala. She just hadn't bargained, says Wilma, on that day coming so soon.

The constables are scribbling. They want to know more about Lala and about the last time Wilma saw Baby alive. She has never seen Baby, says Wilma, she never laid eyes on her while she was alive.

'How you mean, "never"?' questions Beckles, incredulous. 'Not even once?'

'Not once,' Wilma confirms, and the tears dribble down her cheeks. 'I told Stella I would have nothing more to do with her if she went to live with that man. I told her not to come back once she set her feet outside my door.' She nods. 'She went anyway.'

Sergeant Beckles is touched by Wilma's account of her daughter being one of these women who can bewitch a man. He himself has fallen victim to such a woman, a woman who inhabits his dreams while his wife snores beside him. A woman called Sheba whom his good sense should not permit him to love. He understands. He calls Napoleon aside. He is going to visit this woman's husband, he tells him. He is going to find out what drove this man away from his wife and young child so that he was nowhere to be found when this child was kidnapped, that he was not part of the search party when Baby was found. He is going to see why Wilma calls this man a louse. Short of work, what could have made this man leave the two of them in that little shack alone with Baby so young?

Sergeant Beckles tells the constable to start looking for this Adan and get back to him.

He is interested, he says, in Adan's side of the story.

CHAPTER TWELVE

Lala
17 August 1984

Later that morning, Lala is grieving, puffy-eyed, at home, when she is visited by a short yellow policeman. Adan had anticipated this visit, and before he had sprinted back down the beach towards the tunnels to hide, he had held her head between his palms and barked at her about how she should respond, not even releasing her face long enough to wipe the wet from his own face. Do not tidy the room, he has told her, a grieving woman cannot keep a clean house. Do not take too long to answer their questions, but keep the answers short so they are easier to remember. As much as is possible, he has warned her, look them in the eye so they will not think you are lying, but do not stare, especially if the policeman who comes is a man. By the time the yellow policeman actually knocks, Adan is, she guesses, safely ensconced back in the tunnels, in a spot that neither he nor Tone has shared with her yet. Perhaps the same place he has been hiding since Baby was born. She looks around the room one more time, shaking her head when her eyes want to linger on a little Moses basket made of rushes that she had collected from the Salvation Army and then used to hold Baby's cloth nappies and clothing. Her hands are shaking when she reaches for the door handle, her fingers stumble when she tries to release the bolt.

After the policeman cautions her, almost apologetically, because he has been trained to do so, and not because he believes that she has anything at all to do with her daughter's death, Lala tells him what she thinks might have happened. He understands, he tells her, that she isn't sure, that her daughter's death is as much a mystery to her as it is to the police; just tell him as much as she can remember.

So she does. And when she is done, he asks her the things he thinks she should also remember, the things she should have thought to tell him. Things like what time it was when she realised Baby was missing, things like whether she had heard or seen anything strange the night before. The policeman is accompanied by a woman who says she is from the Child Care Board. She has to make a report, says the woman, any time a child dies in suspicious circumstances. It takes Lala a while to understand that the child who died in suspicious circumstances is Baby, that a report is being written about the death of her daughter. It is nothing to worry about, says this woman, but she also has a few questions. This woman is tall, so tall that it almost seems like she has to stoop to enter the house. Her smile reminds Lala of a necessary parting of lips, rather than a pleasantry.

The woman does not extend her condolences or ask whether Lala slept well; she asks other questions. She asks whether Lala breastfed Baby and does not appear worried when she says she thinks so, she often tried. She asks how long the baby slept each night and who would feed her, at night when she woke up, Lala or Adan. She asks how many times per day Lala bathed her, how many times a night she changed her diaper. She asks if Baby ever made Lala angry, if she ever responded to that anger by smacking her. Even once. Lala tries to remember the answers the best she can – details like that are not particularly fuzzy, because in her mind they do not have to do with Baby's death, with the fact her daughter is dead – but because she does not know why she is being asked these things, she worries about the policeman's motives and the woman's tone. She worries whether, should she answer with the first response that comes to mind, she will give them clues to other questions they should ask her, questions whose answers she has not yet rehearsed, questions that will lead them to answers that must remain hidden.

For this reason, and this reason only, she thinks long and hard before answering any of the questions they ask. For this reason only she matches the policeman's expressionless stare while they wait for her answers, watching her turn the black velvet collar of her one good dress over and under and over again with trembling fingers. The woman does not appear sympathetic enough to ask her if she understands clearly, if she wants the questions repeated again.

When they are done, the woman lets herself out and the policeman asks more questions. Does she know anyone who would want to harm her baby? Anyone who would want to harm her? When exactly did she realise that Baby was not beside her on the bed? And where, he asks, was her husband?

The story flows out of Lala's lips without stumbling.

Her husband was away, she says, fishing with friends. Her husband has been away since before Baby was born. The policeman writes it down. And if he thinks her voice too steady for a woman who has lost her only child, her hands too skittish to suggest innocence, or that her eyes fail to sit properly on his, he doesn't say so. He takes her statement in a cursive that he forms deliberately, he calls her ma'am, he asks her if she'd like to stop for a drink of water and says yes when she offers him one as well.

When he finally closes his small plastic-backed notebook and replaces it in his pocket, Lala accompanies him to the door and watches him walk down the steps. She smiles when he looks back at her, smiles again when his feet find the shifty sandy soil at last, and he gives her a final wave, a deferential tip of his hat, before he disappears between the bow-legged squat of the farthest pair of coconut trees.

Lala waits for a full minute to see whether he will return before taking the steps herself, three at a time, almost buckling into a broken shin on the last few. It is only when she reaches the sand that she realises she is sobbing, that she is looking around her wildly, like she knows someone might be watching her. She gathers her composure and looks around more slowly, but the only sound is the scrape and drag of the fishermen launching a boat into the water. They are too far away to be seen or to see her and Lala flies to the left rear stilt on which the house sags towards the sea. There is an arrangement of rocks there but she is too tired to recall whether they are in the order in which she last placed them. She starts digging with her hands, so fast that the sandy soil splatters up into her face, pocks her lips, salts her hair.

It will not take them long to figure out what really happened, thinks Lala, it will not take them long to come back to arrest her. She has to be gone by then.

When she had first buried this tin, it was because she had harboured dreams of a holiday abroad, of saving enough to pay for a visa and a ticket and a place to stay and putting on a good dress and going to the airport and catching BWIA and going to America. The tin was emptied of the Christmas biscuits she'd bought and she'd started to fill it with fives and tens and twenties out of the US dollars she was paid by the tourists, the tips she was gifted for her neat plaits and clean partings and making her clients' hair look like Bo Derek's in *10*. The tin was what her thoughts turned to whenever she wanted something that seemed out of reach – a black velvet jumpsuit with shoulder pads and gold sequins for Old Year's dancing, for instance, or a little motor car so she and Adan could drive around the island on Sunday evenings and buy ice cream and *toot toot* at Wilma when they saw her at the bus stop. Later, when she was pregnant, that tin had held a dream of a beautiful cradle for Baby, the means to call a carpenter and tell him to come and fix the leaky house so her new baby would never get wet when it rained, like she and Adan sometimes did. Although she'd hardly ever actually followed through to buy whatever it was she wanted, that tin meant that the means were always there, if she was ever presented with a justifiable emergency or a goal truly worth the expenditure.

But the tin is lighter than it should be when she finally lifts it free of the soil.

When she opens it, the tin is empty.

Lala makes her way back up the stairs with unseeing eyes, holding the tin in her left hand, groping the wood for guidance as she ascends, stopping to remove the bright red lid every few steps up the precarious gradient to see whether there really isn't anything in there, whether the pictures of a grand English garden and a horse and carriage and a liveried footman on the lid of the biscuit tin really give way to nothing at all. She tells herself a moment later that she must be blind, that it must be this blindness that has fooled her into thinking the tin is empty. It must be this blindness that also refuses to reveal the little money in the hem of her wedding dress, the few dollars she rolled in a bag and sequestered in the third spring her hand reaches from the hole on the left side of the mattress, the coins in the little paper bag shoved into that hole in the floor behind the closet. It must be a sudden blindness, because it cannot be that the money is not there. Or there. Or *there*.

Lala waits for Adan to come back, clutching the empty tin, wearing one of Wilma's stolen dresses, with one of Baby's pink frilly panties in her pocket. She has vowed to keep something of Baby's on her every day for the rest of her life, but that does not temper her decision to kill Adan the moment he walks through the door. It is his fault that their baby is dead, it is his fault that she is hurting, and now it is his fault that she cannot escape, that the money she was saving appears to be all gone. The how of it never enters her mind – how *exactly* will she deprive her giant of a husband of his life? She is not a small woman, she knows she is solid, but she is still no match for a physique so finely honed by tough street living, by hours of practice on a tiny unicycle, by countless sprints to escape the long arm of the law.

She gets up, goes to the window above the sink, grasps a few fine hairs at the front of her scalp and starts to braid her hair, over and under, over and under, until she has two fat cornrows on either side of her head that hide her bald spots, the bare patches of scalp where the hair that Adan once pulled out does not grow back. She has rubbed these patches with the pounded pulp of aloes, with warm coconut oil, with a poultice made of grated ginger and glycerine. The hair still does not grow back. Today she folds a wad of toilet paper into a fat square after soaking it in garlic tea and aloes and grits her teeth and opens her shirt and places it over her nipple. There was a time when she would discover a bruise or a swelling or a flap of broken skin she did not remember getting and it would hurt her all over again. This is not the thing she is feeling now. What she feels now is relief. This is the day she accepts that she will either kill Adan or die trying. And with this acceptance comes a type of calm, a calm that frees her: she does not go and start to make breakfast so he can eat if he comes back home from his hideout, she does not make the bed or tidy the bedroom, she does not hide the knife by the sink in the event that he is in a temper.

When his footsteps sound at the bottom of the stairs, the volume of his whistling amplified by lungs pumped full of crisp salt air, she approaches the door slowly, thinking of Baby. She reaches for the handle. It is better, she thinks, to meet him at the top of the stairs, before he has the chance to come inside and trap her in this small room. At the top of the stairs, if they fight, he can fall from a great height.

She is thinking thoughts like these, thoughts of killing this man she married, when the door rattles and someone other than Adan steps in, flashing a badge at her.

This policeman is a short black man built broad and soft by a well-meaning wife. His bald head shines in the manner of one that no longer even requires shaving. He looks as if he once had a jolly disposition, but too much exposure to the underbelly of life has left him only slightly bemused and matter-of-fact in the face of tragedy. His one condescension to style appears to be his jewellery – a heavy gold home-made link around his neck, assorted bits at his wrists and fingers, a tiny glinting bauble at the top of his right ear. It is this bauble that Lala fixes her eyes on while he talks, which he does in the nasal whine of children after inhaling the helium in balloons, a whine under which a laugh, the type that has nothing to do with humour, lies waiting.

'Sergeant Beckles, ma'am,' he says without greeting, when she is startled by the sight of him in the doorway. 'Now tell me again where you was when you realise the baby was missing?'

CHAPTER THIRTEEN

Lala
17 August 1984

These is the reasons why you baby dead:

1. The first baby, the one you throw away when you was
   still by Wilma because it didn't seem like a good idea to
   have it and it didn't seem real until after you swallow
   the pills and something lumpy fell out and you flush it
   and Adan, who buy the pills off a pharmacist who sell
   people every kind of medication even without a prescription, say you shouldn't worry because it probably
   only a few weeks growing and not a real baby at all but
   that didn't help and getting rid of a baby you don't
   want must most certainly be punishable by losing a
   baby you *do* want because God say you do not get to
   play God.
2. Being rude to Wilma when you was there because she
   is still your grandmother after all, and she take you in
   and raise you up after your mother die, even if she beat
   you if Carson look too hard, even if you couldn't have
   friends over or go to parties or fairs or have a Walkman
   or listen to Soca, because Wilma, for her one part, is
   not a bad person and she still take you in even if you

had to sleep in the little old outhouse in the yard, just like your mother did, while she and Carson sleep in the stone house, even if sometimes at night you used to look out the window and see her there spotting a flashlight in the direction of the outhouse just to make sure you were not in there with Carson or sneaking out to look for another man.

3. Stealing. Fruits from the trays of the vendors in the market, money from Wilma's purse when she let you in the house, Wilma's make-up and creams, Adan's place as the breadwinner of the household and the assorted hearts of several men.

4. Because, despite your best efforts, you are just like your mother.

CHAPTER FOURTEEN

Lala
17 August 1984

At the bottom of the steps to Adan's house is a patch of coconut trees, big trees with ricketed trunks that curve away from each other and find their way back to themselves at the bases of skirts made of fronds. These are not the trees of postcards, not the type you tie your hammock to and lay under with a good book and a rum punch. These trees throw shadows with claws onto the steps and sometimes, when the wind is high, they throw coconuts you have to dodge for fear they could kill you. The fronds of these trees are home to centipedes that fall out while dreaming and land writhing on the steps to Adan's house. When they land, these centipedes do not climb the remaining stairs to the house; they are too wise to head for the inside of this dwelling. Instead, they speed back towards the coconut patch, hoping that Adan does not see them first. The carcasses of the ones he has found litter the steps and he has instructed Lala not to sweep the skeletons up, so that they can be a warning to any of their kin bold enough to approach the inside of his house, where his cutlass sits waiting beside their bed. It is the same cutlass he used to cut coconuts for her while she was pregnant, the one he holds to her neck on bad days, when she could decapitate herself by the simple act of exhalation. Lala remembers how, while pregnant, she had marvelled that Adan had never cut himself with this cutlass while climbing these coconut trees, how when he had jumped out of the tree and back to the ground and scalped a nut to present her with the cool, slightly milky sweet water, his velvet skin was never scraped or swollen. He had never been stung while in the tree. Not even once. You could assume that a man is not really a bad man, thinks Lala, when even nature never sees it fit to punish him.

It is near the perimeter of this patch of trees that Lala watches Sergeant Beckles stoop when he finishes interviewing her. When he straightens again, he is holding a little yellow bootie in his hand. This bootie is spattered with dirty sand but it is clearly a yellow bootie and it clearly matches the dress Baby was wearing when she was found. Lala jerks her head from the window, flattens her back against the inside of the house, does not dare to breathe. She cannot see the sergeant, but she knows that he is looking back at the house, at the very window from which she watched him leave. She knows that he is wondering if he should broach the steps again, ask her a few more questions, remind her that she may need to come down to the station to give a statement. But when she does not hear the door again, when there is no knock to signal that he has come back to question her further, she does not feel relief. She feels, more than ever, that this investigation will not end well for her, that everything is falling apart, that the only thing she can do is leave.

But where can she run? And *how*?

That whole day Lala does not venture out to braid hair. She waits for Adan. She waits until nightfall, when the beach is blanketed in dark velvet and the sky is spattered with rhinestones that glint at her through the window. She waits and she waits and she waits and Adan does not come home and Lala finally falls into a sleep full of dreams in which, inexplicably, she loves him, instead of killing him, in which he escorts her into the carriage on the cover of the money tin and where, inside that carriage, Baby is alive and cooing in her bassinet. She dreams dreams in which Baby's hunger is sated by her heavy, hurting breasts.

But then she wakes up and realises that Adan still has not come home and she is no longer pregnant or nursing and that Baby is still dead. She realises that today could be the day Sergeant Beckles comes back to arrest her, that right now they could be watching her under cover of the coconut trees, and Adan is still nowhere to be found.

Lala suddenly cannot stand the sight of the coconut trees. It is a grey and windy day and missiles from the tree strike violently as she stands by the window, crashing into the side of the house with thunderous cracks, telling her that it is repulsed by its own fruit. Adan has always hated coconuts and had arranged, prior to Baby's birth, to sell what Lala did not devour to Coyote, who hustles them to tourists, tourists who remain delighted by the tropical colours of the little neon straws he sticks inside the soft jelly at the top of the nut.

This morning, when she sees the trees, she shuts the

window and opens the door and peeps outside. She imagines that her daughter has not died, that this might all be a bad dream, the obeah work of one of the many women who want Adan. She imagines that if she closes her eyes and opens them again she will wake up and Baby will be on the beach in her bassinet, amazed by her own fingers, waiting to accompany her mother to plait heads on the beach.

But although Lala closes her eyes and counts to ten, although she says a prayer for a peaceful mind and the protection of the angels and enough of a miracle to make this only a nightmare, Baby is still dead when she opens her eyes, when the last of the prayers leave her lips. Baby is still dead, but the trees, still flinging their fruit, are not.

She resolves, in anger, to cut them down herself. Right now. While they are taking aim at her house, while the wind is whipping their leaves around. Right now.

She has returned inside to look for the cutlass when the door opens and Adan comes in, and with the sight of him, his swollen eyes and the anguish still twisting his lips, comes the knowledge that cutting down the trees will not bring Baby back. Killing Adan will not bring her back. Nothing will bring her back.

She wants to ask him about her money, about where he's been hiding, she wants to tell him about the policeman and the questions he asked her, she wants to tell him that they must run, but what comes out instead is her relief at his return, her desire for his comfort, her need to go back to the time before Baby died, to stay there.

'You still taking the coconuts for Coyote, Adan?'

Adan hasn't said a word, but is now stretched out on the wrought-iron chair where he dozes sitting up. This is something he is accustomed to doing when he is angry – not coming to bed, shedding his clothes at the door of the house and sitting and sleeping in the wrought-iron chair when she is already curled up on their bed.

'I ain't see the cart lately,' he mumbles. 'I don't think it working.'

'You could still get a few dollars for the ones outside. You check by the house?'

Adan's voice loses the quiet rasp of weeping and hurts her ears.

'You think Coyote want coconuts if the fucking cart ain't working?'

Coyote's cart is painted red, gold and green. In an alcove just beneath the handle of the cart he stores a small boom box and a stack of cassette tapes of Culture, Peter Tosh and Jackie Opel. Coyote plays his tapes when he is waiting for people to order coconuts. His music calms him, he says. He has several diagonal slashes across his inner left forearm to remind him of what happens when he cuts coconuts while agitated. When he is approached for a sale, he presses pause and the little cassette player whirs to a stop. Lala once watched a white tourist, blistered red and blissfully happy, order some Bob Marley with his coconuts.

'I don't play no kiss-me-crutch Bob Marley, but anyway, it ain't music I selling,' Coyote had said then, and he cut the coconut so savagely that the tourist was alarmed and Lala was sure he would finally sever his hand.

Coyote cannot stand Bob Marley. It is one of the things he argues about in the rum shop, over ESA Field white rum – this fascination with Bob Marley. Coyote often tells the men in the rum shop the tale of the tourist asking for Bob Marley music. Depending on how many drinks he has had, he received one or all of the slashes on his left arm on the day this tourist asked him this question. Bob Marley wasn't no real reggae star, he spits with a steups, Peter Tosh was real reggae. It is the way of the world that Tosh never get the bligh that Marley did. Most often, nobody in the rum shop takes up the other side of the argument, and Coyote drinks himself into a stupor and refuses to engage with anyone on any other topic. For weeks on end after similar episodes, he blasts Peter Tosh from his little transistor as he trundles it along. On such occasions he refuses to turn it off while tourists are ordering so that they have to shout 'Two coconuts!' at him above 'Equal Rights'. His intolerance for Bob Marley requests is now the sort of legend that even children know.

Adan sucks his teeth from the chair. The day before Baby was born, he had relieved the tree of some of the coconuts. Then they had planned to use the money they got from Coyote to buy Baby's layette for the hospital. Now he can tell that Lala is thinking of ways to pay for her funeral. If he does not take the coconuts to Coyote soon they will dry out and become useless for selling cool drinks to tourists and good only for skinning and grating and making coconut bread and conkies – labour reserved for locals, who have trees of their own. Still, he resents being reminded.

116

'Coconuts can't pay for a funeral,' he observes, 'so stop harassing me about rasshole coconuts.'

'If I still had the money in my tin . . .' she starts.

Adan sighs. 'Wasn't no money in that tin, no *real* rasshole money!'

'What you do with my money, Adan?'

'Oooh! *Your* money, *your* money, Lala? We married, you living in my house but it is *your* money?'

'We need that money, Adan,' says Lala quietly, eyes still on the coconuts. 'I need my money.'

She tells him about the dark policeman, the questions he'd asked her, the laugh in his voice that never made it to his lips in a smile. She tells Adan that this policeman asked her where he was, said that he wanted to talk to him. She tells Adan that she is scared. And he listens with his eyes closed, as if he really just wants to go back to sleep.

'He ain't gonna figure out you make Baby dead,' says Adan. 'The police not that smart.'

'*I* make her? Me one?'

His eyes open and flash warnings of fates so dire that she doesn't bother to finish, swallows the lump in her throat instead, realises a moment later that it has settled into a knot at the pit of her stomach.

'You remember what to say when he ask for me?'

'I tell them you was away fishing with some friends. I tell them we ain't manage to contact you yet.'

He nods because she remembered, because she has said exactly what she was supposed to say.

'It ain't safe here, Adan, we have to leave. We have to go. We—'

'We ain't going nowhere, Lala. We just have to be quiet until everything settle down. You too frighten. Too coward.'

Adan stands, stretches, rubs his fists over his face, as if she is stopping him from sleeping, as if he must now stay awake only because she is bothering him, because she refuses to let a tired man rest. He frowns, as if she has brought him nothing but trouble. Is she not the one who turned up outside the big house on Baxter's Beach and buzzed the gate? Is she not the reason that white lady remembers him? Is she not the same one who caused Baby to fall? He retrieves his vest from the floor by the door and starts to brush his teeth in the little sink under the window at the front of the room, where a red heliconia Lala has placed in an enamel teacup on the lip of the window is now as withered and decrepit as the house itself.

'Besides,' says Adan, and his face flinches with the frustration of remembered spite, 'I got business to finish first.'

'Adan, please, just—'

'Shut up, woman!'

But she can't shut up.

'I could go then, if you want to stay here. I . . . I could go and you could come later.'

'You ain't going nowhere, Lala, you got money to go somewhere?'

'I had money, Adan. You know I had money. I want back my money, Adan. What you do with my money?'

Adan's laughter erupts without warning, mouth wide open, belching mint-flavoured lava. He walks over to her

118

right side, still brushing his white, white teeth with his naked left hand in between his laughter.

'You want back you money?' he sing-songs through cotton, taking her right hand. 'You want back you money?'

Lala refuses to look at him. Her left arm has started to tremble, and she gently curls its fist around the side of her skirt. She is now looking at an aeroplane through the window, just lifting itself into the sky above the coconut trees, en route to another world entirely. In this other world, Lala imagines, coconut trees do not exist, neither do centipedes, nor men who hold your right hand so tightly you could wet yourself.

'Gimme back my money, Adan,' she insists, in a little voice she does not recognise. Her voice is not the roar it started out as in her head. 'Please, Adan, gimme it back, Adan!'

There is a physical state beyond pain, a sort of numbness that allows Lala to remain standing while the flesh and bones of her right hand are forced upwards, so that her wrist looks like it is wrapped in bracelets of warm red. In her mind her bones break with the explosive *pop-pop* of fireworks. Maybe they do, maybe they don't, but at first she is screaming, and then she is in such pain that she is not.

'Bitch,' says Adan, twisting her by the palm so that she spins on her heel and begins to fall to her knees by the sink. 'Tell me what you gonna do if I don't.'

CHAPTER FIFTEEN

Adan
7 November 1970

To tell the story of Adan Primus you'd have to tell the story of a Burger Bee snack box on a Friday afternoon. Adan is ten at the time of this story, and he is already growing into someone a friend should be afraid of just the same as a stranger. He is not only growing tall, but wide, and the short khaki pants of his school uniform look comical on him, like someone stuffed a man into a schoolboy's uniform. It is however not just the fact of Adan's impressive physical build that is worthy of caution, it is the sinister undertone to his actions that would worry anyone who takes the time to watch him.

Adan is a child for whom the suffering of a foe he beats in a fight is a mere fascination. He does not need to be provoked to use his prowess to do harm, this Adan, he often uses it just to see what will happen. When he pelts the neighbourhood cats with rocks until they shriek and go running, when he seeks to reassure those same cats as they avoid him for weeks at a time after, when he plies them with bits of mouldy cheese and drops of stolen milk so that they come closer to him, only to hold them and squeeze their necks until they choke, when he laughs and bobs and weaves to avoid the ire of their unsheathed claws, it is hard for any onlooker to view his actions as just a child's natural curiosity.

'You stop that shite right now, Adan Primus!' shrieks Ms Nancy, from the safety of her kitchen window, when the yowls of the cats make her come running. Ms Nancy shakes her head and reminds herself not to let her children fraternise with this Adan, no matter how many times he broaches her front yard, loudly bouncing a ball or exclaiming as he pitches marbles on the smooth concrete, baiting her children just like the blasted cats. Ms Nancy has tried to warn people about this Adan, especially her neighbour Preta, under whose doting attention Adan's flaws of character take root and multiply. It was Ms Nancy who threw open the doors of her little blue house so everybody on the street could come to celebrate Preta's new baby that she didn't birth herself. Ms Nancy was the first in line with a blue box with a bow to welcome him. But now Ms Nancy lies in her one bedroom at night with her children around her in her little box in the warren built by the government for poor people just like her, and worries that one or more of them will someday turn out like Adan, that someone could similarly be praying to God that their little one doesn't turn out like one of hers. As a consequence, Ms Nancy beats her children for every little infraction, for the simple reason that she has observed that Preta does not do likewise and this sparing of the rod, she decides, is the source of Adan's failings.

Every Friday evening Adan Primus walks to the clinic of the goodly Dr Thompson. He starts walking the moment the last bell is rung at Baxter's Comprehensive Primary School to signal the end of the school day, the throngs of children swarming the street parting like the Red Sea before Adan as he strides to meet his Auntie Preta. At Dr Thompson's little clinic on the corner of a busy street in Tatler's Farm, Adan will wait for his Auntie Preta to finish her work so they can go home. Dr Thompson's clinic is at the side of his house, which is a big stone building surrounded by a large yard with a hardscrabble garden from which Auntie Preta has been gently coaxing okra, carrots, pumpkins and sweet potatoes. Auntie Preta works for Dr Thompson, cleaning and washing and making puddings and golden apple juice.

Every Friday evening when the last patient has left Dr Thompson's clinic, he turns off the light and walks to his car and Auntie Preta and Adan open the back door of his silver Subaru and are carried home, because Dr Thompson is a good man with a soft heart and on Fridays he closes the clinic early and pays Auntie Preta and takes her and her nephew home. Most Friday evenings Dr Thompson's daughter Janey joins them. There is no Mrs Thompson to watch her at home and she is only eight years old. Mrs Thompson decided that she did not admire a man who would waste a perfectly good medical degree on patients from a poor neighbourhood. She had no desire to understand the plight of patients who often begged off her husband's modest fees and left huge hands of bananas and plantains and sacks of sweet potatoes at the back door instead. As it happens, Dr Thompson accepts these potatoes, these plantains, so much sugar cane with the same good-natured benevolence with which he faced his wife divorcing him because of them.

Every Friday evening Dr Thompson drives, with Janey in the front and Auntie Preta and Adan in the back, into the car park at Burger Bee to buy his Janey dinner. Poor Janey has a funny stomach and must have her meals to time. This is the reason that Dr Thompson steers the Subaru into the Burger Bee car park at five minutes to six every Friday and little Janey starts jumping. She will have fries, she tells Dr Thompson, and a burger. No, she will have a roti, a beef and potato roti and a banana split. No, she will have a snack box and a milkshake. Her choices meander, always, back to a snack box and a milkshake.

On our particular Friday, the man-boy Adan sits in the back of Dr Thompson's car with Auntie Preta and watches Janey fidget. Adan thinks that Janey looks like a spider. He longs to pinch those long, long limbs, to pull that lank dark hair, but he doesn't dare in the eyesight of Auntie Preta. All arms and legs, Janey is, a skinny torso and a sheet of long brown hair that hangs on each side of a little heart-shaped face and limpid hazel eyes. Dr Thompson lifts her from the car when he gets out. He comes around to her side and Janey's long, long arms wrap themselves around her father's neck in a way that makes Adan think of the snakes in the science book at school. Janey is carried towards the white-lit windows of the Burger Bee. Dr Thompson has stopped asking Auntie Preta whether she wants anything by this time, or whether she wants a snack box for Adan, or a roti. Auntie Preta always says no. On Fridays Auntie Preta does not cook for the Thompson family. On Fridays, by agreement with her boss, Auntie Preta focuses on the washing and the ironing of Janey's school uniforms and Dr Thompson's shirt-jacs and the washing of the house linens, so on Fridays Dr Thompson buys Janey her favourite fast food on the way to drop Auntie Preta home.

Adan twists around and clambers to his knees in the back seat of the square Subaru and presses his big face right up to the back windshield so he can watch Dr Thompson and Janey walk past the big wide windows and the bevelled glass door opening and closing below a flashing Brobdingnagian bee. Adan watches Dr Thompson enter, remove Janey gently from his shoulders and lift her under her armpits to face the wide smile of the cashier to tell her what she wants. At these moments Adan feels like he is suffocating in the back seat of Dr Thompson's car, as if he will find himself unable to breathe if he does not reach for the chrome handle slotted into the grey velvet panelling and open the door and run.

Adan knows better than to beg Auntie Preta to buy him a snack box of his own. He knows that Auntie Preta is not really unkind, she merely believes it best to bring up her boy to know his place, to understand that weekly excursions to Burger Bee are beyond him and his kin and should remain that way until they can buy their own snack box every Friday, should they ever be able to. Auntie Preta believes it is good training to help Adan to understand that the chicken she will cook on Sunday would have been raised, fed, slaughtered, wholesomely prepared and placed before him without costing the price of a single snack box. But Adan does not understand this and he simpers, he simmers, he sighs. When Dr Thompson comes back to the car with Janey, she returns to the front passenger seat and starts to devour her snack box, putting aside one-eyed Mr Teddy to lick her fingers, wiggling in delight and kicking her shoes against the dashboard.

What happens next occurs at the top of the hill where the road starts to descend into the rough architecture of Baxter's Village. Janey is nibbling the crunchy skin of one of the two pieces of chicken that nestle in her snack box when Adan reaches his long left arm through the space between the front passenger seat and the door and neatly retrieves the other piece. It is so quiet and unexpected a movement that at first Janey does not believe what has happened. Then she protests, loudly, that Adan has stolen her chicken. Adan, meanwhile, is happily eating the golden-brown thigh as if he is oblivious to Janey's protests.

Dr Thompson chuckles. Says it is OK, a kindness that Adan later attributes to the fact that Dr Thompson is a doctor, as if his benevolence is a by-product of his profession. Auntie Preta shrieks apologies at Dr Thompson, at Janey, retrieves the meat from Adan's grasp and proffers it to Janey, who of course no longer wants it, and looks at the bitten thigh in her hand as if she was the one caught stealing. Janey looks close to tears.

On this particular Friday afternoon, when the Subaru sighs to a stop outside their house, Auntie Preta alights from the car with the bitten chicken still in her grasp and says thank you to Dr Thompson. She says she will see him on Monday unless he wants any help with Janey over the weekend, in which case he should call her straight away. She does not mind, says Auntie Preta, babysitting Janey on

125

a weekend, she is such a dear child, no trouble at all, not like her Adan. Dr Thompson reiterates that it is OK, children will do these things, Janey will get over it, next time he will buy Adan something as well, he should have done that because his mind had told him to even when she said no. And then Dr Thompson honks goodbye with Janey still sobbing in the front seat and refusing to wave.

Inside the house Auntie Preta heads to the kitchen to make dinner. As she takes the saucepan out of the cupboard something takes over her. Perhaps it is the thought of Ms Nancy firmly ushering her children back inside their house the moment she sees Adan get out of the car and wringing the ear of the one Adan's age who persists in turning around. Something happens, because Auntie Preta is not one for beating, not her beloved Adan who came to her when her sister died, looking like an angel from heaven, like God himself sent Adan to be a barren woman's joy. But Auntie Preta beats Adan until the saucepan is dented and no longer able to sit steadily on the stove, until her head-tie is undone and her hair is flying around her and there are little beads of sweat above her eyebrows, until Adan is curled in a ball on the floor begging her to stop, although he surely knows that he is man-boy enough to stand up and make Auntie Preta regret ever picking up that saucepan. The fact that he does not, rather than the beating itself, is what makes Adan angry.

'No. Means. No!' Auntie Preta is hitting Adan like the lesson consists of the beats to a song she is teaching him, 'Did. I. Raise. You. Up. To. Thief?' over and over until her lover comes through the door and tries to restrain her.

John yanks the saucepan away and throws it through the back door.

And then Auntie Preta comes out of her madness and starts to make dinner. She doesn't want to talk to John about what happened because the telling will have to end with why she beat Adan, and she is not sure of why that was; it is the first time she has beaten her Adan, or anybody's child, in her life. But she doesn't have to say why to John, who does not look at her this evening when he puts a brown envelope on the table with a few big banknotes that Auntie Preta knows belong to somebody else. John knows that the beating is less about Adan's theft than it is about Auntie's Preta's guilt for having a professional thief like John around the boy. John puts the money down and Auntie Preta picks it up and puts it in her pocket because she wants it but she does not want to have to look at it. Not this evening, not with Adan howling on the floor and the saucepan on its side in the dirt still visible through the doorway.

On this particular Friday, Auntie Preta makes Adan's favourite – long, soft cylinders of macaroni with butter, and floury dumplings with just the right amount of gravy. But Adan cannot eat it and when Ms Nancy wanders over to prove with her own eyes that Preta finally put some licks in her demon of a nephew, Auntie Preta says that Adan no longer likes macaroni, that she will buy some chicken necks and make pelau, that she must find something else to feed her sweet boy. Ms Nancy gives a snort, because cooking to please a ten-year-old child is just the kind of nonsense that demonstrates that Preta has not really become a disciplinarian after all, and returns to her house where she will feed her five with a huge pot of white rice and corned-beef gravy whether they like it or not. No wonder, confirms Ms Nancy, that Adan is the way he is.

The story of the snack box is what Auntie Preta thinks of when people ask her, in her later years, when she started to realise that something was wrong with Adan. By these times, Auntie Preta has started to tell herself that Adan has not been sent by angels to be a crown on her head after all, but by the Devil to shame her face. Try as she will, she cannot give a good answer when asked, she cannot articulate why her Adan has turned out the way he has. Despite her shame, she cannot think of anything she could have done better in raising him. On these occasions, to this day, Auntie Preta thinks of the snack box, although she cannot think to tell you what it was about the incident that was an omen. She cannot articulate what it was about that story that is the explanation for everything.

After the beating, when Adan is bruised and some parts of his belly are strange shades of blue, and he does not eat the dinner Auntie Preta has made for him, John offers to take him for a walk, to buy him something to eat. They walk through Baxter's Village and into Hawks Hall and Adan tells John what happened while they walk towards the Burger Bee. Adan notices how people stare at John when he passes, how they take in his bright windbreaker over a button-up shirt he has not buttoned, his peg-legged khakis with the cuff just high enough to show the world his leather stitched-sole shoes. John wears the kind of shoes that have soles that clip-clop, as if this will convince those who know him that he is not really a robber because he loves shoes that announce his arrival and a robber never would. John is a short man, but not when he wears these shoes. When he wears these shoes John is six feet tall, a thin whip of a man who does not sweat or swear, whose Jheri curl does not dare drip down his neck, who only wears socks imported from England, whose clothes always have the appearance of having just been purchased from the department store in town – brand new, sharply coloured and professionally pressed.

When Adan finishes the story of the snack box, John just nods, and though Adan never says how badly he wanted one at the moment Janey Thompson came out to the car and planted her mouth firmly around the heel of a drumstick, John understands. John takes Adan into the Burger Bee and orders him a snack box and a milkshake, just like Janey's, and then sits quietly in one of the little kiosks inside and watches him eat it.

'It good, right?' he says. 'Is just what you need, ent it, big man?'

Adan just eats.

'Tongue long-out for a little snack box, cuh-dear.' John licks his lips, rearranges the little piece of grass stalk he plucks and places between his front teeth on a daily basis. His gold bracelet rattles with enough bass to let everyone in the Burger Bee know it is real. 'Cuh-dear,' he says again, 'a man should never have to depend on another man for a snack box, ent it?'

Adan is eating his snack box, turning the fried chicken

flesh over and over on his tongue so he can savour its eventual swallowing.

'What you wanna be when you done school?' asks John.

It is exactly the type of question that Adan does not know how to answer. Finishing school is too far away to deserve much thought. He shrugs, breaks the wishbone of the chicken, chews one side into fine grey-brown grounds.

'A man need to be able to take care of heself,' says John. 'Feed heself, clothe heself, sleep at he own house.'

Adan watches John press the lapels of his shirt with his fingertips as if to demonstrate the type of man he speaks of. The shirt is unbuttoned to the middle of John's chest, and dark chest hair peeps through, some of it turning grey. John has been seeing Auntie Preta for several months by then. Some mornings Adan wakes up to the sound of his Auntie Preta giggling in a way Adan hasn't heard before, and later John comes out of her bedroom and goes into the backyard to pee out in the open and pluck the day's stalk of grass. He puts this stalk between his teeth and says, 'What's up, li'l man?' as he passes Adan looking out of the window near the back door, and Adan glowers at him and says nothing. John is not there every night, something Adan is grateful for, because he enjoys the nights he can crawl into Auntie Preta's bed and sleep with her smell all around him. Adan can only sleep in Auntie Preta's bed when John does not come over; when John comes he must sleep alone, which means he can hardly sleep and he wakes up early in the mornings to stare through the back window. In the beginning he hated this about John visiting – this separation from his Auntie Preta – but he is beginning to reconsider his feelings about John now that he is chewing the bones of some fantastic fried chicken in a snack box that John bought him.

'You stick close to me,' John tells him. 'I will learn you how to buy your own snack boxes, big man.'

So Adan does. At the age of ten, Adan is taught how to make a pick for a lock from a broken windshield wiper swiped from a mechanic's shop, how to use a tension wrench, how to scrub this pick back and forth until a lock clicks and opens as if by magic. He is taught to use plastic gloves and to carry a rag pre-soaked in vinegar to clean his fingerprints off handles and door jambs and loot that must sometimes be left behind. He is shown the weaknesses of alarm systems to be found in businesses and big houses and he is taught how to shroud a security camera so it cannot see who is blinding it. For eight years Adan works with John. Even after Auntie Preta and John are no longer lovers, Adan works with John, until the day that John is caught and jailed while on a job and Adan begins to work alone.

His first solo job, at eighteen years old, is Dr Thompson, of course it is. It is nothing personal, this decision to rob Dr Thompson, it is simply that by then the goodly doctor has become so accustomed to the grace and favour of the community he serves that he leaves his doors unlocked and his windows unlatched and this makes him a perfect match for Adan's intentions. By this time Auntie Preta no longer works for the doctor; Auntie Preta works sewing smocked dresses for one of the factories near the harbour and has forced Adan to leave her home, exasperated with his repeated deviance and urged on by Ms Nancy. She gives him the little house near the beach she had inherited from an uncle and washes her hands clean of him, even if she does so with a heaviness in her heart that she takes to her grave.

Dr Thompson does not seem to recognise the gruff growl behind the President Carter mask when he is awoken from his bed in the early morning. He does not remember the ten-year-old version of the hand that holds the gun. His willingness to hand over the contents of his wallet and his safe angers Adan immensely. It is not, as Dr Thompson thinks, the fact that there is little money in the wallet and even less in the safe that incenses the robber. Adan takes it all, using a gloved hand to shove the bills into his pocket, and he is still not satisfied. But then he remembers Janey, who is sleeping upstairs. She has grown even more beautiful, has Janey, she is taller, her hair is silkier, her eyes even more dewy.

Adan believes he should delight in feeding yampy-eye Janey the length of his cock while he holds a gun to her temple to stop her biting him. He should, but he doesn't. It gives him no satisfaction that he is making her eat him the way she did that drumstick so many years ago. And he finds this point worthy of pondering, the fact that he doesn't feel any pleasure. Or even any pain. And when he finally takes the gun and beats her with it until that silky hair is caked with blood, those dewy eyes are pinpoints of terror, and he is holding several of her teeth in the palm of his hand, Adan confirms, with some frustration, that what he still feels is nothing.

CHAPTER SIXTEEN

Beckles
17 August 1984

The black policeman lives by his belly. This is how he knows, while walking away from the house on stilts after questioning Lala, that something is not right – his belly rumbles. It is not the type of rumble that warns of hunger or foreshadows a string of mild intestinal protests against a meagre meal. Rather, this rumble forebodes the type of gastric revolt that sends him scampering to the nearest toilet. Of course, at Baxter's Beach there aren't any. This is how the black policeman comes to spread his generous buttocks six inches above the sand in the centre of a dense circle of seagrape trees, praying that his spit-shined shoes are spared. The revolt sheds the best of the last week's work by his wife – bakes fried flat and fair with just the right measure of cinnamon, fried plantains served with little peppery fishcakes, cassava boiled and slit and basted while still steaming, and tart salt fish pickle he ate with Crix.

Having signalled to him that there is more to this mystery than meets the eye, his tummy settles into a writhing reminder, which, like his ruminations on the evidence, produces nothing of substance.

So a baby is dead. It has been found on the sand by a

gigolo who is a friend of the father. This father is away fishing. The baby is found before the mother has reported it missing to the police. The baby was new, the parents are poor, there are no bruises or signs of abuse. Babies die, he tells himself. He knows this well. They die because they change their minds about facing the world, because accidents happen, because God has his own logic that man need not understand. Sometimes, he knows, babies are killed before they are even born because their mothers do not want them. Occasionally they are killed after they are born for the same reason.

A dead baby, without more, does not mean a crime. But babies are not often kidnapped. Not in Baxter's Beach. Not from dirt-poor people like Adan Primus and his wife, who cannot pay a ransom. When babies are kidnapped from people like these it is because there is someone who wants a baby, and reasons that they can take better care of one. But babies kidnapped for this reason do not then turn up dead. And a baby who is killed is not left out in the open on a beach where it can be found, unless this baby was killed by an amateur. But why?

Although Beckles cannot admit it to himself, he has come to take this murder personally, very personally indeed. He is still smarting that the Whalen murder, the one he was sure he would have been able to solve almost single-handedly, has been handed over to Scotland Yard and the death of a small baby whose face does not haunt the daily newspapers has been left with him. This is why he is careful with this investigation, why he is determined to solve it himself, and as soon as possible.

His belly falls silent, but it is a sanctimonious kind of silence, one that refuses to elaborate after it has already spoken. He cleans himself with some sea-grape leaves and considers the evidence afresh, thinking himself into ever-deepening perplexities as he walks back towards his car. But when he is seated and the car has *chug-chugged* into readiness, he finds that he cannot bring himself to release the brake pedal and drive himself back to the police station. Instead he sits and stares at the wide expanse of powdery pink sand, he stares at the roof of the Primus house barely visible above a clump of coconut trees. He thinks of the mother of this baby, how she jumped every time he made a sudden movement, as if she had something to hide, how careful she seemed to be about answering him, as if she were trying to ensure that the words she said matched ones she had rehearsed. The black policeman thinks he knows this kind of woman, a woman whose word cannot be trusted. He thinks he is in love with one. Her name is the Queen of Sheba.

Beckles first met the Queen of Sheba while he was on duty. It was 1980 and he was still a constable, assigned to the drudgery of the 'Paradise patrol', walking up and down Baxter's Beach and its environs, escorting drunk tourists back to their hotels, taking statements about lost credit cards and cameras, helping out with the occasional investigations of the drowning of visitors who had had too many rum punches too close to their swim.

He had been patrolling the beach on foot around 10 p.m. with Constable Napoleon one Friday night in tourist season when Napoleon was almost knocked over by a black

American man, by the sound of his accent, running like the wind down the beach, hotly pursued by a woman in a pink Hunza jumpsuit, her waist-length ponytail and enormous yellow hoop earrings swinging as wildly as the curses that spewed from her brilliant orange lips. Napoleon had pursued and restrained the man just because he had nearly knocked him down without stopping to apologise, but as it turned out, the Queen of Sheba had wanted them to arrest him anyway – for failing to pay her for her services.

Even now Beckles chuckles when he remembers it – her insistence that she be paid in the face of the American's protests that he hadn't thought he was supposed to be paying for anything. He thought he'd met an attractive woman on the beach, said the American, a woman who was willing to sleep with him then and there because she was attracted to him too.

'Oh, so you "meet" me, then?' challenged the Queen of Sheba. 'Well if you meet me, tell them my name.'

And the American couldn't.

Beckles had admired her spunk much more than the protuberant breasts and behind that seemed to bedazzle her clients. Napoleon, still irked by the rudeness of the visitor but not particularly inclined to write up an assault, had decided to have fun with it, and said he would let the assault of a police constable pass, but only if the American paid the woman. So the Queen of Sheba got her money although Beckles still insisted that she leave the beach, under threat of a charge for soliciting. He told her that they would take her home, and wouldn't hear any of her many objections. They would take her, he said, just to be sure that she reached her destination safely. And so Beckles and Napoleon took the Queen of Sheba home in the patrol car, watched her go inside a little pink two-storey apartment in a block of broken-down government housing and close her door behind her.

The relationship was purely symbiotic at first: Beckles made sure that the Queen of Sheba was safe when she sold her services on the beach, hustling off any clients who seemed too boisterous, too dark, too dangerous for her comfort or his. In turn, she was a source of leads when crimes happened on the sand or in the sea. She seemed somehow to always know the real story behind the crimes the police were trying to crack; she was always in tune to the whats and hows of the crimes committed in and around Baxter's Beach.

Beckles eventually got promoted for his good sleuthing and the Queen of Sheba stayed safe and out of jail. And neither of them said a word to each other to suggest that theirs was anything more than a mere casual acquaintance, neither of them said a word about the other to anyone else. Everything was fine, thinks Sergeant Beckles, until he started to make use of her services himself, until she started switching her usual work spots without telling him, protesting that she wasn't trying to avoid him, she just went where the work took her. Sometimes he wouldn't see her for days, and when he tried to find out where she had been, the Queen of Sheba showed the same spunk she had with the American.

'I don't have to tell you nothing!' she had shouted, just the week before, when he caught up with her for the first time in a fortnight and asked her where she had been, who she had been selling her sex to. She had wrenched away from him trying to hold on to her, threatened to report him to the authorities if he didn't leave her alone. He had told her that he *was* the authorities. He had dropped her hand then, but something had burned in his gut against her ever since.

It is true that he has a wife, thinks Sergeant Beckles now, true that he is unlikely to leave her, but Sheba is the type of woman he would build a house for. He would ensure she would always be comfortable, that she would never have to walk the length of Baxter's Beach again, never have to give her body to anybody but him. He knows that this is a prospect most women would kill for. Sheba's disinterest can only mean she has found these prospects somewhere else.

A man could have the best of intentions, sighs Sergeant Beckles, it don't matter to some of these women. Some women just don't want to settle down.

Lala, he thinks, is possibly one of these types of women, and therefore capable of anything, including the death of her own child.

The sergeant stays in his car until evening, sleeping, thinking, watching, waiting until the sun goes to sleep and he is parked in a soft darkness and he must go home.

The following morning, when his belly tells him to go back to the circle of sea-grape trees, still steaming with his stink, to watch and wait, he obeys it. And when he sees a sun-bleached gigolo concealing himself behind trees and bushes on the approach to Adan's little house, he is not surprised that his belly starts screaming.

CHAPTER SEVENTEEN

Tone
18 August 1984

The beach stinks of stewing moss, sargassum seaweed and the putrefying guts of beached fishes, rotting in the warming air. It is one of those mornings when the water remains hung-over after a night of reckless abandon and has vomited on the sand before seeking to sleep it off. The tourists find that a walk along the shore is less about a stroll on the stretch of pink powder reproduced in the magazines and more the halting stop-and-start necessary to avoid the hidden jellyfish in the seaweed and the spines of sea urchins washed ashore and submerged in the sand and the glass bottle pieces that have not yet been in the sea long enough to be smoothed and dulled by sun and salt and made into something worthy of the treasure-hunting of children.

Tone walks along Baxter's Beach and his feet rely on their own eyes to avoid the stings and sticks and slicings waiting in the detritus. Tone is watching Adan's house as he comes up the beach, acting like he isn't watching it, like he is merely strolling along the sand at this early hour of the morning. In truth, no one would think anything amiss if they saw him there. Everyone knows that men of Tone's genus are fixtures of the beach, an accepted part of the ecosystem that thrives there. But Tone is not a gigolo this morning, Tone is a worried lover and this is why he thinks he might arouse suspicion.

Adan's house is at the very end of the stretch of beach without a calm, clear bay for bathing. There are no tourist women here for Tone to offer hand-made jewellery or a night in bed or a joint or a ride on a jet ski, but the view is beautiful and luxury villas still open on to this stretch. Several of his clients tend to rent these houses, or to own them. It isn't unusual for people to find him walking this beach at any given time of day or night. But it isn't tourists that Tone is watching for; Tone is watching for Adan, and Adan is the reason he bobs and weaves behind coconut trees and vegetation every time he hears a sound he is not accustomed to, instead of continuing to walk out in the open.

Eventually he comes to sit in the ruins of a small fish market, where the fishermen used to beach their boats and blow a conch shell and announce to a bygone village that there was fresh fish to be had on the sand. This village died in the birthing of the big houses, because rich tourists who visit for a few months in a year do not wish to suffer the stink of a market in order to purchase food each day. Only Adan's little old house, rising unsteadily from behind the coconut trees, and the ruins of the market are left. A few tiled stone structures like tall tables are spread across a paved square with a stopcocked pipe at one corner. Tone crouches beneath one of the tall tables, from where he can see the foot of the cement stairs to Adan's house, and looks for Lala. She is sure to come down soon, he reasons. There are clothes to pick up off the line and she'll come down and he'll talk to her, tell her that he's sorry about Baby, offer her an out.

The ruins of a nearby public bath have long since been overrun by a colony of sea-grape bushes that have flourished and become colossal in proportion, with wide flat leaves that remind Tone of the upturned palms of the beggars in town. Tone considers making a break for the sea-grape trees and waiting there a few minutes to be sure that Adan will not return, but ultimately decides against it. What could Adan find amiss about him visiting the house to see after Lala, especially when her husband is in hiding, especially after what happened to Baby? His reasoning makes him bold and he is about to step out of the ruins when he sees Adan approach the stairs. Tone eases back into the ruins, away from the little wooden house. He settles a little farther away, near two fishing boats beached for repairs. He will wait there a while, Tone resolves, he will wait there until Adan leaves and then he will visit her when it is safe.

CHAPTER EIGHTEEN

Lala
18 August 1984

Lala is pretending to have fallen asleep. After he had nearly crushed her hand, Adan had stomped outside to gather the coconuts the tree had discarded, and others he had set aside for Coyote. He was tired of hiding, he had decided, better to get rid of the white woman so he could tie up that loose end and return to his house as a man, live his life in the open. He had grabbed the cutlass as he left the room and from their bed Lala hears it whistling through the coconut fronds and fibre.

At times like this Lala does not know what to do. She is unsure whether she should go outside, near Adan and that whistling cutlass, to dredge the coir fibre in sand and scrub the dirty pots in the salty surf. She is unsure whether she should stay in the bed, curled up as she is, with a throbbing hand and a stinging breast, and try to rest until Adan has left with a load for Coyote. She decides that he may leave more quickly if he thinks that she is sleeping, that she is doing nothing that can further offend him, and so she tries her best to return to the land of dreams, where Baby is alive.

But Lala cannot sleep. And when the cutlass stops its

whistling and she hears the dull thud of his feet on the steps, she turns to face the wall and closes her eyes.

In the foggy darkness of their bedroom she feels rather than sees Adan look at her, senses rather than hears that he is still angry. It is the type of anger that is in search of a release and Lala is therefore unsure about her decision to pretend to be asleep. While she thinks about this she considers the possible infractions: being asleep in bed instead of up doing chores like the good women of the world, her turned back instead of a willing smile, any number of household chores left undone, a dead baby she cannot bring back.

She is facing the wall beside their bed with her hand set carefully on the pillow beside her to cool and her eyes tightly closed and she is breathing quietly, the way she imagines she does when she is asleep. The problem is that the only person who knows what she truly breathes like when asleep is Adan, and the curiosity of whether her breathing is a convincing approximation keeps her shoulders tense.

'I know you ain't fucking sleeping, Lala.'

She cannot turn around. In that moment, the weight of all her injuries falls upon her, those existing and those remembered, and the sheer bulk of them renders her immobile. There is the left nipple that, despite a poultice of aloe gel and breadfruit leaves, still seeps through the toilet paper she folds and positions inside the cup of her bra each morning. There is the knee that has ached her for several months now, that she bandages each night before bed and unwraps on any occasion that she has to leave the house or do something for Adan that will require enough proximity for him to be angered by the evidence of her injury. There is the leaden weight at the bottom of her spine beneath a peeling burn in the shape of the clothes iron.

But in that moment Lala also suffers the remembered horrors – the time when, with Baby still in her belly, she was held by her face at the edge of the cement steps and made to scream why he should not let her go, not let her fall enough feet to split her like a watermelon; the time when he held a sharpened cutlass to her throat so closely that when he at last released her there was the thinnest line of beaded blood across her windpipe; the time he dragged her by her hair up those twenty-five steps, when the clumps of hair that bore witness to her struggle had littered the steps the following day.

Even if she wants to move, she cannot, so firmly do these memories hold her still, so that when a stinging lash falls across her back and her eyes fly open with her mouth in the surprise of pain without origin, Lala considers that the true source of her pain is not the current cruelty, but the fact that she cannot do anything to avoid it, even if she wanted to.

'Get up, Lala! Get to fuck up! Who you think you fooling?'

'Why you does be doing me so?'

'Get. To. Rass. Hole. Up!'

People lie about the first slap. Lala knows you can never trust a woman who can tell you the direction from which the fist first came, because if you are genuinely shocked that first time you are beaten, the only thing you remember is the sting. You cannot remember the direction because you were not expecting it. It is like the stories men like Adan tell about getting shot and not even realising it and your senses have to make sense of the evidence of the aftermath of something your brain still cannot comprehend. Your eyes see blood, your ears recall the report of gunfire, your nose smells gunpowder, you taste bile, you feel a wet red spot. Meaning, you are shot. With that first slap you never know you have been slapped until your senses recover enough to tell you. Any woman who says otherwise is a witch who expected the slap anyway and very likely provoked it. Such a woman is therefore possessed of eyes too wide open to suggest genuine love in the first place.

Lala cannot now remember where that first slap came from, she cannot remember the finer details of what it was about, but she knows that, in the dim light of morning after that first slap, she became Wilma without even thinking about it. Wilma's response to chaos was always to seek order in the things around her.

Lala had started with the bed that first morning she was boxed – she had removed the fitted sheet, the flat sheet and the two pillowcases and washed them, taken down the curtains from the window behind the bed and washed them too. Swept the wooden floor, mopped it, beaten the rug, taken Adan's rusting yellow unicycle from the corner of the room and scraped and polished it until it shone, replaced it and fretted that it would not stand upright, propped it with a rock and tried not to worry that it would roll away on its own, as if ridden by a ghost, scrubbed the rotting cupboards without thought to splinters, scraped the mildew and dried scraps of food from the garbage can beneath the sink, washed the dishes and the curtains until her hands were grey from prolonged exposure to blue soap.

She startled herself when she caught a glimpse of a woman with a black eye in the pockmarked shard of mirror Adan had tacked to the wooden partition in the kitchen, to help him with his shaving. She had stared at this woman, at the purple right cheek and bloodshot eye, and tried to remember whether this woman was someone she knew, someone whose name she should recall.

('Why you so fucking own-way, Lala?')

In the early nights of their marriage, after that first beating, Lala had made deals with God while her new husband snored. If He would only make this the marriage of her dreams, she had offered, if He would only grant them a happy life full of children and laughter around tables at dinner time and matching outfits at the races or the fairs, if God would do that for her, she would forgive Him for taking her mother before she got the chance to really know her, she would forgive Him for subjecting her to growing up with Carson and Wilma, she would go to church, she would forget about Tone, she would not hold these beatings against Adan.

('Rass. Hole. Own-Way!')

Of course she did not leave him. What woman leaves a man for something she is likely to suffer at the hands of any another? Didn't Wilma's neighbour run out of her home and into Wilma's almost every Friday evening once her husband came home? Hadn't she seen the evidence on one or other woman she had known of worse beatings than these? Had her own mother not tolerated such beatings?

Lala had instead focused on the good days – bus rides into town with the setting sun behind them, window-shopping outside Harrison's and marvelling at the clothes on the mannequins, the big Kawasaki that flew past them that Adan said he'd buy himself one day, with an extra helmet so she could ride on the back of the bike with the wind making those long, long braids whip against her bum. Any outfit she wanted, said Adan, once he had the money, any outfit at all.

When the ability to move returns to her, it returns so forcefully, so decisively, that she is out of the bed and behind the chair before her thoughts have asked her feet to stand. But movement alone does not bring memory with it, and, as often happens at times like this, she cannot remember his name to call him, to make him stop.

'What happen? What happen?'

'Why you couldn't just leave Baby? What kind of woman you is, Lala, to let go Baby so?'

'I didn't let go Baby on purpose! I sorry, I didn't mean to let she go!'

She pleads from the corners of their room for his forgiveness, she tells him she is sorry.

'Please,' she says, 'I did not mean for our baby to die, please.' But she cannot say that name, the last thing his mother gave him before dying, the one appeal that might stop him. And when she is sobbing on the floor at his feet, and she has resigned herself to the strike that will finally kill her, when she has already welcomed the peace death will bring, the possibility, perhaps, of seeing Baby again in one or other of the places where dead people go, he sucks his teeth like she is not even deserving of his beatings and retreats to his chair and his Bible, and she sees a path straight to the door and she escapes, running down the cement steps without thought to the risk of breaking her neck, so free she feels she is flying.

Down the beach, the pink man with the big gruff dog is crying. He is bent almost double over the green wrought-iron railing that delineates his piece of Paradise and he makes deep sobs that somehow still sound as if he is making it up. What can a man such as this have to cry about? Lala slows down, wipes her own tears. Betsy is on her side, shuddering and frothing by his feet on the patio. The pink man is wearing the same black shorts he wears every day to take Betsy for her walk and his toes are covered in the sand that dusts his patio like pastry flour scattered on a flat surface in the work-up to a pie. Lala has previously wondered whether these tourists do not mind how this powdery sand must stick to everything, making it impossible to house-clean, how it must make everything slippery, how it surely infects with the memory of wetness and salty skin and swimming a space meant to be dry and clean and stationary.

He does not seem to see Lala running, nor does he startle when she stops. He is oblivious to everything but Betsy suffering beside him, trying to drag herself upright every few minutes, struggling to lift her head to nudge his thigh, pawing the railings and whining, wondering why he does not save her.

A woman Lala has never seen before comes off the beach in a sarong that shrouds her and a large straw hat that might be the reason for the shadows that cover her eyes. She pats the back of the pink man, letting her hand linger until it hardly leaves the surface of his skin and sort of squirms there, flopping about in a series of useless shivers. With her other hand she holds the hat firmly on her head and she shouts at no one in particular to call a vet, for Christ sake, even as she grimaces at the slimy green froth that trails perilously close to her slippered feet.

When Lala reaches them she notices that the woman's slippers have jewelled straps that glimmer, even in the pinky grey before the full spill of sunshine. She notices how the woman looks at her and is suddenly conscious of the warm trickle of blood on her cheek, the seaweed cloak on hands and hair, the throbbing in her teeth that mimics her heartbeat.

The woman says, 'My God,' but she is no longer looking at Betsy, she is looking at Lala, and Betsy breathes her last and the woman removes her shades to have a proper look and the pink man sobs harder. The woman takes her hand from his back and only then does he raise his head, wipe his eyes and look at Lala.

'My God,' the woman says again, 'what happened to you?' and she starts to walk towards Lala. 'Were you robbed?'

She keeps coming closer, even though Lala is shaking her head, looking back down the beach, warning her to stay away. The pink man wipes his eyes, he is coming too. Lala looks around, trying to decide what to do, where to go. This is when she notices that the patio on which Betsy has died is attached to a big pale blue villa, and that this villa shares a guard wall with one adjacent to it. This other villa is not blue, it is white, and the wooden fence that tops the guard wall is familiar to her. It is one she has seen just recently.

'I can help you,' says the woman. 'I can go inside and get Rosa, she will know what to do.'

'No,' says Lala, 'no. I am OK, it is OK.'

'Hey!' the woman is saying, when Lala starts to run. 'Come here! Let us help you!'

Lala is running fast, but not so fast that the pink man cannot catch her, and eventually she finds herself sitting on his patio near the stiff shadow of his dead dog. Up close he is nothing like she expected, although it is difficult to say how. Up close, the pink man's hand is burned brown, with little blonde hairs like brush bristles sticking straight up and out of his skin. When the bristles come near Lala's face she jumps, and when she makes to run away, he says:

'Relax, I am not going to hurt you.'

He runs his fingers along her neck and *hmmms* below his breath.

'You have some nasty bruises there,' he says, 'but I don't think anything is broken. Who did this to you?'

Lala doesn't answer.

The woman with the floppy hat and jewelled sandals looks at him and he at her and then they both look at Lala.

'Do you want to go to the hospital or the police?' the woman asks quietly, and Lala shakes 'no' and accepts some water in a wine glass from the brown bristled hand. There are perhaps no other kinds of drinking glass in this villa. Lala's mind is racing. The man says, drink slowly, your throat must be sore. And she is not sure whether he means from the swelling or the screaming. When she hands him back the wine glass and stands up to leave the patio, she notices that a single fly has already found Betsy's body, that soon there will be others.

Lala is thinking about the police. If these people call the police, it will just draw more attention, she is thinking, it will just give them cause to ask her more questions about Baby. She does not need policemen asking her more questions about Baby. She needs to get away from the police, from Adan, from these people, from this beach. And in order to do that she must seem as if she *isn't* running, from any of them. When she finally runs, decides Lala, it must be a run that will take her to another place entirely, a place from which she will never return. Where can she run to now? She cannot run to Wilma, whose house will not feel like a harbour. She cannot run to Tone, who has no place of his own to take her, no totem strong enough to keep her safe from harm.

She looks out at the sand beyond the patio and sees her baby, whose image then melts into a crab, scampering off the sand and towards her feet.

Soon Lala is sprinting again, back to where she came from, and this time the brush-bristled hand cannot hold her.

'I sorry, Lala,' Adan tells her that evening. 'You know I sorry.'

She is wrapped in his big broad arms and her face is tickled by the hair on his chest and he is talking to her above her head so that she has to imagine his repentance etched across his features.

151

'Is just . . . Baby gone and I, I couldn't save she, Lala. I couldn't save she after you drop she.'

He kisses the top of her head, strokes the hair from which her braided extensions had once been forcibly removed. She has stopped plaiting it in styles that cover the bald patch where he yanked out her hair from the root. It is hard not to flinch when his hands reach that spot, it is hard to pretend that she has no memory of that hurt, even if she cannot remember what was the issue that had led to it, but Lala does not flinch, she does not shy away from those hands in her hair.

'I know, Adan,' she says. 'Is all right.'

'I can't even get the money to bury Baby,' says Adan, 'I can't even get she bury.'

Lala's thoughts return to her tin, but she says nothing. It makes no sense to bring up the tin and how its contents could have helped to bury Baby. It makes no sense to agonise in her own mind about how the money in that tin could have helped her now.

'I going help, Adan. It have more people coming to get braids, I going save the money to bury Baby.'

He shifts restlessly and stops stroking her hair so that she wonders where his hands are, what exactly they are doing.

'We need more than you little money,' he says. 'Baby deserve a good funeral, a proper send-off . . . is not she fault that . . .'

And then he is weeping, sobbing disconsolately in a way that stuns her, a way that she has not heard since they met, a way that makes her unsure about whether she should lift her head and look at him or wrap her arms around his torso or tell him again that he is OK, that they will both be OK, even though she knows this is not true. She stays still, barely breathing. She does not hold him. She does not look.

A soft rain starts to fall, the kind that leaves little spears on the windows, like arrows pointing out the direction of the wind. He cannot do another job on the beach, explains Adan when he is calmer. The police are on high alert since the white man was killed, more of the inhabitants of the houses have hired security guards, some have fitted their guard walls with barbed wire, a few more have surely by now also purchased guns.

A job in the village is unlikely to get him the money he needs for an undertaker, unless it is a commercial job, and he can't do that type of job alone. There is just this job with the weed, says Adan, that is the only way he can think of to get the money to bury Baby. He could ask Tone what he think about this new thing with the weed, but he can't get Tone to come and meet him and talk about it. Tone ain't no real hustler, Tone was always just a soldier, grouses Adan, just waiting for Adan to tell him what to do. He pauses, clears the hoarse from the back of his throat.

'Tone acting funny to you, Lala?'

'Tone?'

'Yeah, man acting sketchy couple months now. You ain't notice how funny he acting when he come around? Even before Baby come, I was to ask you if you ain't notice.'

'He acting the same as always to me,' Lala says softly. 'I ain't notice nothing different 'bout him.'

153

It takes her great effort to keep breathing normally but Adan does not let on if he thinks anything amiss. He eventually unfolds the embrace within which he has wrapped her and says he is going out. He can't just lie down and relax when his baby can't even get a decent funeral, he says, in a way that sounds like an accusation: he is a man, and *as man* he going and figure out how to pay for the funeral she deserves.

Lala watches him stand, put his shirt back on, shove open the door and step into the damp air. She stares at the door for a long time after he has gone. She shivers. She doesn't have much time.

When Lala answers the door half an hour after Adan's exit, her face is masked with the mourning she believes it ought to wear – the innocent kind – in anticipation of the police again. Adan would not be back so soon, he would not knock, and she is not expecting anyone else.

In the way of all people guilty of extreme sin, the proof of her wrongdoing has started to be mirrored everywhere: in the number of times she has heard or seen the word 'murderer' since she held her dead baby in her arms on the beach, in soap opera plots and on the front page of newspapers. She is haunted, too, by the body of her daughter – in the soulful eyes of a crab in a hole on the beach, in the cries of a little baby a client brings to sit next to them while Lala does her hair, a baby who stretches her toes in her pram until her bootie falls off to expose Baby's triple-jointed toes.

She is convinced also that supernatural beings are

conspiring on her daughter's behalf to make her understand that she will pay for her part in her death. She
understands that it is a wicked duppy who placed the pink-
labelled can of formula sitting in the cupboard just behind
a few cans of beans, because she knows she has thrown
out all of Baby's milk. It is this duppy, or another, equally
malevolent, who infuses the peculiar sound the paper bag
of flour makes when she is making dumplings and it hits
the floor with the same sound she heard when Baby was
dropped. There are demons, she knows, who sprinkle the
house with the smell of the Cussons baby powder she often
dusted around Baby's neck and chest, although she is certain that there is no one in the house besides her and she is
not using baby powder.

Her guilt seems to sit on her, so that she is sure that
others must immediately recognise that her hands are not
clean, that she is at least partly to blame for her daughter's
death. And this is why she is expecting the police to come
back to arrest her, why she masks her face when she
answers the door, because only a face free of guilt can
assist her if it is that dark policeman on the other side of
the knocking.

But it is not the dark policeman. It is Tone.

'Why you come back here again?' is what she howls at
him, even as her face crumples and she weeps her relief.
She is still howling as he holds her, kissing her nose right
there on the step, kissing her forehead, licking the tears
from her cheeks, patting away her relief as she cries, 'Why
the fuck you keep on coming back here?'

CHAPTER NINETEEN

Mrs Whalen
19 August 1984

Rosa is not having it. She is not tolerating any more non-sense. All of this pining not good, says Rosa, she can understand the loss, yes, but you ain't the only body who ever lose. It is terrible, yes, but you have to get up, get out, start over. God take Mr Whalen, Him didn't take you. While she is saying this, Rosa is stomping around in the dark of Mira Whalen's bedroom, flinging back the blackout curtains until the room is flooded with blinding sunlight and Mira Whalen cannot see anything but the faint shadows of the swinging flaps of skin beneath Rosa's upper arms projected onto the far wall.

Up until today, Mira Whalen has forbidden her to do anything but change the bed linen, and Rosa seems determined to make up for lost time. Rosa is picking up the bedding off the floor. Rosa is clearing the bedside table of glasses of stagnant tap water and empty pill packets and crinkly Kleenex stuck into position by Mira Whalen's snot. Rosa is replacing the cordless telephone on the stand so that its red eye is relit and Mira Whalen feels again like she is being watched. Rosa is putting the cricket bat that stands between Mira Whalen and death on top of the wardrobe, almost out of her reach entirely.

'No!' says Mira Whalen. 'No, you know you're not to touch that . . . No!'

But Rosa shoves the bat a little further back so that it is completely hidden from view.

'No?' asks Rosa. 'No?' and all the while she keeps working and routing: the empty bottles of fine rum, the mugs in which cocoa has clotted and coalesced into a sticky brown gel that myriad spores of fungi now call home, the tear-stained photos of Peter hastily shoved under the bed so that the children won't catch Mira Whalen looking and get upset. 'You is not the first God make a widow, you is not the last.'

Rosa is coming for her and tugging the robe off her back and saying that it smells worse than the people Rosa serves meals to at the Salvation Army on Sundays after church. Rosa runs hot water and says, come here and sit in this here tub and let me clean you up, and there is something in her face that pre-empts the firing Mira Whalen wants to give her. This something will accept nothing but surrender, so Mira Whalen gets into the tub and lets Rosa scrub her skin and her hair and lets the steam poach her insides and sear her skin and decides that she will determine tomorrow whether she will fire Rosa or not but she knows she will not because a new person would not know her and they would not remember Peter and the children might not love them.

Rosa is not gentle with the scrubbing, she does not check whether the water is just the right degree of hot, she does not brush gently around the teeth that Mira Whalen bares for her, in deference to the tender gums that hold them there. Rosa rubs the loofah like she is scrubbing stains from a floor that will not let them go and Mira Whalen is sweltering and her skin feels like she is being stung by a thousand wasps at once and her back is turning red where the loofah has lashed it but she does not shriek the way she wants to, she whimpers instead and she is at ease in her whimpering because Rosa ignores it.

You need to get outside, says Rosa, you need to come back to life. God take Mr Whalen, Him didn't take you. You think he would want to know you pining away like this?

Mira Whalen closes her eyes. Just yesterday she had ventured outside, just a little walk on the beach, and had seen the neighbour's dog die, had seen a woman too ter-rified to report an assault she had suffered. Mira Whalen does not think she could muster the energy to go outside again. Mira Whalen doesn't think she could muster the energy for anything.

If only she had someone, she thinks, someone she could call, other than Martha, who would come and sort every-thing out for her. But she doesn't have those kinds of friends in Wimbledon. Even after six years, the friends are all still Peter's.

Rosa tells Mira Whalen she need to hurry up make funeral arrangements. She tells her it has been a whole month – she need to call back the people who been calling, the police who call to tell her the autopsy is finally done, the body can be released, the head-doctor who want to know why Mira Whalen miss the appointment this morning, she need to sort out the little children, the poor peeny children, is not their fault them father dead. The mother call yesterday, Rosa tells her; she, Rosa Omarilla Watson, tell her that Peter dead and she should come for her children. Right away she should come for them. Don't look at me that way, says Rosa, is the gospel truth I telling and Mrs Whalen know it. Somebody have to tell her that pining away in the dark all day not going change anything, and God must be did decide it might as well be her, Rosa Omarilla Watson, 'cause she is the only body like them telling Mira Whalen that this is bare foolishness she doing. Mr Whalen already dead, she plan to kill herself too? She call her Mr Watson, says Rosa, and he coming right now to take Mrs Whalen to the appointment with the head-doctor. Right now he coming, says Rosa, right now self.

This is how Mira Whalen comes to be *chug-chugging* downtown in the back of Rosa's husband's plastic-windowed Datsun, in clothes that sore her skin and are, to her surprise, now two sizes too big. Mira Whalen is aware that her outfit has been put together by a three-hundred-pound domestic who prefers to wear cheap polyester skirts in bright colours that she has purchased from the coolie-man and pulled up over long breasts she leaves bra-less. Mira Whalen understands that this means she must look like shit, but she doesn't know because she hasn't looked before leaving. Mira Whalen looks now, while Rosa's husband is listening to cricket, and the drone of the commentary is just the type of silence Mira can settle into. She is wearing a satiny emerald-green jacket with shoulder pads, a yellow skirt and white satin pumps and stockings, and underneath Rosa has dressed her in new black lace panties because she says that you must wear new, fresh, clean panties to a doctor's appointment, even if this is not a doctor who needs to examine anything under your skirt.

13 January 1983

Peter Whalen had a thing about panties. This is how he came to know that Mira Whalen was having an affair – her panties had told him. Mira had come back to the house in Wimbledon late one night when Peter had, extraordinarily, made it home from work early. He'd bought her excuse about a late hair appointment, but then he'd turned playful, started to relieve her of her clothing and her handbag had dropped and coughed up a rolled-up red lingerie set he'd never seen before. Mira Whalen hadn't been particularly inclined to lie about how she came to be carrying around a soiled red lace corset, matching panties and stockings, so she'd simply whispered 'sorry' and steeled herself for the worst. As it happened, the worst part of what had come next was not how her husband had raged, but how he had cried.

If she'd been able to talk to Peter about what had caused the affair, she'd tell him it was nothing he had done. Rather, it was her body's stout refusal to carry his baby. The third miscarriage was, she thinks now, as the Datsun crawls through the traffic on the tiny streets toward town, the start of everything. This is what she would tell Peter if she could speak to him, if he was here sitting beside her, if she was finally able to have *that* conversation with him about why she had spent her afternoons astride a twenty-year-old art student with a penchant for older women in tarty red lingerie.

3 September 1982

She is hosting Sam's fifth birthday party when a wine-soaked strawberry slips out of her. This is baby number 3, the subject of three months of constant prayers God has chosen not to hear. They are nearing the end of the party, she is in the middle of the lawn, handing out loot bags, when she realises what is happening, asks a clown to hand out the rest, and makes for the bathroom. In the bathroom, she does not cry. She decides against telling Peter until after the party, she decides to make a brave face for little Sam and returns to the loot bags. It does not make any sense going to the hospital right away, she already knows what the doctors will say and she does not want Sam's birthday to be associated forever with this. She spends the rest of the afternoon organising the piñata and showing harried moms with squirming toddlers to the bathroom and fetching punch for the clown, who is of decidedly bad humour as he waits in his top hat for the time slot for his show.

It is only after they have waved goodbye to the last guest and Peter has returned Sam to his mother's Victorian terrace, where he will have another birthday party tomorrow, that Mira Whalen tells Peter what has happened and is taken to hospital.

After she is no longer pregnant, and she is at home and

brooding, Peter is the same as he always is – he brings her cups of cocoa in bed, he rubs her feet and sings her love songs while she cries, he breaks the news to his friends and those neighbours she can't bring herself to greet at the door. But although he does all these things, something cracks within her. It is something that did not crack when Martha said, on being told she was pregnant with baby number 1: 'That poor woman, you being pregnant so soon after Peter left her.' It is something that did not crack with the demise of baby number 2, but it cracks now, a tiny fissure she does not immediately notice, which yawns, over time, into a chasm she tries to fill with shopping trips and maniacal workouts at the gym, and too much alcohol at the wrong time of day . . . and an art student named Fred for whom she sits naked in response to the ad he placed for an artist's model.

Fred paints her in his flat, in fat, round strokes and bright, bold colours, which she takes to mean that he sees her as the mother she so desperately wants to be. It is because of how she thinks he sees her that she agrees to stay a few minutes for coffee after her sitting one evening; it is why she agrees to go with him to a jazz club on an evening when Peter is again working late. It is because of all this that she finds herself in Fred's bed one lazy Wednesday afternoon in December, with the icy cold glaring at them through the windows, wearing nothing but Fred and a fleece blanket he must have bought in a thrift shop.

What she would tell Peter, she thinks now, as Rosa's husband gets out of the driver's side and comes around to her door and opens it, and stands there with a little transistor to his ear so that he will not miss even a moment of the cricket, is that it didn't matter. It was nothing he should have worried about. It should not have shadowed everything after that, it should not have been allowed to cast doubt on everything before. It just was what it was, it was all about her, it wasn't anything he had done and he shouldn't still be cross about it. He needn't have tried to make her bread pudding or carry her luggage or do family things they hadn't focused on before. He had been perfect as he was.

She would tell Peter that she couldn't remember what Fred looked like, for one, could not remember if she enjoyed sex with him or not.

This is what she tells Rosa's husband now, because he is a man and he would understand these things – that Fred did not mean anything, that she cannot even remember if she enjoyed sleeping with him or not. The fact that she cannot remember it, she tells Rosa's husband, demonstrates the reality of that relationship because she remembers most everything about Peter. The way he ran his right hand through the thinning lock at the front of his forehead when he was tired, or flabbergasted, or angry. How his voice broke when he sang 'I'm Every Woman' for her birthday because it was her favourite song by Chaka Khan. The way he patted her knee when she needed reassurance. Everything. You are a man, explains Mira Whalen to Rosa's husband, you should understand what I mean.

20 August 1984

The following afternoon, the first Mrs Whalen comes for her children. She sweeps on to the rear patio because, in the way of these houses, the only visitors who can enter from the front patio are those who come, like salt air, right off the surface of the sea. As it happens, Mira is on the rear patio, staring at the service gate, wondering if she should change the locks or add another foot of brickwork to the top of the wall so that the house cannot be seen at all from the road, when the red Datsun crawls up the street and slows to a stop.

At first Mira swallows panic, because she believes that this car means the return of the robber, but it is a muted panic, something she feels through cotton, because she is smoking a spliff, and she was never a spliff-smoker before now, and this is the effect that ganja seems to have on her – this muting of painful things just enough so that she can endure them. The panic dissolves into giggles, because she is watching a woman alight from the little red car, and ganja wisdom tells her this is the first Mrs Whalen, and because it reminds her of childhood cartoons where a huge clown disembarks a tiny vehicle for the sake of a few laughs. The first Mrs Whalen is decidedly not huge but her dress is large and billowy. She does not wear the paint-smeared jeans and T-shirt of Mira's imagination. The undersides of her nails are not smeared with greasy acrylic pigments. Her hands are not coarse from stretching canvases and miscalculating the distance between her finger and the staple gun, not like Fred's were.

The giggles coalesce into a hollowness inside her stomach.

The first Mrs Whalen refuses a cup of tea or a glass of mauby or to come inside. She does not want to share a

164

piece of Rosa's renowned great cake or be served a square of warm cassava pone or a few slices of avocado bought for more than they are worth from the wiliest of the market vendors in town. The first Mrs Whalen just wants her children and keeps the taxi waiting, its engine continuously clearing its throat in weak riposte to the roar of the waves.

It is an old taxi, one of the ones you find if you come out of the arrivals hall, past the shirt-jacketed airport taxi drivers with their gleaming white machines, past the buses and coaches awaiting the tour groups. The Datsun would have been one of the pack of unlicensed taxis circling the perimeter of the airport, with raucous drivers shouting their best fare offers. You would have to have been aware of the big difference in the fares of these taxis and the licensed ones to know to take one, Mira thinks, and she suddenly understands that the first Mrs Whalen has visited the island before, that the home she is visiting was once her own. That she must have stood on this very patio in this very house, with her husband, when her husband was still Peter, and watched the very road that Mira, in clean pyjamas freshly washed by Rosa, is staring at now. Mira is suddenly grateful that Rosa scrubbed her skin and shampooed her hair. She imagines that the first Mrs Whalen would have been horrified to turn up and find her dishevelled and smelly. This makes her laugh harder than ever.

Rosa comes, her round face beaming at the sight of the first Mrs Whalen, her soapy hands embracing her without a second thought by either of them. Rosa does not hug

Mira with soapy hands. Rosa did not hug Mira at all before Peter died. The children come shrieking, and join Rosa in embracing their mother, and Mira feels the old knife in her gut, only just dulled by what she is smoking.

The reunion is long and tender, smattered with the mother's apologies, and then Beth and Sam go to pack their things with Rosa while Mira Whalen smokes pot on the back patio, looks at the wall, at the taxi, at the cavernous doorway into which the children have disappeared, at the huge enamel ladybug the first Mrs Whalen wears on her ring finger now, in place of a wedding ring. It is silent on the patio. Mira Whalen does not know what to say to the first Mrs Whalen. What to say to her was generally Peter's job. Peter is dead.

Mira first knew the first Mrs Whalen by her voice. When Peter had called her from his hotel room to tell her that he was leaving her for an island girl he'd met on a business trip, Mira had sat silent in his bed and listened to this voice screaming through the receiver. The voice was more anguished then than angry, and Mira had moved over to the bathroom to brush her hair rather than listen to it, but later conversations had been filled with invective: when Peter came to the island to visit, when Mira travelled to Devon to meet his family, the morning after they married in the registry office in Greenwich. In the subsequent years she had never once set eyes on the woman. The embodiment of that voice is not what she had expected.

For one thing, the first Mrs Whalen is petite and thin with a lilting Irish accent that yawns over her words when she introduces herself. Mira Whalen is distracted by the beauty of that accent; she is so distracted that she cannot hear what the first Mrs Whalen is saying. The first Mrs Whalen has chosen to wear a bright emerald-green dress of many layers of chiffon with straps so fine it seems impossible for them to hold up so much cloth. She is wearing a wide-brimmed yellow hat; her skin is the kind of pale and peachy that must be smothered in protective creams or it will protest the sun by flushing deeply and flaming persistently, even after the required basting in over-the-counter sunscreen. A few stray tendrils of frizzy red hair threaten revolt from beneath the hat. The first Mrs Whalen appears to be in the pink of health and not in the least bit bereaved, but she does not appear to be gloating or resentful. There is no sign of bitterness when she talks, the words dancing out of a slightly open smile. The ladybug travels over her cheek as she tucks a stray tendril of hair away. The waves crash from the other side of the house. The spliff blazes and crackles. The taxi coughs and is turned off, the driver realising that the collection will take longer than his gas tank might allow.

When Beth and Sam return with Rosa, they are carrying the little suitcases they had used for hand luggage on the trip to the island, the only bags that Peter had not tried to lug with him while they had waited for a taxi, one of the licensed ones. The first Mrs Whalen hugs the children hard when they return, ushers them towards Mira to say goodbye.

What Peter had said about her would be important at a time like this, thinks Mira, if only she could remember it. It would help her to understand what the woman is likely to be saying through those thin unvarnished lips, to respond in an intelligent manner. Mira knows the first Mrs Whalen owns an art gallery in Camden, that she is a much better art dealer than the artist she first wanted to be, but not much else. Peter did not talk much about her during their initial courtship on his frequent business trips. By the time Mira had moved to London, all traces of the first Mrs Whalen had been removed from the house.

Peter had not mentioned her habit of taking off for an ashram in India for two months at a time whenever he had the children for the long summer sojourn on Baxter's Beach. Mira had always imagined her in a draughty old studio in Camden, splashing her frustration over huge canvases laid flat on the floor.

From the woman's facial expression, it would appear that she is offering her sympathy.

'Thanks,' says Mira. The first Mrs Whalen sets the ladybug to flight again. A headache blossoms from the centre of Mira Whalen's brain, unfurls behind her eyes and ears and blooms, crowding out her thoughts.

The children hug her but their eyes betray relief. They are looking at their mother and the waiting taxi, which has coughed awake again. Beth gives Mira a kiss on her cheek and has to be coaxed into another one. Sam reaches up to be lifted and sobs into her neck when he gets there. He was only two when she married Peter. He calls her 'Momma Mira', he comes to her to be comforted when he falls, but this is his real momma, whose name does not need to be qualified when he calls her. Mira thinks she puts the spliff down and clucks comforts at him, she thinks she rubs his hair and his back. She thinks she tells him she will visit. She wonders if she can demand to see him again. She wonders whether she should be surrendering them so easily, whether Peter would have wanted her to protest that she hadn't been given notice, hadn't been properly informed that the first Mrs Whalen would sweep into the back patio and take back her children so soon after Peter's death when she knows very well that Mira Whalen doesn't seem to be blessed with a womb that can have any.

Rosa is the one who tears little Sam away. The first Mrs Whalen shepherds the children across the street and into the car, says something to Rosa, who is going with her to help them settle into the first Mrs Whalen's hotel. They will spend a night there, and leave for Camden tomorrow.

The gate closes, the car leaves in a flurry of waving hands and grim goodbyes and Mira Whalen is truly alone, a fact she finds funnier than ever.

CHAPTER TWENTY

Lala
20 August 1984

If we were to look for Lala, and if we were to find her on the flank of Baxter's Beach, knuckle-deep in the hair of a stranger, if we were to walk up to her and ask her whether she knows the frowsy beach bum, the one at whom our island women chupse, the one the memory of whom makes some tourist women breathe faster, we would notice first how she keeps her gaze on the head in front of her when she queries, 'Who?' as if she is deliberately avoiding our eyes. Her fingers would not slow down, not then, they would keep weaving hair at a speed that would seem incapable of measurement: *overunderoverunderoverunderover* . . .

We might describe Robert Parris (also known as 'Tone') first in physical terms, because his form – rusty, shoulder-length locks, average height, slim build, sinewy and strong – is what is first obvious to anyone who looks at him. We would explain that we are talking about the one whose toenails are washed white as surf, whose skin is salted with the fine white dust of a living made on the beach. We would explain that the hair on his head and hands has become the gold of the sun, so that, like the sun, we would not see it if we look at him straight on.

When Lala still feigns ignorance of his acquaintance we could refer to his quirks – the shark-tooth necklace he wears around his neck and kisses before he ventures into the water, the way he slaps the surface of the sea with his jet ski so that the older swimmers startle and the younger ones spit obscenities, the tendency he has to take the unruly locks at the crown of his head and squeeze them to get rid of the salt water while bent over at the waist.

And because Robert Parris is a subject that must be avoided at all costs, we would hear Lala again say 'Who?' even as her fingers slow their speed on the hair in front of her. (*Over. Under. Over. Under. Over. Stop. Over.*)

And it is only after she realizes that we will keep asking until she answers – after we have described him in such a way that it would be more suspicious if she said she does *not* know him – that we would find the small brittle smile of recognition.

'Oh, *Tone,*' Lala would say. 'Yes – yes, I know him.' And her hands would start to trip over themselves, to drop the silken strands of flaxen hair before her so that she will have to start the cornrow all over again. (*Over. Stop. Over. Under. Stop. Over. Stop. Under. Overunderover-underoverunder. Stop.*)

If we were to push further, to ask *how* she knows him, her eyes would fall from the hair in which she has tangled her fingers and land on her feet, where a fly would be broaching the sticky-sweet memory of a drop of sno-cone dried on her toe. And her eyes would stay there while we reassure the tourist between Lala's legs. This tourist would now be closing her book, gathering her towel, saying she

171

can come back when we are done, hesitating with a half-done head when we tell her it is okay, she can stay, this will only take a few minutes.

Perhaps prior to the death of her baby, Lala's smile would have widened and her 'Why you want to know?' would *not* have led to more probing while she plaited corn-rows with such tenderness that her client would have started to doze off, her hair now being plaited in the land of dreams.

Before the death of the baby we might have said we were asking because we have seen the way he looks at her when he lands on the beach with a roar of the jet ski and the water only just rejoining behind him, the way she avoids looking up at the sound of this roar as every other pair of eyes on her stretch of sand does. Had we not been aware that she was wedded to another man, we might have told her, we would have taken this Tone for her husband. Were we not aware that this Tone sells his body to the tourist women on the beach, we would believe that his body is hers, so studiously does she avoid devouring it with her eyes in the way her client cannot help doing.

But this is not before the death of Lala's baby, this is after. This is a time when we do not talk to Lala, when our good hawkers hesitate to refer tourists in need of braids and beading to her, although we know she is our best. This is a time when we have all heard how Lala can lunge at a crab in the middle of cornrowing and try to kill it with her comb. We have heard how the wailing of babies on the beach can make her howl, and leave her too upset to finish her client's hair. This is a time when some of us, unsure that Lala's mind is still steady, refrain from asking her questions about anything, for fear we might further unsettle her.

But unlike us, Sergeant Beckles is going to ask Lala his questions, despite the death of her baby and the fact that she is unlikely to be truthful in her answers. He is not everyone on the beach, after all, he is a sergeant of the Royal Island Police Force and he has conducted a covert surveillance operation and he has seen this woman kissing a man she is not married to on the steps of her husband's house a few weeks after her baby died in mysterious circumstances. Sergeant Beckles has a job to do. This is why he persists in his line of questioning, why he takes his time with the asking. He does not allow Lala's lowered eyes or her client's squirming or our quiet stares to put him off in the least. This is why he takes a seat on the sand, removes his spit-shined hard-shoes, leaves his socks on and swats the fly approaching Lala's big toe with one swift, smooth movement of his hand so that she realizes that he has killed it only when he opens his palm to reveal a fly carcass he flicks away without a hint of revulsion, because he is a policeman and he has seen much, much worse.

'You know what I forget to ask you the other day?' Sergeant Beckles says to Lala when he is seated and smiling, despite the gnawing hunger in his stomach, despite the rumpled, slept-in uniform. 'Is my fault really, is why I can't ask you to come down to the station to answer these extra questions, you understand, 'cause is me that forget to ask you!'

He chuckles, a chuckle that says *We're all human,* we all

make little mistakes from time to time, you can't grudge a person a few mistakes.

(*Over. Stop.*
Under. Stop.
Start. Stop.
Stop.
Over. Underoverunderoverunder. Stop. Start. Stop.)

'Let me tell you something about policemen,' he says. 'We suppose to ask you all the questions up front, *brisk brisk,* and only ask more questions later if something else come up. Nobody want to be coming back to go over the same thing all the time so. But investigations go on and if there is new information . . .well . . . is you I trying to help, see? So let me ask you this question I shoulda ask you the other day.' He chuckles again, runs his fingers through some dry sand and dusts them. 'How you come to know this one they call Tone?'

CHAPTER TWENTY-ONE

Lala
9 July 1979

Lala meets Tone on her thirteenth birthday.

On that day she wakes up apathetic. She feels no happier than the day before, no more comforted, no more hopeful than on any other day. She recognises that this indifference to birthdays does not happen in the pages of the Secret Seven and Nancy Drew books she devours at the rate of three or more per week, and therefore, on this her thirteenth birthday, in recognition of the fact that she has outgrown these books, Lala stops reading Enid Blyton. It is consequently no special injury when she is *not* presented at breakfast with two instalments of Malory Towers, wrapped in the slightly crumpled sepia-coloured tissue paper from which Wilma cuts her dress-making patterns. In her fervent prayers to God in the weeks leading up to this birthday, Lala has begged for these specific books wrapped in precisely this way, these books at the very least, but now she waves away the fact that God has not answered her prayers. As a matter of fact, she tells herself, it is better this way, it saves her having to explain to Wilma that she no longer reads Enid Blyton.

When Wilma realises that Lala has entered the kitchen,

she comes to stand next to her, places a hand on her head and administers prayers. And on this birthday, for the first time ever, Lala performs a mental eye roll at the repeated mention of God. She opens her eyes on the amen, without uttering the word herself, and her gaze lands on two golden-brown bakes on her plate, awaiting a ladle-measure of salted cod to become her breakfast. She sits silent at the kitchen table, on which a square of heavy transparent plastic draws sweat from her elbows to the soundtrack of sizzling saltfish. She thinks of all the gifts she could have gotten, if her mother was still alive and celebrating with her – a Walkman, perhaps, or a boom box or a pair of hot-pink LA Gear sneakers.

Wilma wipes her hands and points at the head and shoulders of a mannequin sitting on a chair in the corner. Lala recognises it – it is the stand that Wilma uses to fluff her wigs and repair her hats, but this mannequin also has fine brown hair of its own.

'For you,' says Wilma. 'You can plait her hair.'

Wilma has noticed how Lala turns the hair of her dollies into elaborate braided creations, how she experiments with her own hair when Wilma will let her, how she sneaks into Wilma's room and runs her fingers through the silky wigs Wilma keeps there. Lala says thanks.

Carson farts from the pantry off the kitchen, which Wilma has turned into his room to spare him having to walk up the stairs. The stench that follows is familiar. Lala knows that Wilma will wash Carson by wheeling him into the backyard, cutting the clothes off of him with her sharp, sharp scissors and turning the garden hose on him so that

176

he screams under the blast of the water, the shock of the cold and the bite of a wind that wails at 6 a.m. She will lift him like he is cotton on to a wooden chair with a low back to which she has had the neighbourhood handyman affix wheels repurposed from a child's tricycle, salvaged from the dump. She will wheel him over the kitchen's flagstone floor, down a piece of plywood fitted like a ramp, on to the gritty dirt of the backyard. When the pipe creaks on and the hose stiffens, but before Carson has been stung by the shrapnel of icy water in the verdant green shade of breadfruit trees his ancestors planted with their own hands, he will scream. He will scream in high-pitched exclamations reminiscent of the way the men who play dominoes by the street light effuse after a joke or a sweet six-love, except that Lala will not miss the undertone of terror in Carson's hollering. It is something she sometimes hears in her nightmares.

'*Woi! Woi! Woi!*' Carson will scream, but in Lala's dreams he is asking '*Why? Why? Why?*', a rhetorical demand to know what evil he has committed to deserve these insults, this cruelty in his old age. On this, the morning of her thirteenth birthday, Lala will tell him.

Wilma's wiry hands throw the ladle into the sink, unhinge the apron from her neck and waist and are rigid by her side as she walks into Carson's bedroom.

'You is one dirty old man is wuh!' she protests. 'You mean you ain't know yet to find the potty, Carson?'

As recently as the previous birthday, when Lala was younger and still innocent enough to think Carson faultless in this whole sorry business of his ignominious shits, she had explained them away by telling herself he couldn't help it. Until Wilma showed her how, if promised a beer for keeping the bed linen clean, there would be no such spontaneous soiling of himself. Wilma had shown this to her the last time Lala cried when Wilma had hosed Carson off to his hollers of '*Woi! Woi! Woi!*'

The porridge that Carson will eat starts to burn and the sweet scent of hard spice becomes the smelly scorch of any burning bark. ('*Woi! Woi! Woi!*') Wilma drops the hose, rushes in, replaces her apron before lifting the saucepan with her bare hands (because Wilma is a woman of order and the apron comes first), burns her fingers, drops the little copper pot she knew was bad for porridge but used anyway. She slaps her arms against her sides, stamps her feet, calls for Jesus, asks for the Lord's mercy, receives neither and snaps at Lala to please wash Carson while she remakes his porridge. Wilma is now also worried that she will be late for work.

Lala rolls her eyes when Wilma's back is turned and her grandmother's bony hands are scraping the charred and gummy cornmeal from the bottom of her new copper pot while an iron pot of water awaits the new porridge. She pushes back her chair so the legs rake against the stone floor and looks with longing at the two bites of saltfish still sitting on her plate. (*Woi! Woi! Woi!*)

The skin of Carson's back is rashed with goose bumps when Lala picks up the hose. This skin is paler than it used to be and it has started the slide towards the grave that is characteristic of the mortally ill, the dying and the elderly and that is most pronounced in those who are all three. Lala goes to the pipe, turns it so far left that it locks into full force and she cannot turn it back again, even if, some-where deep inside of her, she wanted to lower the water pressure. She does not.

The fine-featured girls in Enid Blyton get birthdays with something called blancmange that sounds delicious even to say. They get frosted cakes and sandwiches with pink and yellow cheese pastes and friends who come around with presents and freshly washed faces at 3 p.m., thinks Lala, but *she* gets to hose shit off her crazy grandfather, whose wilted totie worms from a nest of patchy pubic hair that resembles the coat of a dog with mange. (*Woi! Woi! Woi!*) She gets to scorn a beloved breakfast because she is suddenly aware of how its colour matches the faeces speck-ling Carson's slashed-up clothes and the tricycle wheels on the makeshift wheelchair. (*Woi! Woi! Woi!*) This is what she gets. She tightens her fist around the hose. She aims.

'*Woi! Woi! Woi!*' screams Carson. '*Woiiiiiiiiiii!*'

'Why? Because you is a nasty, dutty old man,' spits Lala under her breath. 'Because you is a nasty, shitty, mudda-cunt old man.'

When Carson is bathed and bedded again, and Wilma has shovelled him as full of freshly made cornmeal pap as she can before she is forced to leave, Wilma and Lala and the half-mannequin head to work. Work, when it is not mak-ing dresses for women and girls, when it is not raising and slaughtering and selling her chickens, when it is not feed-ing Lala or caring for Carson, or cleaning the house, is cooking for a madam called Mrs Kennedy in one of the big houses on Baxter's Beach.

179

Wilma isn't fond of the idea of taking Lala to work with her, but as it is, Lala is already too big-boned and breasted to be trusted alone at home. Aunt Earlie has died, and there is no other relative with whom Wilma can leave her granddaughter while school is out for summer. The memory of what happened to Esme does not allow her to leave Lala at home with Carson, even if he is old and feeble and cannot remember his own name sometimes now. Wilma realises that it cannot be helped and therefore settles into stoicism. It is the first day of the summer holiday. She has cautioned Lala to be quiet to make Mrs Kennedy forget that she is there, to make sure and not speak unless spoken to and not, under any circumstances, to use the people's bathroom if she has to make number two.

While they wait at a big wooden gate, Lala watches the veins that web the back of her grandmother's knees, the softness of her ankles above the *slap-slap* of her slippers as she taps her impatience and waits for the door to open, the tumble of curls under her hat, the highlights in her wig glistening like the strands of gold Rumpelstiltskin spun for the King. Lala wonders what Wilma will do now that she has given her the mannequin, how her grandmother will fluff her wigs into fullness.

The gate swings open and Wilma smiles at a white-haired woman with the soft, slightly wrinkled skin of a rich woman who actually wears the expensive creams sampled in the magazines, a woman who buys those bottles by the dozen.

'Wilma! We were wondering what happened!' exclaims the woman in a voice that does not move a single register above or below politeness. They are under a pagoda festooned with purple bougainvillea and the buzzing of bees and Lala's hand is heavy in Wilma's as she is tugged into the house – she does not want to be stuck in this house every day of her vacation. For this reason, she broaches the welcome mat reluctantly, wishing she could stay under the pagoda and be stung and stung and stung on the big bones of her face, just so she will have a good reason to scream. The thought of having to watch Wilma do chores during the eight-hour wait until they can go home again is worse than the fact that she did not get the something she wanted for her birthday.

Mrs Kennedy is wearing white linen culottes and a pale grey denim shirt with a crisp collar and diamonds at her ears and her neck and her wrists and her fingers that look like they have captured rainbows inside of them and are not the dull white of the stones in the costume jewellery Lala convinces Wilma to buy her from the itinerant vendors when they come.

'Little issue at home,' explains Wilma, 'all fixed now . . . I sorry.'

'Not a problem, Wilma,' says Mrs Kennedy. 'And who have you brought with you?'

Lala nods hello with a joylessness the woman does not seem to notice.

'Mrs Kennedy, this is my granddaughter, Stella.'

'Stella! How delightful to meet you!'

Lala believes that it is her home-made gingham dress, gently flared to a perfect tea length and bordered in anglaise, the matching ribbon that restrains her pressed hair, her cheap Chinese slippers worn with socks, it is these things that make this woman think that she is younger than she is, that make her think it is OK to speak to her as if she is some little child. So she does not return the greeting, even if she knows that Wilma will wring her ears for it later.

'Come in and make yourself comfortable,' says Mrs Kennedy. She starts walking Wilma through the menu for the afternoon: Wilma will clean the house in preparation for Mrs Kennedy's party and Wilma will bake a cake that Lala would kill for and Wilma will remember to ask the gardener to cut the pink roses to decorate the table because they are Mrs Kennedy's favourite and she will make and serve green banana pickle because it is Mrs Kennedy's favourite thing that Wilma makes. And it is not even Mrs Kennedy's birthday.

Lala finds the boy at lunchtime. She has taken her mannequin head with its straight brown hair and she has drifted out of the garden and up the beach and then into a cool alcove covered by coconut palms and sea-grape trees. She is looking for a quiet place to sit and plait her mannequin's hair and the comfortably breezy spot is the perfect respite from a very hot day. This is where she finds the boy. He lays on his belly adjacent to a stone gutter where plastered cement restrains a dribble of green waste-water from soaking into the earth before it reaches the sea. The water smells horrid; she can't understand why the boy would hold his nose so close to it, can't believe there is something so valuable to him that bearing this stench would be better than suffering its loss.

This is how Lala meets Tone, neck over the edge of a gutter like he is looking for something he has lost, pants below the swell of his buttocks. Heavy with the guilt of what she'd done to Carson just that morning, she feels her heart move at the sight of him, the thought of what could have happened to end with him there, ass exposed and bleeding. The boy is crying, letting the snot stretch down into the algae below. Lala has never seen a male cry before, except for a fat little baby at Wilma's church. Even in his moments of anguish, Carson screams but his eyes remain dry as bone. It is one of the reasons her grandmother ignores his screams – the dry eyes betraying the lack of emotion behind the bellowing. He does it for attention is what Wilma says when Lala pleads with her to stop, you don't know what he is really like.

Lala watches the boy cry a few minutes before she can bring herself to speak to him.

'Hey,' she whispers, 'you good?'

He doesn't reply; she wonders if maybe he is high, one of those parro teens who lets mature tourist men buy them with money. Wilma has told her about this type of sale and purchase by then, warned her that it is the worst kind, a horrible thing, although she has not deigned to describe exactly what it is that the parro teens offer and the mature tourist men buy.

'You OK?'

Still nothing.

Lala considers leaving to call someone, the police, maybe, someone at the Kennedy house, but she fears that in so doing Wilma will find out that she hasn't after all stayed in the room to which she has been exiled for the day, hasn't observed her strict admonitions to remain indoors, reading, out of sight of Mrs Kennedy, her guests, and Wilma, serving dainty desserts on silver platters.

Lala looks at the boy, takes in his exposed behind, blood drying in iridescent swathes of brown that crack and peel under the gaze of the sun. She puts her mannequin head and her beads down and runs the few yards to the sea and catches some seawater in an empty soda bottle and comes back and washes away the evidence with salty beach water and worries that there will be sand in her socks that she will have to explain to Wilma later. And, unlike Carson, with Tone she warns him first that the water is coming, that it might be cold, that it might smart. With Tone she pours gently and holds his hand to help him to his knees and wipes his eyes with the edge of her skirt. She asks him to just stay there, says she'll be back with some salve and a towel. The boy doesn't say anything, but makes muffled gurgling noises like he is trying to swallow his own tongue, and tears continue to pool at the corners of his eyes and drizzle onto his cheeks although his expression doesn't suggest that he is crying at all. Lala knows that kind of crying; it is crying born of anger, rather than hurt.

When Lala comes back, he has pulled up his pants, the water bottle is empty, his face is clean and he is throwing stones into the canal. Lala has found an antibiotic cream in one of Mrs Kennedy's cabinets, has stolen a leaf off an aloe plant from her garden, and now she sits next to him, pounding the two together with a smooth sea stone because that is how Wilma tends Carson when he gets a sore that will not heal and she believes that this will help this boy.

'You want me to call somebody?'

He shakes his head, no. The stones ping when they bounce off the concrete walls of the canal, plop and sink when they land in the wobbly moss leeching on to its middle. Lala can't tell whether he is trying to hit the concrete or the moss. She finishes pounding. The sea-grape trees do not cackle, the waves do not whisper near the shore, the seabirds do not squawk.

'You want me to put it on?'

He looks at the potion. He is crying again.

'I won't look,' she explains, and when he is still sullen, 'Or my grandmother know a nurse-lady live near town. You could go there, I—'

'Don't need no nurse!'

He is so fierce in his refusal that Lala jumps and wonders whether coming back to tend him was a good idea. She'd guess his age at fifteen if pressed, although his height and build mark him as younger. There are all sorts of stories, she belatedly remembers, about girls who do not follow the warnings of good elders and find themselves in the company of males they do not know. Stories Wilma has told her. She begins to worry that she is not safe.

'Help me up.'

She stares at him, suddenly unable to move. He sucks his teeth, wobbles on to his hands and knees, grabs a branch and pulls himself up until his body weight is borne on his right knee.

'Don't tell nobody 'bout this, you hear?'

185

His voice is menacing and she recoils and nods, mute.
'Please,' he says, softly.
He stands without the branch. He starts to limp away.
The salve stays on the stone beside her.

The next time she sees him is a few days later, when he is working in Mrs Kennedy's garden, using a cutlass to hack at a sweet lime hedge with the savage ease of a man free of concern for his own safety. He is wearing several layers – a long-sleeved polo shirt that might have once been green but has been washed into grey, a pink T-shirt and above that a bright blue polyester button-down. He is wearing long green pants and rubber garden boots and nothing in his walk suggests that he is the same boy from the beach. But it is him. Somehow it makes her indignant that he does not look up when she speaks to Wilma, does not acknowledge the source of the shadow that falls on him when she walks past on her way to the beach with her mannequin, does not seek a few seconds when she is unaccompanied to give her the thanks he denied her that day by the gutter.

CHAPTER TWENTY-TWO

Lala
21 July 1979

Carson falls off his bed and is hospitalised again. As a result, every evening when she has finished the housework for Mrs Kennedy, Wilma boards a bus to Baxter's General and Lala is alone. On these evenings, she does not go straight home like Wilma warns her to do. She walks towards the house as long as Wilma is watching and then, when the bus is almost a speck in the distance and Wilma is no longer watching, she makes her way to the beach and sits and plaits the hair on her mannequin. There is something about the beach, about the quiet crash of water, that soothes her, something about the wide expanse of blue that makes her feel she is free. On these evenings at the beach, she watches Tone skim the surface of the sea on a silvery board while her hands work their magic. At first he does not acknowledge her, but one evening, a few weeks into the summer, she starts to make her way home and accidentally leaves her mannequin head on the sand, and he calls after her, runs to her holding the perpetually smiling head in his hands.

After that he grunts hellos each evening that he passes her seated on the beach in inappropriate gingham dresses, plaiting and beading the hair of a mannequin with glassy eyes. And a few weeks later he asks if she would like to visit his mother, who sells the best beads, better even than those sold in town. His aunt sends them in from America, he says; some of those beads have not reached Baxter's Beach yet. By then, a few tourists have stopped beside her to admire the patterns in the braids of the bodiless mannequin; one or two have asked whether she would do theirs. Lala is flattered – the professional hair braiders litter the beach, women whose false nails *clack clack clack* as they descend the plaits they weave, like spiders, out of air. She is now beginning to think of braiding and beading as something she could do to get away. Something that will earn her enough money to escape Carson's awful shits and Wilma's suffocating guardianship for good. The best and brightest beads might be a beginning.

Lala is doubtful of Tone's motives and doesn't have money to buy beads, but she agrees.

They go to meet his mother. The mother is friendly but she doesn't get up, and Lala spends most of the rest of the meeting wondering why her apparent friendliness does not prompt her to her feet in the presence of a stranger. The mother is a squat black woman who buys and begs for discarded clothes and sits in her veranda all day, shredding them into long strips to be sold to seamen. While she strips, she talks about finishing her house. It is a house made of unpainted wood, swollen by rain and dark with age. At the back of the house the wooden structure has been encased in a concrete and steel frame, which is the skeleton of the new house she is building. This is the house she will leave for her children, Mrs Parris says, Robert included. It takes Lala a minute to realise that Tone is the Robert of his mother's imaginings. The house is for Robert and his four brothers, says the mother. She imagines them, all five of them, living there together into old age; she prays her five boys all get good wives to sweep it clean each morning. Her scrawny chickens strut and cluck through a mound of building sand she has bought which is stored by her step and births blades of grass and green things. When she suggests that Robert take Lala to the kitchen to pour her a cool drink of guava juice, Lala whispers:

'You tell she what happen?'

'No.'

Lala thinks this is what it must mean to be trusted by a man – to know things about him his own mother doesn't, things he would not want anyone else to know. His mother smells of uncooked rice and the many perfumes of the mystery donors to the Salvation Army from whom she begs these clothes. The scissors she uses for cutting are large and sharp and are attached to her apron by a chain and a manacle. It reminds Lala of Wilma. Of Carson.

While she sips, Robert goes into a bedroom to fetch the beads. The beads are brought out on a wide flat wooden tray. There are neon beads and Lucite beads and beads that look like braided gold and wooden beads and cowrie shells and clasps made of gilded wire. Lala's fingers find and fiddle with the best ones, turn them over and over and peep through the middles where there are holes waiting for hair.

'They nice,' she says. 'I will ask my grandmother and come back.'

Later, when the mother leaves to buy vegetables, Lala notices her atrophied left leg, which seems to wish to draw itself into her side, to curl up in a foetal position. This leg ends in a foot that claws the floor like talons and a heel that never touches the ground and is smooth and yellow. The talons are long and painted red and Lala tries not to stare. After his mother leaves, Tone presses a bag of gold-braid beads into her hands, silences her protests about not having the money to pay for them, tells her she can have them, the mother would not mind.

Carson deteriorates and Wilma's time at the hospital extends beyond the bell to signal the end of visiting hours at seven o'clock. Carson needs to be cleaned and fed and watched and the overworked nurses at Baxter's General do not mind if a wife wants to reserve these tasks for herself.

Lala hears Wilma's admonitions to stay at home and in her books until she gets back, but listens instead to her heart. She finds herself standing on the road with her chest thudding each evening that the bus exits her line of sight for Baxter's General, and then she runs back to the beach until she is breathless.

They go to see *Rocky* at the Globe Cinema, where Tone has a friend from schooldays who will let them in for free. They sit in the balcony, in the more expensive seats despite the threadbare red velvet and the peeling gilt columns that separate them from the gallery. From this heady height they pelt the moviegoers below with popcorn and candy, a trait of bad breeding that Wilma would surely whip her for, and a source of extraordinary delight for Lala as a result. Lala looks at their feet propped on the backs of the seats before them, his neat ones in Reebok sneakers she's seen on posters in town, her huge ones in the jelly flats Wilma has forced her to wear with her frilly socks. He does not say anything when she takes hers down to remove the socks. He does not blink when she puts them up again and, sockless, pushes them closer to his.

One evening, Wilma leaves a little late and Tone, worried about why Lala hasn't appeared, walks to the bus stop instead. They don't have a lot of time before visiting hours are over and Wilma will be back, so Tone says he will take Lala somewhere close by, somewhere she hasn't seen before. When they reach the mouth of a cave beneath the huge nose of a rock face, Lala hesitates. Tone takes her hand, coaxes her forward, tells her not to worry, stick close to him and she will be safe.

On this evening he takes Lala for the first time to the underground tunnels that traverse the earth beneath Baxter's Village. He tells her that his family has known about them for generations. These tunnels were built many years ago by soldiers stationed on the island to guard it, he says; they were intended to stop the flooding that accompanied each rainy season. It took some time before the English soldiers realised that the flooding encouraged mosquitoes to breed, and they bore the yellow fever that killed the troops in their numbers. Before that, they just knew that the rain fell, the earth flooded and soldiers died, and so

191

they built the tunnels to alleviate the flooding and to keep the soldiers' thoughts off death and firmly on the mathematical mystery of digging beneath the ground.

He don't show anybody else these tunnels, Tone tells her, they are his and his alone, his special place he goes to think about . . . things. And he is quiet as if he does not want to speak aloud about what those things are. The tunnels belong to him, he says, nobody know them like he does, but if she not scared, he will show her what they are like. Lala says she is not scared.

The tunnels are one man wide and two men tall and they are dark and dimly lit in parts where they open into caves above ground. Tone walks just ahead of Lala, who holds his hand tightly; it is the only solid evidence that he is in the deep dark with her other than the sound of shifting pebbles as he moves forward. They stop when the tunnel opens into a damp cave where the roof *drip-drips* water.

It is here, standing up, that Lala sleeps with Tone for the first time, or so it feels in the few moments after sex. Afterwards, she remembers sweat, the saltiness of his neck and the starchy stiffness of his T-shirt in her mouth when she bit into it, but otherwise she thinks she understands why the act is likened to dozing. She remembers it as a dream – the sensation that they had been forever squeezed together in that tunnel, and as if, unless she was stuck to him in just that way, a part of her would always be missing. She remembers coming out of the tunnel a changed person, sure that she must be walking differently, that Wilma will know as soon as she drifts through the door from the hospital that, despite her vigilance, Lala's virtue has been lost. But Wilma doesn't know, doesn't notice, and aims her anger instead on the gold-plated earring that, much as she has warned her, her granddaughter has managed to lose.

Tone soon starts ditching the summer job in Mrs Kennedy's garden. He takes to surfing all day instead, lies on a surfboard and paddles out on it every morning when there are good waves and then stands up and dances on the surface of the sea right in front of the Kennedy house while Lala watches from the upstairs bedroom to which Wilma has banished her. This morning ritual soon becomes an all-day obsession, and sometimes, although she has gone to great effort to come to the beach looking for him as soon as Wilma's back is turned, she is forced to be content with being seated on sand that assaults her face and hair and makes her worry that Wilma will know where she's been.

One day she sits on the sand alone and Tone does not appear. He is not in the sea. He is not on the sand. Lala goes home before Wilma returns, worried sick that something has happened to him. Although she visits the beach each evening after that when Wilma goes to the hospital, she does not see Tone again for three months, and by then Carson is better and she can no longer get away as easily.

Eventually she ignores Wilma's warnings and takes to long walks, for the sake not of meeting Tone but of being free to do anything she wants. When Wilma discovers she is missing, she often waits for her at the gate of her little stone house with a switch in one hand and a Bible in the

193

other. Lala does not mind. While Wilma is trying to beat her granddaughter full of good sense, Lala thinks of new styles of braids and beads and the one-armed sister girl who lost her arm in that tunnel. It is because of the one-armed sister that she does not allow these lashes to deter her from escaping Wilma's stone house whenever she feels like it. It is for this one-armed sister that she tries to find and explore tunnels and dark places anywhere she goes for the next two years.

On one of these occasions she chooses to visit a fair. And it is at the fair, amidst the gay stalls and gruff music Wilma has forbidden her to listen to, amidst the creak of a merry-go-round and the hawking of snow cones, and lucky dips and donkey rides, that she meets a giant on a unicycle who, despite the magic of his art, looks like he would rather do nothing but spend his time talking to her. The giant's name is Adan.

CHAPTER TWENTY-THREE

Tone
13 September 1979

When Tone's fifteen-year-old body has mended itself and he no longer winces when he goes to the bathroom, no longer jumps each time he walks the road and a bush rustles, no longer watches the ghost marks of black and blue hand-prints on his arms with incredulity, something starts to eat him. It is this thing that Tone responds to when anyone offends him, instead of the actual wrong that has been committed, and his response is therefore often disproportionate.

Fish Brown tackles him during a football game one afternoon and holds his arms behind him in the same way that Tone repeatedly suffers in his nightmares, landing on top of him while Tone is face down in soggy grass. For this Tone gifts Fish a broken nose and three lost teeth. Tone is unaware that he keeps on punching long after he has stunned Fish Brown into submission. It is not that he does not feel his fists pound Fish's flesh like the movement of his mother's mortar; it is rather that somehow he does not understand that the firm pillow he is punching is a person, and that this person is Fish Brown – skinny, bow-legged Fish with the perpetually open glare of the species after which he is nicknamed. Tone only stops after he has been punching for a while and Fish's eyes are white orbs of surprise in a bloody pulp of face and Ma Tone's screaming reaches her son's ears through a mist.

Ma Tone has run the length of the fence that separates her house from the playing field, to find the entrance and stop the fight. One of her other sons has fetched her because, he said, Robert and Fish had words and Robert get that look he get when he about to lose his head and nobody can hold back Robert when he lose his head, everybody tried and Robert just keeping on punching the same Fish Brown he thick-thick with since primary school days. He says it with such amazement, such admiration that his brother could be more powerful than the many who tried to keep him off the other player, that Ma Tone rises on her one good foot before he is finished and runs despite the awkward gait her condition dictates. She rounds the piss-wet wall of the cricket pavilion some politician has had built to ensure that boys like her son are kept out of this very type of trouble, and screams at him to *STOP! ROBERT, STOP!* although the rusty-haired monster crouched over a prone and bloody Fish Brown does not look like her Robert at all, it looks like something darker, something she can only restrain with an appeal to the Almighty. So Ma Tone drops on her one good knee before she reaches her son's side and pleads the blood of Jesus over the demonic force that has possessed her son, *sweet Jesus, please.* And this is when Robert comes to himself and hears his mother praying and sees his good friend Fish Brown, against whom he has no beef that he can remember, choking on his own blood with Tone's two red-dipped hands compressing his throat. Ma Tone runs to her son then, grabs him against her chest, holds his face in between her palms and searches his eyes for the sweet, slow-to-anger child she once knew.

'You all right, Robert?' she asks him. 'Robert, you all right?' because although she cannot guess what it is, Ma Tone understands that her son's sudden violent disposition means that perhaps *he* is the one who is suffering something and not the swollen and broken Fish Brown, coughing blood unto the grass of the playing field.

'I all right, Ma,' Tone tells her, but he is twisting his face away from her gaze to stop her seeing the cause of his anger so that the effort she must make to keep it steady between her palms is a fight in itself, one that she is not winning.

The police come with the sirens silent but flashing and in the pulsing winks of red and blue, Ma Tone tries to search her son's face for what ails him until two policemen step out and drag the boy away from her grasp and her gazing. It is not, as the police think, the fact that her son is being dragged away from her and to the station that causes Ma Tone to wail. It is the tiny glimpse she gets of something in her son's eyes just before she lets him go, something that she hasn't seen before, when her panic at his being pulled away from her causes him to allow their eyes to meet. This tiny glimpse is all Ma Tone needs to know that there is something she does not know. And that this not knowing is very dangerous indeed.

After his arrest, she tries her best for him, Ma Tone does. She empties the money bag tucked beneath her breasts to pay for a lawyer, she buys him the best dress slacks and tie she can find for his court appearances. She begs the family of Fish Brown not to press charges until they cross the street when they see her coming and refuse the gifts and money she sends by envoys. Despite these efforts on the part of his mother, Tone is sent to the Government Industrial School for Wayward Boys for three months. When Ma Tone visits him there, he persists in not meeting her eyes, except when she tells him the girl came to ask after him, the girl he brought to visit. When she says this, he looks straight at her, and his eyes brighten, before darkening, clouding over again.

'And what you tell her?'

'I tell her you gone 'way,' mumbles Ma Tone. 'I didn't know what else to tell her.'

'Is the best thing you tell her,' Tone assures her. 'Is better than she worrying about me in here.'

On his release he is rewarded with the reputation of a ruffian who is not to be messed with, he is ignored by teachers in school, given a wide berth by the bullies in the street and chosen first for football teams in games that somehow then dissolve before they even get started because nobody wants to offend Tone by not choosing him but nobody wants to risk playing with him either.

Within three weeks of his release, a drunkard heckles him one day on his way to the beach, tugs his surfboard and tries to insult him by saying his ass is round and wide like a woman's. This drunkard is flung so far into the air that villagers report for years afterwards that he is lucky to be alive, and Tone is returned to the School for Wayward Boys – this time for over a year.

Tone leaves school with no certificates and the Thing He Cannot Name still gnawing at him. A friend of Ma Tone suggests he try renting jet skis to tourists, as he is so at ease in the sea, and puts him on to Capitan, who has several jet skis and hires them out on a concessionary basis to seaworthy young men who need to make a dollar. But then Tone is robbed of the fee for a ride on his machine by an Italian tourist, who spits in his face when Tone insists he pay him. At the end of what happens next, the tourist is hospitalised in critical condition for several weeks and the newspapers report almost daily on his condition and, later, on Tone's trial. When the man recovers, the newspapers show him at the airport, heavily bandaged and vowing never to return to Paradise. It is not like they say in the magazines, the tourist tells the newspaper, these people are still like savages. The magistrate tells Tone that it is men like him who are hurting the country, who drive the tourist dollar away and make bad for everybody.

Please, Ma Tone begs the magistrate before sentencing, please, my son, my son not the same. Something happen to him, he is not the same boy and I try and I try but I can't see the something. He is a good boy, begs Ma Tone, have mercy, Judge, he is really a good boy. But the magistrate says he is tired of hearing these mothers come into his court and say their sons are good boys. Boys who assault and batter others and cause them serious bodily harm are not good boys, the magistrate says, and he scolds Ma Tone until she is weeping and snivelling like a child in the gallery of the court and Tone is in danger of succumbing to the Thing He Cannot Name right there in the dock.

And then the magistrate jails Tone for three years.

Tone enters prison believing the Thing That Eats Him will now be able to swallow him whole. He spends each day in prison looking over his shoulder, fearful of a hulking monster he has not seen, rather than the hundreds of ones that he *has* seen, the ones that surround him. The other prisoners recognise that he is a man who is haunted, so they give Tone the one thing that is in very short supply in prison – they give him space. So sure is he that he will not leave the prison alive that Tone writes goodbye letters to the two people he loves most in the world and keeps them among the few papers he is allowed. Tone writes a letter to his mother and one to Lala but he doesn't have the heart to send either and eventually, when he is tired of watching the shadows grow short in his cell, he tears up the letters and flushes them down the toilet.

20 August 1984

The prolonged hibernation of the Thing That Eats Him might be why Tone did not recognise the dark that obscured his vision and flooded his body that moment on the steps of Adan's house when he spilled kisses on the forehead and nose and lips of the woman he loves and felt her flinch when his soft lips landed, feather-like, on a spot made sore from Adan's beating. While Lala spewed hatred at him, even while surrendering herself to be held, Tone had felt that unaccustomed heat start warming the soles of his feet and making its way up his legs and arms. He did not recognise it at first, because he had not seen the Thing

That Eats Him for so long that he began to be unsure that it had ever existed.

Ma Tone had told him that she had prayed while he was in prison about that darkness within him; she had declared that her prayers had been answered with such passion that Tone now admits a latent belief in the power of her merciful God. Still, he felt the Thing, lurking, when Lala told him that day on the step how Adan beat her. He felt himself start to be swallowed by this thing that day when he saw Lala wince because he was hugging her too tightly, when he watched her weep because his chest had rubbed against her mangled breast, the tears that rushed to her eyes mirroring those then pooling in his own.

But Lala had rejected him that day on the steps. She had not wanted to hear him when he told her to come away with him. She had returned his kisses, his hugs, and then she had said that she was already married to Adan, that trying to visit her like that would just get them both into even more trouble. They were no longer little children, Lala had told him, they needed to grow up, move on. Adan would eventually settle down, she had explained, and stop beating her. All marriages have these rough patches, Tone shouldn't think that he needed to save her.

When she said that, Tone almost did not recognise her, as if some imposter had clothed itself in her body and forced her lips to say things Lala never would. He had been given cause to wonder whether she was even the same person he had met on the beach all those years ago. Whether this was some little fantasy he had carried in his head in prison, something to keep him warm at night, not something that should be bothering him now.

In the two days since they met on the steps of Adan's house, he has watched from his jet ski while Lala spends hours on the beach, plaiting heads for US dollars. Word has reached Tone about how she jumps from behind the hair of her clients and goes chasing crabs on the sand, about how she howls for Baby when people pass her with children, leaving heads half done. Any time they see each other on the beach since that evening on the steps, Lala and Tone do not speak. It is as if their entire meaning, one for the other now, is the keeping of secrets, it is as if they both know their friendship is now doomed. What are secrets but things we want to forget? Why then would we keep the acquaintance of others who remember them?

22 August 1984

The Thing stays silent two days later when Adan meets him in the tunnel with the announcement that he intends to go back home. It has been long enough, determines Adan; if the police had wanted him about the white man's murder they would have come looking for him already. He is tired of visiting his wife in secret and then retiring to the hard floor of some facking cave at night. He is tired of laying low during the day. Bad man no 'fraid police, says Adan, bad man no 'fraid nobody, as man.

They need to sort out the next job, says Adan, them need to talk about it.

This is how Tone comes to be sitting in the wrought-iron chair beside Lala and Adan's bed, smoking a joint with the man he has served faithfully since boyhood, watching the same big hands that bruise Lala stretch towards him with a spliff.

Adan still jumps with the sound of feet ascending the steps to his house. He still nods to Tone to tell him to be ready in case it is somebody they cannot welcome; he is still palpably relieved when he sees that it is only the Jehovah's Witnesses, and not Sergeant Beckles and the soldiers of Babylon come to take him in for questioning.

The Witnesses want to talk about the parable of the bread and fish, the miracles marked in the Bible. Bitches on Baxter's Beach was making bread out of big rock for years is what Adan tells them; what make you feel they need a Bible to tell them how all of a sudden? Tone watches one of the Witnesses step forward and smile. This Witness has not heard what Adan has said, he has heard how Adan has said it and has therefore concluded that what Adan needs, more than anything, is the love of the Jehovah he serves. This Witness is a frail old man in a stained fedora who walks with a stick. When he extends a small, thin magazine, it shakes so much that Tone can hardly make out the image on the cover until he takes it in his own steady hands. The image is of two lions, a male and a female, resting their heads in the laps of the stupidest black people Tone has ever seen.

Adan chupses long and hard, takes the tract from Tone, says thank you to the Witness, closes the door without checking to make sure the old man makes it back down the stairs unharmed, throws the tract in the trash, and gets back to rolling another spliff. Adan doesn't have any problems with people who believe in the Bible, he says, but he doesn't have time for Witnesses, for reasons he considers so obvious he doesn't bother to articulate them.

'I got to get this thing sort out so we can bury Baby. I know you know the tunnels good, good,' says Adan. 'Nobody ain't going think to look in them tunnels for nothing so.'

Tone had not intended to be there, talking to Adan about his latest master plan, but Adan had insisted and he didn't have anything better to do right then, so here he was.

What happen to him that he getting on sketchy so, all of a sudden, Adan wants to know, and Tone is washed by a guilt he has not felt up to this point. He repeatedly denies that there is anything unsaid between him and Adan, he forces his eyes to stay on Adan's until Adan looks away first.

In his head, Tone admits that it is a good plan. The garrison tunnels stretch from the historical fort like the legs of a many-tentacled octopus. They have been mostly unused for the three hundred years since the fort was abandoned by the British. There are only a few people in his neighbourhood who know about them, mostly older people, and they have chosen to use them only as the home of the fictional monsters who inhabit the nightmares of children. Children are therefore kept safely away from their depths, but Tone has long become unafraid of nightmares and he knows the tunnels like the fingers of his right hand. One of these tunnels ends in a cave on the beach into which a boatload of marijuana can easily be deposited and there are several caverns that converge into underground rooms big enough to hide a few hundred pounds until it can be sold.

Tone understands that in Adan's head these few hundred pounds are the key to his future. Before Baby died, the weed was the means to a new house, a proper one that wasn't so weather-beaten and decayed, a warm, dry place where you could raise a girl baby and keep a wife. Now the cargo is the means to a decent funeral for that same baby girl, repairs to the house where he keeps the wife who killed her.

'We could even go in and move it once or twice, just to make sure.'

'Uh-huh,' says Tone, inhaling the lit spliff. He is beginning to regret taking Adan to the tunnels to hide after the robbery.

'As man, is just the money now for the boat man and the consignment,' Adan reasons. 'Is just that little money I gotta fix up.'

Tone is thinking about Lala.

What he remembers most about the Lala he first met was that she was always humming. Even when she was listening, in the quiet spaces between whispered conversations in the tunnels, in the yard of his mother's half-house and on Baxter's Beach, she would be delivering little melodies under her breath. It was as if a happy little child lay beneath that bullish build, a child whose belly was full, whose clothes were dry and who was therefore free to sing while it explored the world. He spent months looking for that child, trying to coax it out of her, but up to the time they ended, he'd never found it. She managed to keep it away from him, singing deep inside her.

Even when he met her, the outward Lala was big, bigger than he was, with shoulders like the ones on the swimmers at the Olympics. Lala was not a fat girl. She was not the soft, pillowy sweet of Pammy at the convenience store, whose touch felt like grace when she handed Tone his change. She was not the tall, thin and willowy of his friend Rocky, who worked the beach behind the Holborn Hotel. Lala was a big body on a big frame. A frame that said 'solid'. A frame that said it did not need anyone to carry bags on its behalf. As it happens, Tone would have carried them anyway. Lala was quiet. He used to watch how she kept her eyes in the books her granny bought her, hardly looking up when he passed her on the beach. Tone had been intrigued by all that solidness surrounding a voice that barely squeaked when she spoke, a spirit that preferred to sing. Tone had fallen in love with her silence and the promise of liberating that hum beneath her breath. The man who could release that hum, Tone had thought, the man who could turn it into a song, elevate it to a shout, *that* man was a man indeed.

Lala had been the reason he turned up in the early hours of that morning after they had dropped the baby. He had been making his way home after a night with one of his regulars – a middle-aged German woman who never seemed to style her grey hair, clip her toenails or shave her pussy. She was one of the clients with whom he could never spend a whole night, could never allow himself to wake up the next morning and look at those toenails, that face, and admit what he had become, but she was also one of the ones who paid him handsomely, one of the few who took her holidays in the summer because it was not the height of tourist season. Tone has fewer clients in summer and therefore more time to spend with her.

Tone had been thinking as he walked. About maybe going home and getting a board and catching a wave. About Lala. About whether he should work the jet skis that day. About Lala. About whether Adan had hurt her after he left with Jacinthe. About Lala. And his feet had taken him to the sandy soil at the bottom of the little board house of their own volition. And then he had become transfixed by a screaming he recognised as the anguish of the humming child.

When Tone had run up the steps that morning, Adan and Lala were bawling so hard that neither of them heard the door open or saw him come in. By then they had passed the stage of trying to shake Baby awake, of gently tapping her cheeks, of lifting her eyelids and blowing into them. They had passed the initial winded sobbing of surprise, of scrambling to find wallet and bag and a hat for Baby, who, though still warm, was clearly already dead. They had passed the stage of wrapping her in a blanket against a cold she would never feel and almost bumping into themselves on the way to the door. They had passed the stage of coming back in when they realised they could not walk to Baxter's General and there was no bus at 3 a.m., passed the panic of rummaging for change to use the payphone at the top of the hill and then, remembering that emergency calls were free, racing with Baby to the kiosk to call the ambulance. They had passed the despair of finding that the kiosk had been robbed of the receiver and cursing the murderer who had taken it, all the while running back to the house, patting Baby, cooing to her, assuring her that she would be fine. They had passed the point of putting Baby on the bed, lifting her neck and blowing into her mouth the way they had seen on TV, taking turns between blowing and screaming and crying and bawling and blowing and calling a baby who would now never answer them.

They had passed these points and were simply draped over a dead baby on a bed, bawling.

Who knows now why the first thought that came to Tone on rushing through the door was hiding what had happened, trying to make sure Lala was free of blame by faking a kidnapping? Who knows how he managed to convince them that it was best to let people think that someone else had taken Baby, that that someone had probably killed her? Who now can question the logic of enlisting a man who had spent so many nights under arrest to help them to avoid arrest themselves? In what had seemed like minutes, Adan had been returned to the tunnels and Tone was racing to Baxter's Beach, placing the little body by the rocks a short while before Lala ran up and down screaming for help, saying her baby was gone.

'You hearing me?' repeats Adan, when Tone does not answer the first time and it becomes evident that he is not.

'Uh-huh.'

'If I get de man to bring it in from Vincy, bring it to the boulders, we can move it in to the tunnels, store it and sell it off. Send back and pay the Vincy people, everybody happy. Nobody gonna think to look down there,' says Adan, 'no police gonna figure out to look down there.'

Adan stares at Tone with the wide-eyed amazement of discovery, a facial expression that has stayed with him since he was a mere child, since they were nothing more than little snotty-nosed boys running barefoot on the rabland behind Ma Tone's house. Tone was one of the few children allowed to play with Adan, for no reason other than that Ma Tone spent too much time seated inside with her rags to know what Adan was really like. As a matter of fact, it was Ma Tone's house that scarred Adan. It had been the early days of Ma Tone's bid to make their wooden chattel house into something permanent and immovable. The concrete bathroom had just been built, and the wall that was, in Ma Tone's mind, the first wall of a kitchen she'd seen in a book extended proudly along one side of the wooden house. This wall had a window already fitted, rolled out each morning and then closed each evening like all the other windows in the house, but it had nothing else – it did not support part of a roof, or meet perpendicularly to other walls to make a room. Adan, unaccustomed then to the new spatial dynamics, had rounded a corner in hot pursuit of another neighbourhood boy and collided with a corner of the rollout window in the wall that enclosed nothing.

Tone remembers how this very same Adan had fallen to the ground as a boy with a forehead gushing blood. He had been taken to Baxter's General but had been kept waiting too long. The cut could no longer be stitched by the time they were permitted to see the doctor. It was Tone who held Adan's hand as the man-boy screamed while the cut was cleaned and examined by a student doctor. It was Tone who had earned Adan's trust by keeping that secret forever after – that Adan, the man-boy, the big bad bully of Baxter's, had cried like a motherless child to have his cut washed and a tetanus shot administered. Adan and Tone had become even closer friends after that.

The cut had scarred, a curvy correction mark that now reminded Tone of a curled-up centipede, and had swelled and stretched as Adan grew.

'Is a good plan,' Tone admits now, absently. Adan smiles a wide smile that exposes two even rows of bright white teeth.

'As man,' says Adan, 'just gotta get the money to pay de boat man now.'

Tone feels the muscles in his neck contract, despite the weed. Once Adan starts to talk this way, he knows it means a job is coming – hot jewellery to sell on the black market, perhaps, or a forged cheque to take somewhere to be cashed. Tone tries to steer clear of talk about jobs since his stint in prison. He's found far better ways to make money, he has no need of these types of jobs any more. Still, it is summer, the season for tourist families and budget travellers. The beach is not rich with the older visitors, the women who pay him, until it starts to really get cold in the climes they are from. In the winter season, the lights in the big villas blaze every night and Tone is harder to find, less available to Adan's hustles.

'If Lala didn't come and get me that night Baby born, I

woulda had that money already,' Adan complains. 'I know it had some good money in dey.'

'Uh-huh?'

'One o' dem rich white men,' Adan explains, 'dem ones always got a safe somewhere. Had to left before I get anything.'

Tone checks a Tissot watch gifted to him by one of his customers and makes as if to stand. He doesn't want to hear about this job. Adan understands.

'If I could get the money, you could meet the boat? Help me get dat thing through the tunnels?'

Tone nods.

'Nobody ain't gonna think to look in them tunnels,' repeats Adan, 'as man.'

Tone has never told Adan about Lala, about how he knows her. Somehow it did not ever seem like something he should say, and so Adan still thinks that Tone first met Lala when he introduced her to him as his wife. Tone remembers himself, newly released from prison and still shocked to shivers by the idea of walking the length of the road without feeling as if he was doing something wrong. He had walked out of Ma Tone's half-house and down the street that day of his release, checking off the landmarks against the memories he had returned to, every day, when his mind needed to escape his cell and the three other men in it. He remembers the tentative smiles of children who might have been warned not to turn out like him, the encouraging words of neighbours who had watched Ma Tone suffer and wished him a life on the straight and narrow for no reason other than that they wished her a life free of further sorrow. He remembers the wary eyes of the bad boys warned not to test him, the quiet defiance of those who thought him overrated, convinced one fist from them would knock him flat but still not particularly inclined to try. His feet had led him past their stares to Adan's little shack on the beach, and that was where he had found Adan, and Lala, newly pregnant, cleaning and dusting his partner's house.

He could not have told her then that he had dreamed of her and her solid, good-natured silence on the many nights in prison when he had been kept awake by the discomfiting proximity of snoring men. He had supposed that he could not really call it love, that thing they had had when they were young. It couldn't compare to what she had with Adan. On the day he had found her again he had offered his congratulations, observed the little thin gold band around Lala's wedding finger that bore Chinky's trademark gaudy style, took in the gentle swell of Lala's stomach. When Adan had introduced her as his wife, he'd said 'nice to meet you' like he didn't remember who she was, and she, following his lead, had returned the greeting. Later, after he had returned home to Ma Tone's and gone to bed, he allowed his mother to think that prison had so broken her son as to make him, a grown man, bawl into his pillow like some inconsolable little boy.

CHAPTER TWENTY-FOUR

Lala
27 August 1984

In the end Lala pays for the funeral with money she has begged off of Wilma. Lala does this after she visits the funeral home early one morning and the attendant tells her that there is another option if they are finding it hard to pay for a funeral. The government can bury Baby, says the attendant, they wouldn't have a service and everything but it would be free. Or the body can be incinerated at the mortuary, since it is just a tiny little baby.

Lala is so distraught by these suggestions that she has to be given a glass of water and time to collect her wits before she can leave the funeral parlour. When she comes back she approaches the beach with a vengeance with her mayonnaise jar of plastic combs and her little packs of beads, but no one comes to have their hair braided. She makes herself brave and she asks, but the women she approaches do not want to convert their bobs to braids, and the women who might have chosen the beauty of braided hair no longer trust Lala with their heads.

That very same afternoon she says she is going out, just to buy a Coke from the convenience store, while Adan and Tone are planning. When she leaves she is dressed in a skirt that Wilma would approve of and an appropriately modest black blouse, and she takes the bus to Wilma's house and she begs her.

'Please,' she reasons against Wilma's stony face, still full of the remembrance of being ignored on the beach when Baby was found, 'please, I need some help to bury Baby.'

The begging reminds Wilma of Esme, of those times she came back to her mother's house, asking to be allowed to stay. Wilma remembers that Esme might still be alive if she had taken her in, if she had refused to allow her to return to Rainford, and it is this memory, this guilt that makes her put her shoes on at last and take Lala with her to take the bus to the bank in town, where Carson's pension has been building for a moment such as this. Wilma feels a weight lift from her shoulders when she withdraws enough for a send-off they can all be proud of. Their hands touch when Wilma hands Lala the money, and Wilma presses the crisp wad of currency, folded in half, into her granddaughter's grasp, folds the young, fat fingers over the head of the island's first premier on the surface of the upper-most hundred, and smiles, as if Lala has done something good.

But when Lala returns home and presents the money to Adan, a storm gathers within his countenance; he is not pleased.

'Somebody tell you ask you grandmother for the money to bury Baby, Lala? You ain't feel that I could get the money to bury my own daughter?'

Lala is contrite. 'We have to pay it back,' she says, 'it is just a little loan so Baby can have her send-off. I know you could get the money, Adan. That is why I borrow it, I know you could pay it back quick-quick.'

He seems appeased, just barely, and she retreats to the periphery of the interior of the house, well out of the way of any sudden malevolent sentiments that might arise in him against her.

Baby has the best – a tiny white coffin with gilded handles and curlicued angels, printed leaflets with her picture on the cover, a pink satin dress. Wilma sits in the front in one of the pews reserved for family and reads a psalm and accepts the condolences of her neighbours. Adan is drunk and boisterous the entire time, asking those who join them to mourn if they like the casket, if they see the little angels on the side, if they can guess how much it cost to have this casket, these angels. He had those little angels made special for his Baby, says Adan to anyone who will listen, his baby must have the very best. *My poor sweet baby girl.*

During the interment, he stands with a group of his friends, asking Jacinthe, who is present to pay her respects, when she is leaving the country and going back to the cold. Adan asks whether she will be available later to go somewhere and have a drink with him. He needs someone to talk to, says Adan, he needs to talk to her.

When the little coffin is wheeled towards the burial ground he is quiet and does not participate in the hymn-singing. There are mourners whose numbers reflect more, Lala supposes, the notoriety of Baby's death than any real sense of personal loss. Adan has few friends, Lala fewer. Still, the church is packed, the locals spilling from the

215

small wooden gospel hall into the street, sweating and stinking in the mid-afternoon sun, jostling each other for a better view of the dead baby's father in a hastily made suit, of the mother too distraught to stand and of Baby, laying stiff and plastic-like in a long pink satin dress. It has taken Adan and Lala over a month to have the funeral, whisper these mourners, and it wasn't just the police investigations that caused the delay, it was that they had no money to pay for it. This, say these mourners, is the real tragedy of Baby's death, not that she was kidnapped and killed by strangers but that her own parents had been unable to afford to bury her. They point out the father, his crisp white sneakers, his thick rope chains of Italian gold. Some parents, say these mourners, do not understand priorities.

Behind the gospel hall rise the mountains, skirted by foggy fields of green banana, dotted here and there by gaily painted galvanise roofs that resemble the far-flung tiles of some broken celestial Rubik's Cube and not the impossibly perched homes of mountain-dwellers at all. It is towards these houses that the mourners look when their noses catch the scent of coming rain. It is away from them that their feet run when their eyes confirm it, and soon it is just Wilma and Lala and Adan and his soldiers and Jacinthe and Tone and a few stragglers left standing in the sopping grass and the sticky soil and the weeping clouds as the coffin is lowered into a little hole smaller than Adan's bed and Baby is gone forever.

After the funeral there is a wake at Wilma's but Adan and his friends do not attend. Wilma is a bitch, Adan tells them, he not going anywhere around her or her house. And in this unspoken command they understand that they are not to venture to the wake either.

Jacinthe ain't no regular woman is what Adan tells the fellas who congregate with him after the funeral, under the last street light before a dark stretch of beach, slouching on raw plywood benches hammered and nailed to the base of a big dunks tree. The tree is too tall, too old, too hardscrabble for the spines on the bark to cause them any real discomfort or for the thinning branches to provide any real shelter, but it is a cool, clear night and shelter and comfort are not what they need.

After Adan talks about Jacinthe he grows quiet and nobody seems to know what to say and nobody wants to say the wrong thing because, after all, Adan has just buried a baby girl by a woman who is not the woman he is now speaking about with such unaccustomed adoration. The wise among them are aware that in this strange light, at these conversational depths, fights are started and slights are shared and none of them wishes to cause or be caused any offence.

They had stood beside Adan and watched her – a caramel-coloured bird of a woman with a head of blonde-streaked curly hair – take her place with the mourners at Baby's funeral.

Ragga does not know Jacinthe, other than what he has heard, neither does Shotta, but they have now both heard Adan speak about her under the street light and the fact that she merits a mention within this congregation makes her, without more, worthy of reverence.

217

Jacinthe ain't no regular woman.

Tone mentions to Shotta and Ragga that he had seen Jacinthe several weeks before, sitting in the kitchen of one of his clients, drinking tea and smoking a cigarette and laughing the same loud, brash laugh she'd always had. He doesn't mention that when he saw her there were two lines of coke between her and the client. That she was shaking the way that addicts do, as if they are living at warp speed and vibrate with the sheer effort of staying still. He doesn't mention that he took her back to Adan's house, to remind Adan that she was still within his reach if he wanted her, to remind Adan that he wasn't meant for Lala, to remind Lala that she wasn't meant for him. This, Tone is convinced, is what caused the fight between Adan and Lala. This is why Baby is dead.

Shotta is lounging on the bare aluminium bones of a beach chair, its plastic strapping missing in the way of those things whose loss can never be rationalised, the how of which can never be explained with logic. Shotta has the disposition of a sloth. When you see him sitting, or sleeping, you could think that he is dead, but Shotta is not dead. Shotta only comes alive when a gun, like the key to a wind-up toy, is slotted into his hands. Then his steps are so nimble, his movements so deft, so speedy, so sure, that he is hard to reconcile with the supine skeleton in the creaky beach chair.

'Jacinthe is good people,' confirms Adan.

'You gotta keep good people near,' Shotta booms. He has the voice of a giant, for a man so puny. He has an uncanny charitableness for a killer.

Rat returns and bumps fists with each man before emptying his pocket of the red bottle caps of the local beer he has arranged with a shopkeeper to collect every evening at the time when the shopkeeper cleans the bar in preparation for the night's patrons.

'How things?' Ragga asks him.

'Sufferation strong,' whines Rat. Rat is counting beer caps for a competition for which the prize is a car. He is determined to drive this new red car to this very spot after it is presented to him, to give the boys a ride. Then he will sell it and buy a ticket to Australia, where he plans to watch kangaroos and marry an Aussie girl because he likes the way they talk from a film he watched at the cinema once. Sometimes at night he dreams about these women, talking to him in that easy sprawl, welcoming him to Australia. Rat has worked out that selling this car will just about get him enough money to get there, to set himself up so that the girl doesn't think he is using her. So he can still buy himself a shirt and pants and make himself a plate of pelau if this girl takes her time in inviting him home to live with her once he gets there. Rat has surmised that long hours at the chicken-processing plant, or on the docks at the port, or painter work or mason work or waiter work or work driving a maxi taxi covered in graffiti will not get him to this Aussie girl, so he does not bother with these options.

'What Jacinthe doing back here?' Rat wants to know, above the *clink clink* of bottle caps dropping like coins into an empty ice-cream container. 'She come for the funeral?'

'She was here before the funeral. Just come for a visit,' Tone says, 'just passing through.'

He does not relay how Jacinthe had told him, as they negotiated the goat-foot vine on the approach to Adan's house, that she had come back because her father had begged her to, because he thought she needed help. It didn't matter, Jacinthe had said, she hated New York. She had thought that in New York she would find her mother, and years after arriving there she hadn't been able to find her. Moreover, she always felt like she needed to wash her hands, her face, her hair once she came inside her apartment from outdoors, as if she was polluted just by standing in the street there.

Adan is kicking the soles of his sneakers against a patch of nut grass. These sneakers were once so white that they seemed tinged with blue against the deep velvet of his black black skin, but the rain during the burial and the resulting muck have smeared them in ugly shades of brown and grey and he is trying to clean them off again. White Reeboks with dress pants are all the rage and he bought himself a new pair with Wilma's money – the brightest, whitest pair he could find – to say goodbye to his baby girl, but now he is marvelling at how easily they were soiled once the rain fell, how unlikely it is that they will ever again be quite as white as they were when he took them out of the box. Some things, Adan is thinking, can never be made new again.

'In truth?'

Shotta's raw local accent belies that he was actually born in Guyana. It is a peculiar ability he has to embody so utterly the essence of wherever he is living. Listening to him, you would think he has been on this block since birth.

He hasn't. He therefore does not know about the high-brown, half-white girl Tone and Adan met when they were teenagers, daughter of a prominent local businessman. He does not know about that day they were in town, hustling locals to pay them five dollars each to arrange for tourists to help them buy perfume and leather shoes duty-free, when they first met her. Jacinthe had skipped school and chosen to pass the day in town instead, haunting the perfume and make-up counters at the department stores until the school day was done and she could congregate with the other children in front of the glossy storefront of the Norman Mall. She'd removed her grammar-school tie, let her shirt ride outside of her skirt, coloured her lips with a Revlon sample. She'd bumped into them, asked for a light for her cigarette, this schoolgirl, and Adan had given her one. Adan had tried his lyrics on her, just to see if she would bite, if he had the same effect on her that he had on almost every other woman who met him without knowledge of his proclivities, but Jacinthe had stood back and watched them and laughed. A derisory laugh, like they were beneath her.

'A duty-free hustle?' she'd snorted. 'Charming.'

They'd become friends in one day, listened wide-eyed to her stories of vacations in exotic locations abroad and servants who made her bed and rides in her father's Mercedes like they meant nothing at all. What she really wanted, said Jacinthe, was to find her mother, who'd gone back to America when she was a little girl. She didn't hear anything from her, she missed her. When the day ended with them walking Jacinthe to the gates of her school in time to be collected by a driver, they'd felt like they'd known her for ages. And right before they said goodbye, Jacinthe had reached under her blouse and produced two Zippo lighters she had shoplifted and handed one each to Tone and to Adan. A memento, she'd said with a wink. And Adan was in love.

'I wouldn't come back here if I had a chance to get away,' Rat says. 'I didn't coming back at all.'

'It ain't like that for Jacinthe when she here,' clarifies Adan. 'Jacinthe father got nuff money, she could do anything she want.' He says it with an element of pride, as if the promise of her inheritance of wealth somehow reflects well on him.

'I still didn't coming back,' says Rat, 'not me.'

Tone drags on his spliff. When he had seen Jacinthe that day at the client's, he had convinced her to come with him to see Adan. He'd trusted that whatever attraction they'd had for each other would have reignited naturally, that Adan would have used his lyrics, his charm and tried to pursue her. It would have been a matter of time before Adan and Lala would have ended, Tone had thought then, Baby or no Baby. But of course that wasn't how things had turned out.

And now, thanks to him, Baby is dead.

CHAPTER TWENTY-FIVE

Lala
5 January 1984

How do you learn to love a man?

You first ask yourself this question when you are a new bride. These are the days when Adan's robberies buy you clothing to replace the awful dresses Wilma made. He buys you neon-yellow denim dresses and orange suede ankle boots with kitten heels and studded leather belts you can wear across your hips when you go with him to the dance hall to hear Alpha 24 and watch bad boys bob and weave to their best approximations of the music of their ancestors while wearing their fortunes around their necks. These are also the days when Adan first demonstrates his ability to box these clothes off of you, to tear these dresses and beat you with the heels of the very booties he first presented in a bow-topped box.

On the night you first ask yourself this question, you braid your own hair in fat box braids piled high on top of your head and you allow it to fall in heavy plaits down your back. You are wearing a little acid-washed denim jumpsuit that strains across a thickening belly and ends in a miniskirt you keep tugging back down your thighs, and a pink undershirt you have slashed and re-fastened with

safety pins because this is the style. On this night you are
still filled with heady joy each time you glance at your left
hand and see Chinky's handiwork, its tiny diamond cast-
ing rainbows across your eyes. You are still inebriated with
the exultation of being free to dress this way, in clothes
Wilma would disapprove of, bought for you by a husband
and not just a boyfriend she despises.

On this night you have ironed Adan's tracksuit and fretted over how to navigate the cuffs and collar so that they
will sit perfectly on wrists you are only just learning to
fear, and then you watch as your husband gets dressed,
splashes himself in cologne, puts on the bright white sneakers you have spent the better part of an afternoon rubbing
with White-X.

When the two of you arrive at the pasture on which
Alpha 24 is hosting their New Year's dance, Adan is
swarmed by a bunch of his friends – women in fishnet
jumpsuits and miniskirts and gold hoops that eclipse the
movement of their jaws as they chew Chiclets gum. Men
who call Adan *big man* and *governor* and touch their own
bling-encrusted fists to his and nod. And in this group of
laughing, drinking, dancing buddies stands Tone, quietly
sipping a soft drink against the gaily branded side of a stall
that vibrates in time to 'Pass the Kouchie'.

How do you learn to love a man?

You may think you learn by doing. So after you have
pressed your husband's clothes and whitened his sneakers
and walked with him to the dance in your kitten-heeled
orange booties, you might tramp those suede booties
through the damp grass to fetch him his drinks, his food

and his Fanta, and then you might stand in front of him, allow it to seem like you are in his care, with your eyes perpetually on his cup to see when he might be in need of a refill. You might think that the flutter in your stomach when you watch him, the beauty of his black black skin and white white smile, and a broad high brow beneath a brown Kangol, is the love you are learning by doing all these things, it is the love you are meant to have and it will cushion the bruises the better you become at it.

How do you learn to love a man?

You might think you learn by obeying. So after your husband has had one too many gulps from a flask of whisky, you do not say anything when the laughter gets louder, the jokes get bawdier and he seems less immune to the fawning of vultures dressed to look like peacocks. He tells you to go home, you need your rest and the music might be too loud for the baby, and he rubs your belly and says he will send one of his soldiers with you to keep you safe on your walk there. You do not say anything when the soldier he summons is none other than Tone, the strong young man you first met by a gutter, a man who now wears the brooding countenance of a gathering storm. You do not tell your husband that he should not send you with this particular man; if he knows what is good for him, he should require you to stay by his side.

You struggle to keep up with Tone through the rickety stalls of galvanise and plywood from which vendors hawk fried fish and fishcakes and American hot dogs in fat yellow rolls of bread. He pays no mind to your rounded belly and even less to the glimmer of Chinky's rough-set diamond in a gold band that used to be part of a chain Adan stole. No, Tone walks apace through the narrow alleys and road-ways towards Baxter's Village and the beach and the house you have recently moved into with your husband and hardly looks behind him to make sure you are keeping up, and though you are nearly panting from the effort of stay-ing a few paces behind him, you keep your eyes on your orange booties, marching one in front of the other, being splattered by soft mud and scraped by rough pebbles and rocks and wood. When he takes you through an alley so narrow that a two-foot stone blocks the path, you have a dilemma. You don't have a choice but to climb over this stone but you can't because the miniskirt will not allow your legs to lift that high, and though you had resolved, when he disappeared years before, that you would never again call this boy in such a way that he can think you need him, you start to stumble and you have to take your eyes off the booties and call this name you cannot forget.

'Robert.'

How do you learn to love a man?

You might think you learn by speaking, because of the warmth that fills your chest and escapes your lips when Tone helps you up and over the rock. When he asks you about your husband, about how you met him, the day you married him, the day you moved into his house on the beach, you talk and your body fills with heat. This warmth is the proof of your love, you consider, and speaking of it makes it stronger. It is to this love for your husband that you credit the heat in your chest when you speak, and not the memory of other days with this boy who is not your husband, whose arms hug your own and heave you upwards, over the obstacle and onto the part where the path is again clear.

The rain comes and the heat does not fizzle and this boy tells you that there is an entrance to the tunnels just close by this path you are on, do you remember the tunnels? And the warmth leaves your chest and fans up across your face and down and perhaps love is indeed obedience because when he asks you if you would like to try to run the rest of the way to Adan's house on the beach or to follow him to that entrance, you tell this boy yes, yes you would like to follow him to that entrance, you would like to shelter in those tunnels.

But of course you do not only shelter in those tunnels, you do not only listen to the rain and wait for it to end. In those tunnels, you understand that you do not learn to love a man, because for the right man there is no need for the learning, the love is the most natural thing in the world. You understand that if you must learn to love a man, he is probably not the man you should be loving.

And this is the reason you shriek your joy so that it echoes through these small, dark passageways and fills them with light. This knowledge, you tell yourself, and not the hands and the tongue and the thighs of Tone beneath you on the ground in these tunnels, is why you are singing. This truth that only the girls who dare to enter the tunnels are able to find out.

The thing is, how to love a man is only clear in the dark of the tunnels. When you exit them, when your husband comes home in the dank of the early morning and he is drenched in the stink of a vulture, when you remove the same sneakers you earlier cleaned for him, now smeared and sullied with wet mud; when you remove the same tracksuit you pressed, your mind snakes its way back to the question of how best to love him, because he smells like weed and another woman and you are thinking perhaps there is something you are doing wrong. And he does not have a mother who can show you how best to love him and you do not have one who can tell you what to do. And you do not know how to deal with the memory of your husband's friend, his right-hand man, loving you in the deep dark of those tunnels, so you push that memory away and you try to avoid this friend when he comes to see Adan and soon he starts to avoid coming to see Adan and he starts knocking before entering when he does.

And you wish you had someone you could ask, someone you could confide in, but you don't, because you cannot confide in Wilma and because Esme is dead.

It is at times like these, although you've never really known her, that you miss your mother more than ever.

CHAPTER TWENTY-SIX

Esme
20 December 1968

There are things she will tell her daughter about love when she is grown, promises Esme while she is tramping across the dew-wet blades of grass on the pasture that leads to Wilma's house, just after five in the morning; things it is best for her to know, important things. While she is marching, Esme watches her feet, which seem to know exactly where they are headed, even if her heart does not want to follow. One of the things she will teach Lala, vows Esme, is what to do when you have a man who does not love your children. And then Esme vows to tell her daughter never to find herself in that position in the first place.

The feet only pause when they pass the banana patch and Wilma's cold stone house comes into view. They hesitate before moving off again, more slowly this time. Wilma, it turns out, is waiting, arms akimbo, beside the okra trees, her face as cold as the limestone with which her house is made.

'Morning,' says Esme, when she is within hearing range, and when Wilma's silence makes her doubt that she spoke aloud she says 'morning' again.

'What bring you now?' says Wilma, looking at the

sleeping child burdening Esme's slight shoulders. 'Why you waking people so early in the morning?'

Esme will tell her daughter that the affection of others cannot be depended upon, even if they gave birth to you. She will tell her, she vows, that loving a child does not come naturally, not for everyone. This wisdom, Esme will explain, is why she did not leave Rainford at the first sign that he was unable to love Lala. She adjusts the bundle on her shoulder. Lala is asleep, and at two years old already looks set to dwarf her mother's slight frame and fine features. Lala's thick legs hang heavy down the front of her mother's torso, her chubby arms are locked around Esme's neck; every so often she stirs when her leg is boxed by the two bags Esme packed in a huff. Esme can feel the wide damp spot where Lala's soaked undies have wet her good dress. She remembered to change her clothes before running, she chides herself, but not her toddler's wet underwear.

'We just want to stay a few days, until I can get by Auntie Earlie,' Esme begins.

'And why you must go and take your trouble to your auntie?' wonders Wilma. 'Old women don't deserve their rest?'

Esme shifts from one foot to the other and Wilma eyes the wet spot and relents,

'Come,' she says, 'I suppose it is OK just for a few days.'

That night they sleep in the sewing room, on a makeshift mattress on the floor. Carson, it turns out, is away visiting family in Canada, but Esme is already planning how she will leave, what she will do next, and she knows that she is not wrong when, days into their stay, Wilma starts to complain about how Esme keeps the sewing room, how Lala's play threatens to upset the dress forms and the in-progress dresses pinned there. Wilma starts to complain about how the sewing room is no place for a little child – she might swallow a pin or something – and she only has the two other bedrooms, one of which is Carson's.

Esme understands.

A few days later, when Rainford's little Forsa finds the street in front of Wilma's stone house, Esme does not protest. She does not take very long to pack their things, to pull the dress forms back to their position of prominence in the middle of the sewing room in a space newly cleared of their makeshift bedding. She tells Wilma thanks, Esme does, and she walks to Rainford's little car and deposits Lala in the back seat despite her crying, resolved that she has made her bed and now, alas, she must lie in it.

Rainford tries at first, of course he does. Esme imagines that he wants to love her Lala, but we struggle, she thinks, to love anything that is not a reflection of ourselves. This struggle is human, and so is Rainford. She tells herself that this is why she does not act when his awkwardness of manner in the first few months after she and little Lala move back in ossifies into a habit of ignoring Lala altogether, although Esme tries her best to have her toddler clean and combed and cute when Rainford parks the Forsa in front of the little stone house in the city where he has rented three rooms for them. It is why she does not protest when Rainford suggests she let Lala spend the weekend with Wilma, just so they can have some time alone, despite everything Esme has told him about her mother.

Esme does not act when Rainford, gently, suggests that perhaps Lala should be sent to live with her grandmother permanently, despite everything that Esme has told him about Wilma and about Carson. It is because she understands this thing about love that Esme does not say no, she doesn't pack up her clothes in a temper and take she and her Lala away, she doesn't ask the Cuban to rent them a room in her warren again, but she does not pack Lala off to any other relative, either. Instead Esme tucks her daughter more firmly against her bosom when Rainford is around, shields her from his harsh barks, and sings her name in the hope that her daughter will never forget precisely how it should sound from the lips of anyone who truly loves her, the tone that reflects the real reverence of the singer. She sings her baby's name and she sings silly songs about escapes she never speaks of aloud. But that morning when he strikes her Lala in her face for once again wetting their one good bed, Esme loses her empathy. She runs back to Wilma.

'It is OK,' she sings to Lala in the sewing room, 'it will be OK.'

And Lala, with the innocence of childhood, believes her, snuggles her big baby body to her mother's slight frame and hums to herself, trying to imitate the sound of the name her mother sings to her.

But it will not be OK.

When Rainford had first suggested that Esme come live with him, she'd considered the invitation an answer to prayer, even if it did not come on the tail end of a marriage proposal. It never occurred to her that it would be

232

something she would pay for, least of all with her life. Within two hours of the offer she had packed up her white Spanish blouse, a gift from the Cuban, some second-hand skirts she'd inherited from Wilma and a little crystal candle holder the sailor man had given her. Then she packed her baby.

The Cuban had watched her, mouth stuffed with cigar, fist stuffed with the rent she'd insisted on for a month's lodging not received, bosom stuffed with the scarves she said kept out the cold. The Cuban had stood with Esme and the baby and waited for the Forsa to shudder to a stop at the top of the alley and wait for them. The Cuban's house was one of those with a door that opened onto a side street; it did not pretend to be the kind of place you wanted to enter through a front door and so it did not bother to have any. Esme had held Lala tight against the white ruffles of a blouse made for dancing, watching Rainford light a cigarette and come walking down the alley while the Cuban made deals with the Orishas under her breath.

By the time Lala is old enough to want to discuss dilemmas like marriage proposals, Esme is already dead, so she cannot warn her. Had Esme been alive, she would probably have relayed to her the way in which her own heart sank when, four months after that second run to Wilma, when Esme had again returned to Rainford, he had arrived home, climbed out of the Forsa with a small box in his hand and asked her to come inside. Esme would have relayed how her protests that she had to stay outside a little longer to catch the light while she finished her chores had all been in vain.

She would have told her daughter that she had already decided by that time that she would never marry Rainford, so that the absence of his asking, up to that point, was more of a relief than anything else because it freed her from the burden of saying no. She would have relayed how, as Rainford professed his love, she had kept her eyes on the ixora bush she had planted in the little hardscrabble patch outside of the rented rooms. It had just begun to flower, Esme would have told her, and she'd been outside tending to it, talking to it and congratulating it on this feat, when the Forsa had honked into earshot and then into her view. She would have told Lala how Rainford's face had been full of glee as he kept his hand on the horn to the annoyance of the neighbour, who had come outside and was sharpening his cutlass when Rainford at last alighted the car with a box wrapped with ribbons that trailed from his hands and ended in curls that bobbed and glinted in the afternoon sun.

Esme would have relayed how slowly she had followed Rainford back inside, her heart sinking with the realisation of the coming proposal. She would have told Lala how her hands trembled as she took off her apron, removed the scarf with which she kept her hair restrained so that it would not carry her sweat to sting her own eyes. She would have told her that this is not the reaction of a woman in love, for whom marriage is a natural progression of that love. She would have told her that when a proposal is right, what a woman should feel, above all, is safe, like she has found a soft place for landing. She would have told her that the thudding heart and trepidation meant that this was not the marriage for her.

If she had lived, Esme would have explained to her

234

daughter why, despite all this, she did not say no, why she had stood in the cramped bedroom she shared with a man she did not love and watched him get on one knee and present her with a box with a thin gold band crowned by a single small diamond he had slaved the better part of a year for. She would have said to her that she did not wish this for her own daughter – the responsibility of having to say yes to a man for whom this proposal was the singular objective of several months' unrequited affection. She would have explained that she had said yes so her own daughter would never have to.

Esme would have relayed that this realisation on her part was no mere instance of cold feet. It was nothing so transient. She would have explained that she had dis-covered that living with Rainford gave her the sensation of being unable to breathe, as if she had been shut tight in a box from which there was no escape. Within this box, Esme might have said, there was the semblance of bliss – Rainford was faithful, his eyes did not waver from hers, he brought her the money he earned from selling household items and encyclopedias door to door, he helped her with the cooking and the cleaning and took her, and little Lala when he could stand her, to the Burger Bee in Bush Hall for chicken and chips and vanilla soft-serve that flopped to the left and was melted not even five minutes after it had been put on the cone. But, she would plead with Lala to understand, this was not enough. Esme did not wish to run her life like a well-kept clock. Eventually the afternoon ritual of readying the house, herself and her daughter for her intended's arrival wore on her.

And so it happened that Esme started taking afternoon walks with Lala in the hours before Rainford came home. And it was during these afternoon walks that men who had previously met her in the brothel would call her name, remind her that she made them weak, that there was nothing they wouldn't do to have a woman like her.

One of these, a man by the name of Plucka, is more persistent. He does not merely call at Esme as she is passing with Lala in a pram the latter has far outgrown, he walks up to her, admires Lala, lifts her out of the pram and onto his neck and talks to her in words children understand while Esme pushes the empty stroller by his side and they walk while he tells jokes that make her laugh and laugh and laugh.

On a few of these evenings Rainford comes up the hill in the Forsa just as Plucka is removing Lala from his shoulders, depositing her in the little garden with the ixora bush, saying his goodbyes. This does not bother Rainford unduly on the first occasion it happens, does not rile him on the second, but by the third time he is irked by the sight of this man, a coarse, rum-drinking hulk of a man, walking beside his fiancée with his stepdaughter hoisted on his shoulders. He is irritated by the sight of his little stepdaughter, already built like the bypass bus, laughing and laughing at the attention of one Plucka. He brings the Forsa to a stop with a screech of the tyres and is out of the driver's seat in a huff.

'Esme!' he scolds. 'You ain't got nothing better to do than walk about with nasty rum-drinking men?' and his voice is high, carries far, embarrasses her.

'Keep your bony ass quiet, Rainford,' is what Esme replies. 'You feel you is more man if everybody hear you?' and her many bangles rustle and ding.

Lala remembers watching the ixora flowers, the bees that buzzed around them, while the adults quarrelled. She cannot recall Plucka asking Rainford to excuse him, that he did not mean to disrespect him or his wife. She cannot recall this incensing Rainford even further – that the interloper would apologise while his fiancée would not. She cannot later recall the stinging slap that Rainford delivers to the side of her mother's face, cannot know how it makes the baby in her stomach jump, how it makes her knees buckle.

Lala would not now remember Plucka saying, 'You didn't have to do that, my man, we was just walking,' as if the punishment could be legitimately applied in some circumstances but just happened, at that instant, to be unwarranted. Lala might not now remember these things: the way Plucka just walked away shaking his head, while Rainford dragged her mother inside by hers and started to beat her, while young Lala stayed outside in obedience to her mother's screams to her not to enter.

Esme would have told her daughter, had she been given the chance, that the marriage proposal of a bad man is an invitation to lose your way; only an idiot accepts such a proposal. Had she lived, she would perhaps have told her this while fiddling with the wedding ring on the ring finger of her left hand, because, as Lala has heard, Esme marries Rainford on a wet December day. It is while they are walking back to the house from the gospel assembly where they exchange vows that Plucka whistles at Esme as she passes the rum shop. Perhaps it is the effect of one too many glasses of rum, perhaps it is his last hurrah before surrendering his admiration of a woman now married to a better man than he thinks himself to be, perhaps it is Plucka's way of telling Esme that, marriage or no, she is still the whore who used to live in the Cuban's brothel in town and sell her sex for the price of a coco-bread-and-cheese. Whatever it is, Plucka doesn't stop there.

'You coming in to give the boys a last li'l piece before you go home, Mrs Ramkissoon?' taunts Plucka, and Rainford is too incensed, too embarrassed, to do anything but walk ahead of his wife, go into their house and close the door. Esme tries to get inside, but the door is locked, so she stays in the veranda and begs to be let in, the few wild flowers in her wedding bouquet already beginning to wilt and wither worse than the curls in her hair.

'Open this door, Rainford,' Esme hollers. 'Open the rasshole door, man.'

Lala has never been told how her mother cursed Rainford, how she threatened to take them both back to the brothel, or to go somewhere where he would never find her. Lala is instead repeatedly told the story of what happened after Rainford opened the door, when he chopped up his new wife with a cutlass before drinking the bottle of weedkiller she tended to use to keep the crabgrass from choking her ixora.

Given the choice, it is not the story Esme would have told her.

CHAPTER TWENTY-SEVEN

Lala
3 September 1984

On the day she had begged Adan to take her with him, to let her come and live with him in his little house by the sea, Lala had not been told the story of Wilma's marriage or Esme's courtship; she did not understand that, for the women of her lineage, a marriage meant a murder in one form or another. This ignorance was why Lala had asked Adan, had practically begged him, to marry her and take her away when she discovered that she was pregnant for the second time, this time with Baby.

She tells herself now that she was tired of telling Wilma untruths to get leave to run down the road and meet him under the gnarled and wizened branches of a dunks tree, to listen to him sing her beautiful songs made entirely of her name. She tells herself that it was not the fear of what Wilma would do, what she would say when she found out that Lala was made of the same slack stock her mother was. She tells herself that it was not the thought of having to raise a baby in the house with Wilma and Carson and the ghost of her dead mother that made her run. She tells herself it was love, only love that had motivated her then. She could have stayed with Wilma, she supposes, Wilma would perhaps have allowed it. But somehow she can never decide if to stay would have been better, if her suffering would have been any less. If by staying she would have doomed Baby to the same life she herself had had. If perhaps, for Baby, that would have been a fate even worse than her eventual death.

Adan had not wanted a baby at first, had not seen himself that way encumbered. But he had watched Lala begging him with the spines of the dunks tree spread behind her, and he had relented. A baby was a blessing, he had reasoned, it said so in the psalms. He had waited under the dunks tree while Lala gave Wilma the news, stuffed her things into a stringy market bag and grabbed her mannequin and a few of the dresses Wilma had accepted from Mrs Kennedy and came back to meet him again. And they had walked together to the little house, where he had cleared a drawer of his things and given her the room to unburden the string bag.

And when she had lain down next to him that first night and spooned her back into his chest and drawn his arms over her stomach, while he had settled and snored, she had felt something, something he appeared to have felt too. This something sent him to Chinky, the ghetto jeweller, the very next day with two pennyweights of stolen gold to be melted and refashioned into a wedding ring.

A few days after the funeral, Lala is looking at this wedding ring when she comes in from braiding at the beach. She has managed to braid only one head, a middle-aged tourist lady too drunk on rum and sunshine to listen to other beach vendors and braiders and steer clear of Lala. One head is not enough, and this is why she is staring at her wedding ring. She is wondering whether she can ask Tone to sell it for her, tell Adan it has been lost at the beach, use it to help buy her ticket.

It is already dark by the time Lala pushes the door to the house and the door finally groans and falls off its hinges, corroded by rain and the resulting rust. She frowns, props the broken door back with her bench and immediately runs back downstairs in response to a sudden drizzle. When she comes back up, she takes a galvanised tub of washing inside with her, balanced on her right hip, as her grandmother might have done. Lala is panting ever so slightly because it has only been a few weeks since she gave birth and even less time since the baby died and somehow her body is still sluggish, so that the effort required to drag herself up and down the stairs to wash clothing in the galvanised tub leaves her heaving when she returns to the top and the Pepsi Cola sign.

Adan does not look up. He is on the wrought-iron chair by the bed, a chair he once salvaged from the garbage of a rich tourist. The chair is wide, its arms curve inwards and are embellished with intricately wrought grapes and leaves. He is deep in his Bible, is Adan, and his lips move swiftly and soundlessly over each verse. He is saying his psalms. He can spend several hours in a day doing this, especially in the daylight hours before a night-time job for which he requires a special blessing. The vehemence with which he is praying suggests that there is a job tonight, that it is big one. There is a little backpack by the door, Lala notices, in the same deep black as the shirt and pants that Adan is wearing. The sight of it makes Lala stumble on her way to the sink but she does not say anything, she does not wish to anger him.

He turns the pages of the grubby red-backed book, lifts a satin ribbon stuck to the spine and brings it down between the two new pages he has landed on. Adan does not need the Bible to say these psalms – psalms for protection, psalms for prosperity, psalms to fool and foil the police – but he refers to it anyway as he recites them because it is something he has always done, something he learnt from his Auntie Preta.

Lala tries not to look at him while he stutters over the old English of the King James Version, while he closes his eyes and crosses himself and kisses the cover of the book in his hand. Something about it causes her such fury she bites her lip until she draws blood. Adan will not discover the fat, soft craters on the inside of her lower lip, because Adan no longer tries to kiss her.

'You eating, Adan?'

Adan's eyes stay on the psalms. The waves crash and bellow on the beach. The rain starts to drum above.

She puts down the tub, picks up one of his bright white shirts to fold it, puts it back, walks ten feet to the kitchen, picks up a knife to peel a potato, remembers that she does not trust herself with knives, puts the potato back, picks up an enamel cup, opens the cupboard below, drags out a sack of rice and swirls the cup through it. This is the sack of rice she bought months before, when she was heavily pregnant, on a day when Adan was not at home and a friendly fisherman stopped mending a net to lift the sack to the top of the stairs for her. This sack of rice is still almost full.

'You eating, Adan?' she repeats.

Adan looks at her, there with the enamel cup in her hand, the cup brimful of rice. He stares at the cup in her hand, and his lips keep moving over Psalm 51. Lala can tell, even though he makes no sound. He does not like to be interrupted when he is saying his psalms. He does not want to be jinxed on the eve of a job by her interrupting the psalms he is saying, so he does not answer her.

Lala sighs without thinking. She makes a loud sound that reminds her of tearing paper. She watches Adan's lips stop their caress of David's words and she sighs loudly again, for a different reason. She watches her hand jerk, sees the cup fall, the rice scatter, watches the pages of the Bible flutter, sees the psalms of David submerged.

This time Lala is sure she is dying. It is not like before – she doesn't hear her bones break, nothing snaps or tears, there is no slow leak of life in little red rivers of blood. This time he simply holds her neck and squeezes it. Not talking, not quarrelling, just concentrating all his energy on the curve of his palms at her throat. Eventually, she can no longer speak, and she finds that the loss of a voice is a lot like drowning. He squeezes so hard that the whites of his eyes grow larger, and bulge, and little red veins pop and bleed inside them and this, more than anything, is what would make her scream if she could.

She is trapped. Like an animal. So that the ten small

paces to the door and the steps and the sanctuary of the wide-open beach, even these ten small paces are impossible. Ten paces that were taken for granted yesterday as she went to buy beads or bread or to beg the forgiveness of a man perched on a boulder, forehead in his hand so that his scar was hidden.

He squeezes, and her eyes grow dark, fog over like the surface of the sea on a rainy day, a sea beneath which she sinks further into silence. Dying, finds Lala, is something like surfing a rainbow with very bright colours in all shapes and forms, dancing out of a point that is perpetually spilling them so that you are forever moving forwards on swathes of billowing reds and blues, but never really getting anywhere, just forever travelling towards a tiny hole where all the colour originates and where it ends. She wonders whether this is how her daughter must have felt when she was dying – the glorious, giddy kaleidoscope hurtling towards a hole that inexplicably remains the same distance away. Lala thinks that if, perhaps, to die means the eternal roller coaster of colour, the giddy dance on blues and greens and reds and purples, then, possibly, to kill could be a kindness.

And on seeing that fact made plain on her face before him, Adan frees her throat and lets her go.

Lala is still on the floor coughing when Sergeant Beckles arrives at the doorway. Sergeant Beckles wants to talk to Adan. He is smiling when Adan steps into that small space at the top of the stairs. This smile has everything to do with his new theory that Tone and Lala conspired to murder Baby. That Adan is an innocent man. Watching them kiss on the steps was the first clue, and the calm of his full belly supports it.

This morning, Mrs Beckles made him roasted sweet potatoes in garlic and thyme, dusted with cinnamon and a puff of cayenne powder, enough to awaken his salivary glands but not enough to irritate them. The wife boiled and pounded lentils with tarragon and coconut milk, she soaked a few tender beet leaves in brine and then poached them with small silver onions she grew herself. When she presented the meal to him, he ate with the guilt of the tasting slave, sure that he was afforded this luxury solely by virtue of his household position and not because of any genuine intention to feed him the gold of his wife's patch of ground. She watched him eat silently, as she always did, not allowing herself his leftovers until he had cleared his plate and had seconds, and then she ate her cooling peas without pleasure, spooning them hurriedly into her mouth so that she could wash the dishes quickly enough to catch the sun before the threatening rain could ruin the wash loads waiting to be hung and dried. The policeman had been struck by the sight of her there, sitting in a corner of the kitchen on an odd half-bench he had built in the early days of their marriage, when he had still thought that that type of industry was required of him. His wife held on to that bench, despite its progressive decay, each day since he had come to understand that it was not.

'Come,' he had said to her, 'come and sit at the table.'

And she had, holding her empty bowl with the muddy streaks of lentil sullying her conscience every time she looked at them. She looked at them often while he spoke, while he thanked her for a meal she had barely tasted. She nodded when he said he thought they should get a washing machine. She sighed when he mentioned that a colleague's mother had died. She seemed relieved when he finished eating, when he said that she could go.

The policeman notices now that Adan does not stand in front of his wife at the top of the stairs. He does not draw her to his side when Sergeant Beckles scales the last step and is face to face with them, there on the little stone landing from which the eyes can sweep down a dizzying depth before landing on sand and sea. He notices that there is no banister that a woman could hold on to while walking down with washing or up with bags of the building blocks of family meals. For the first time he feels sorry for Lala.

Sorry, however, does not excuse a murder.

'I did just want to ask a few questions, a few last questions,' he explains, when Adan ignores the discomfort of the three of them squeezed into a small landing at the top of a treacherous flight of stairs, when he does not suggest that the policeman come inside and speak to him or that he can follow him down the steps and talk, man to man, on the sand. Adan waits for the questions without nodding to signal that he welcomes them.

'Your wife did tell me you was away the night she had the baby. Where was you?' It is a question neither Adan nor Lala expects; it catches them off guard and they both teeter, there on that small landing.

'The night Baby come?' echoes Adan, perplexed enough to seek a repetition. The policeman smiles, steadied by

lentils and coconut milk and enough potatoes to keep him
full until after he goes home for his second meal of the day.
Lala looks around wildly. She is sure that she did not tell
this policeman that Adan was not there with her, pacing
the floors at Baxter's General, when Baby was born. She is
desperate for him to somehow confirm that his question is
an error, that he is more concerned with the baby's death
than that morning she drew her first breath. But the policeman is sure. The question popped into his head at the
bidding of his theory of the crime, ushered in by the sage
direction of his happy belly. When he solves the case, he
resolves, when they make him a station sergeant (instead
of just a sergeant) and give him a station to supervise, he
will thank his wife for supporting him and she will wring
her hands and try to avoid attention and deny that her
coconut-pounded lentils have cracked each case his career
has ever presented. He will have forgotten about Sheba by
then, resolves Sergeant Beckles.

'The night Baby come,' he repeats, 'where you was?'
And Adan adopts the look Sergeant Beckles has seen so
many times before in his career of twenty years: the look
of the criminal reminded that his humanity, and not his
criminality, is the source of his logic, which is why even a
non-criminal can follow it.

Adan stutters, 'I was in de hospital when she start have
baby. I had to leave was to do something for a friend of
mine.'

The policeman writes, painstakingly forming each
word, repeating to be sure his is a verbatim record of
Adan's account.

'And how long you was away fishing?' asks Sergeant Beckles.

''Bout a month,' says Adan.

'She say she had to walk to the hospital,' presses the policeman, 'you was already in the boat?'

Adan is unsure if this is a question meant to trick him. If after he answers he will be presented with the reasons why his answer cannot be true.

'You know how it is,' explains Adan apologetically, ushering Lala back inside with his eyes. When she is gone and the door closes behind her, he says, 'I wasn't on the fishing trip yet, I was by my outside woman.'

Sergeant Beckles' thoughts turn to his Sheba and her continuing reluctance to court him. An outside woman is something every man in Paradise understands, so Sergeant Beckles nods and continues scribbling.

'What about the night Baby died?'

'I was doing a li'l work on a fishing boat,' explains Adan. 'Me and my cousin went out fishing. I didn't even know Baby did dead.'

The sergeant nods. 'Your wife did tell me. Very sorry for your loss.'

Adan nods, drops his head.

'The gentleman that find the baby on the beach,' Sergeant Beckles continues, 'what more you could tell me about him?'

Inside the house, Lala's eyes are running over the outline of everything. She is searching for corners, sharp edges and pointed implements. A knife is shoved beneath the mattress and the bit of plywood Adan had slid over the springs to help her back when she was pregnant with Baby. The ice pick she had used to carve ice for Adan's drink the night before is chucked atop the wardrobe. The corner of a side table is covered in a cloth she'd intended to finish for Baby's bedding. The heavy tawa is put at the bottom of the broom closet and covered with rags used for cleaning, the obtuse angle of the television antenna is removed swiftly and shoved into a garbage bag and the television powered off so that Adan will not be further angered by the snow on the screen. She can hear him talking in low tones, the halting cadence of his speech suggesting that he is thinking carefully.

It is the way of the world, she believes, that her innocent observation that there was nothing that stood out to her as strange before Baby disappeared (the very night of her birth she had walked the beach without worry) could have led to this line of questioning. Her observation that day Sergeant Beckles had questioned her had led him to question why a woman so heavily pregnant had been left home alone. She'd thought nothing of it then, nothing at all. But now . . .

The enamel cup would sting if the lip caught her head at an angle but the metal would cool the heat of a blow and the bruise could be easily explained away because for a marking it would likely be unremarkable. She removes the teacup with the wilting heliconia from the window and scrambles to find a way to cover the little star-shaped tap installed in a corner. It is a small sink, no more than a foot and a quarter square, that Adan had salvaged from one of the big homes on Baxter's Beach. It is why he didn't feel any guilt about robbing these people, he had explained, one night when he was talking, the things they threw away. Anybody who would throw away things like that deserved to get things taken.

It is when the door closes behind her husband and she hears Sergeant Beckles descending the steps that her eyes fall on the umbrella she forgot to hide. It is the way of the world that that is the first thing he reaches for.

Adan is enraged. That she told Sergeant Beckles he'd left her alone the morning she delivered the baby. What kind of husband she trying to make people feel he is? That Sergeant Beckles had the nerve to come to his house, HIS HOUSE, and try to make him feel like he had to answer his kiss-me-ass questions. That Baby is dead. It must have been something she said. *Thwack. Thwack.* Bitch. What did she tell the police? *Thwack.* Stop screaming and answer. Does she know what they do to people who talk to police where he come from? *Bang. Crash. Whir.* Fucking. Rasshole. Bitch. What did she tell the sergeant? What? She want him now? She want the sergeant? *Whizz. Sing. Slap.* Fucking. Rass. Hole. Whore. What did she tell him? He ought to kill her. Did she ever see him gut a fish? He ought to slit her belly like a blasted fish. If she keep it up, he will. Like a fucking fish. Blasted. Ungrateful. Murdering. Bitch. Ain't she know she is the one that kill Baby? As good as if she take her two hands and stop her wind. *Slap. Gurgle. Choke.* See how it feel? See how, bitch? If she think he going to jail because she is a fucking murderous bitch murdering her own baby, she lie. Why she had to pull the baby? Why she didn't just let him show her to Jacinthe?

Everybody want to see him go to jail. Everybody. Fucking Sergeant Beckles must be looking to ask him about the robbery by the old white man place. Not Baby. Sergeant Beckles don't really care about Baby. Poor Baby. Baby didn't deserve to die. Why she kill her? The fucking young bitch by the white man probably give Sergeant Beckles his description. He should have killed her one time. Fucking bitch. *Choke. Choke. Wheeze.* And why she had to ring the bell in the middle of everything? Blasted fucking own-way bitch. He gonna go back and see that bitch in the big house, want to send him to jail. He ain't done with her yet. He gonna go back and finish the job properly and he ain't doing a fucking day for it either. Not a day for that white woman and not a day for her. Fucking. Rass. Hole. Baby-killing. Bitch.

CHAPTER TWENTY-EIGHT

Sheba
4 September 1984

The whores who work the Holborn Hotel are aware, for the most part, of its many pretences. They know, for example, that the verdant green that stretches across the tiny 'walled garden' in which guests are invited to have high tea is in fact a carpet bought second-hand from the entity that managed the National Stadium and is made of a plastic bristle that itches without mercy if you happen to drop a biscuit and drag your hand across the turf to look for it.

The whores know, similarly, that the Grand Foyer, which the advertising booklet suggests is supported by magnificent columns made of indigenous limestone, is nothing more than a large room with a mirrored wall, and that the columns have been covered by the owners in a textured plastic trowelling manufactured on the island. The whores know as well that the nightly rates advertised in the letters of introduction Ganesh Hanu painstakingly types and sends to each member of the Association of British Travel Agents each month are fluid, and that, when the desires of a new client cannot be sated by a few quick moments on the beach, Mr Hanu can be convinced to rent a room for an hour or two if you speak to him directly and do not burden Mrs Hanu or sour-faced Hiram, their acne-riddled teenager, with the seedier aspects of humanity.

This knowledge is why the Queen of Sheba had laughed, at first, when she saw a man walking the rocks on the rough side of Baxter's Beach at 3.30 a.m. on the morning that Baby was discovered. At the time, the Queen of Sheba had been sitting astride an Israeli endomorph called Ru, in a ground-floor room of the Holborn Hotel, trying to mask her disinterest in his tentative efforts to talk dirty. She remembered that one time that Mr Hanu, in an attempt to attract the membership of the Ghost Club of London, had typed up a letter that said the hotel was haunted.

So in the wee hours of 17 August 1984, when the Queen of Sheba had looked out of the tiny barred window of the ground-floor back bedroom Mr Hanu tended to use for rentals by the hour and had watched the half-moon glow on a Rasta man with a baby in his arms, the first thought she had was that she was *not* in fact seeing a sun-bleached surfer in baggy shorts holding a tiny baby that flopped when he sought to tuck it more carefully into the crook of his arm, and this was why she had laughed, wondering whether Mr Hanu might have staged such a scene to please the members of the Ghost Club of London, who must eventually have answered his many invitations.

To the soundtrack of Ru's ribald talk of peaches and prunes, the Queen of Sheba had watched the Rasta put the baby down among the rocks. At that moment, the Queen of Sheba stretched herself upward, leaving Ru perplexed, to put her face right up to the bars of the little window. The Rasta had reached down and seemed to tuck a blanket

253

around the baby and then, changing his mind, had picked the infant back up to wrap it in the blanket instead. The Queen of Sheba had noted that the baby was motionless in the way of those already dead. When the Rasta put the infant back down on the rocks and started to walk away, Sheba had started to shake with the realisation of what she was observing. She had remained oblivious to Ru's mounting desire, his fast and feverish movements beneath her. When the Rasta had paused to gaze around the beach and confirm that he was not being watched, the Queen of Sheba had ducked down into Ru's underarm hair with a small exclamation, which worked surprisingly better than dirty talk to get Ru the relief he had been after.

Later, when the underside of her left breast had been warmed by the stack of US bills Ru had paid her with, the Queen of Sheba had joined the search party on the beach. She had watched the Rasta run back and forth, marshalling volunteers forward to the very rocks he had tucked the baby under. She had watched him, although she knew that *he* knew that it would lead to the baby. She had puzzled over the possible reasons for this and ultimately had decided it was not her business. The Queen of Sheba had therefore walked away from the crowd when the search was over, dissolving into the beach crowd with the acquired skill of someone accustomed to living in shadows. She had observed Sergeant Beckles start to stop people to ask questions about the discovery of the baby. The Queen of Sheba had not been able to stand the sight of Sergeant Beckles. This fucking two-bit kiss-me-ass policeman had been threatening to arrest her since she had started avoiding

servicing him, and she had started avoiding servicing him
when it became clear that, for Sergeant Beckles, what she
gave him was more than a mere servicing. The thing is, the
Queen of Sheba had thought then, she wouldn't have minded
servicing the foolish man every once in a while, but something about the things he made her do just turned her
stomach too much more than the promise of his money
excited her, and the way he took a simple exchange to mean
they were meant for each other made her doubt his sanity.
As a matter of fact, it made her skin crawl.

The Queen of Sheba will tell you that Sergeant Beckles
catches her at a weak moment when he turns up in the early
hours of the morning at the tiny apartment for which she
pays the government twenty dollars per week. It bothers
her, she will say, that he finds himself at her house, in uniform, in full view of her two children just leaving on their
way to school on the first day of the new school year. The
Queen of Sheba would not say 'intimidation', but should
she be questioned, should the meaning of the word be
explained to her, she might be hard pressed to deny that
that is exactly what she feels when she hears him banging
on her door, shouting her name at the top of his lungs. Sergeant Beckles says that he is on his way home from a
stake-out. That is how he says it – *stake-out* – in a way that
makes the Queen of Sheba think of livestock being put out
to graze and not of TV episodes of *Matlock*. The case of
the dead baby, he says, and he looks at her like he expects
her to be impressed. The Queen of Sheba is not impressed.
She knows that he is lying, that the little exaggerations of

255

his investigation are meant to dazzle her in a way that the shining metal stripes on his sergeant's uniform do not. She fidgets in her furry bedroom slippers, keeps wiping the sweat off the palms of her hands and into the fabric of her red nightshirt, made to look like the jerseys worn by baseball pitchers in the United States of America.

'Open the door, Sheba,' says Sergeant Beckles, when she is still looking at him above the taut security chain that keeps the door open just a sliver.

'How come you here?' wonders Sheba. 'How come you here at my door?'

Sergeant Beckles' voice assumes the high-pitched whine Sheba mimics with the other whores when he is not within earshot.

'I could come in, Sheba?' He smiles, and the look on his face allows her to understand that he truly intends to make her work in her own house, the one place in which she has, up to this point, refused to be anything other than a mother and a daughter and a friend.

'I ain't feeling so good today,' the Queen of Sheba pleads with Sergeant Beckles. 'I ain't feeling so good at all.'

'We could just talk,' Sergeant Beckles cajoles her, while the hair flares out of his nostrils in a way that tells her that talking is the least of the things he has in mind.

'I don't know . . .'

The Queen of Sheba holds on to her side of the doorknob and looks back towards the inside of her house when the knob starts to rattle with the force Sergeant Beckles begins to apply from the other side. She has turned to stare at the poster of a pastel-pink poodle on the door to the single bedroom where she sleeps with her children when she allows herself the luxury of actually sleeping at night. The Queen of Sheba loves poodles; raising and breeding them is what she dreams of doing once she has retired.

'Open the door, girl,' insists Sergeant Beckles. 'Open it!'

'I tell you I ain't feeling good,' the Queen of Sheba protests. 'I ain't taking no clients today.'

'Oh-ho!' Sergeant Beckles grouses, and the doorknob starts to give way in Sheba's hands, to come away from the cavity in which it is situated. 'So I is just a client now, eh?'

'That ain't what I meaning,' explains Sheba. She looks at her son's new Walkman on the bed, noticing that he has taken off the earphones in a huff because she said he could not take it with him to school. She sees that the cassette is still playing, that the earphones still vibrate with the bass of the Jamaican dancehall her son had dressed himself to. The Queen of Sheba would tell you that she watches the tape whir in the Walkman and wishes the sergeant away.

'So what you really meaning, then?'

And when she does not answer, 'What you really meaning, girl?'

The Queen of Sheba will tell you that Sergeant Beckles pushes the door open so roughly that the imprint of the knob is stamped on the upper part of her right thigh for a week afterwards, and that the chain preventing the door from swinging wide open comes away from the spongy wood of the door jamb with one shove of his shoulder. She will tell you that when he comes inside he stands so close to her that she feels she cannot move, and that she has already resigned herself to the feel of the hot air being blasted from his nose on her face as he speaks, to the nausea she will suffer through what will come after.

'We ain't friends no more, girl?' Sergeant Beckles wants to know, as he lifts the red nightshirt and pins her against the plywood partition. 'You and me ain't friends?'

The Queen of Sheba would tell you that, though she is scared, she doesn't understand why. After all, Sergeant Beckles was once a client. It isn't like she does not know him, it isn't like he hasn't positioned her against a tree behind the Holborn Hotel in just this way at least ten times before, it isn't like he does not already know the precise number of palm lengths from the middle of her thighs to the perimeter of her panties, the specific angle at which her legs need to be parted for him to fit himself between them. The Queen of Sheba would readily admit that she has no reason to be scared. It isn't like Sergeant Beckles has ever harmed her, not really, it isn't like he hasn't turned a blind eye to her and her clients on one or other occasion, it isn't like he hasn't done her favours before – like releasing her when a rookie policeman who didn't know any better arrested her and brought her in to the station.

As she cannot explain her distress, the Queen of Sheba concludes that she isn't distressed, not really, that for some reason she isn't being her sensible, practical self. This is why, when the Queen of Sheba ends up sitting on her bed after the deed is done, feeling the sergeant's slime seep out of her and on to the bed on which her children have left their damp towels and the tumble of clothing they searched through to find the twin of a single school sock or a washed and unpressed T-shirt for games, her one thought is to get

Sergeant Beckles out of her house as soon as possible. Because somehow the Queen of Sheba cannot rationalise for herself that Sergeant Beckles has done her anything wrong, and if he hasn't truly wronged her, then she knows she is foolish for feeling as she does. She does not wish to continue to see his face to be reminded of precisely how foolish she is.

Sergeant Beckles, however, is in no hurry to leave. Instead, he strips himself of all the rest of his clothing, save his socks, and stretches himself out on her bed, shoving aside her children's clothes, to doze. Even after he wakes himself a few minutes later by his own snoring, he remains seated at the foot of her bed, naked as he had been born, watching the poster of the poodle on the open bedroom door and theorising about the case of the murdered baby. The CID in the city hasn't cracked the Whalen case as yet, even with the help of the mighty Scotland Yard, but Sergeant Beckles knows that it is coming. He feels like he is racing against time, like he must solve Baby's murder before he can be blindsided by news of the arrest of Peter Whalen's murderer.

The Queen of Sheba will tell you that what she really wants at that moment, what she truly intends to do from her heart, is to get Sergeant Beckles out of her house, away from the big pink dolly house she had bought for her daughter, which stands in the corner of the bedroom with majestic purple spires and its family of perfect little dolly people, like a portal to another world. She wants to get his eyes away from the pictures of the children on her dresser, the picture of her mom, the picture of her from a few years

259

before in baggy jeans and an LA Gear T-shirt and a face free of the shadow of the knowledge of just how evil men can be. She wants to wash the smell of him out of her sheets and shirt. That is all she wants, the Queen of Sheba would say, that is her only aim – what she does has nothing to do with Tone.

She has nothing against Tone, she will emphasise, nothing at all to hold him in mind for. As a matter of fact, she and Tone could even be called friends, at least co-workers. She would tell you that he used to shout her when he passed her on the beach and she used to shout him back. Tone never give her no problems, the Queen of Sheba would say. Matter of fact, Tone is one of the few that made her feel that good men still existed. Never brought her any nasty talk, never acted like he knew what she sold on the beach at night, never gave her a 'good morning' that sounded like it differed in any respect from the one he might give to his mother.

Nevertheless, good man or no, the Queen of Sheba admits that when she realises that the one thing preoccupying the sergeant's mind this morning is the solving of the baby's murder, she understands at once what she has that will cause him to get dress, to scurry back to the station and strategise and leave her alone.

She ain't no informer, the Queen of Sheba would say, her mother ain't raise no snitch. It is innocent the way that she tells Sergeant Beckles what she saw on the night the baby died. She ain't mean to point a finger at Tone, the Queen of Sheba would explain, she don't want him locked up or nothing. That ain't how ghetto people does live.

CHAPTER TWENTY-NINE

Mrs Whalen
4 September 1984

'I wondered if you'd like to come by for a drink' is how it starts, the day after Mira has Peter cremated. She is flying out two afternoons hence with Peter's ashes, she is taking them home to Wimbledon where his sisters have arranged a memorial service. She is relieved to be leaving the island behind, unsolved murder case or not.

The cremation was a small ceremony, in the chapel attached to the crematorium, for Rosa and Mr Watson and the neighbours on the beach. Mira remembers that Grayson, who has turned up at her front door to invite her over, was there.

She hopes it will end with 'No.' But he persists.

'Look, it's nothing but a drink.'

Mira looks hard at him, in his customary black sports shorts with his chest uncovered. She notes his ginger-snap curls of chest and back hair, netting swarthy, sun-damaged skin. His body is not muscular, he rather looks like a wrinkled barrel in black bathing shorts. He rather looks like Peter.

'Thanks, but I don't drink.'

Mira tries to close the door but Grayson stops her. Her

eyes sting under the onslaught of sunlight. Mira has not slept; she'd been to the auto-mart around 2 a.m. and Jack hadn't been at work and all night she had, absurdly, worried about him. The store attendant who was there did not fold the bag the right way to protect her box of raisins. She had been afraid to ask whether Jack had been fired, whether something terrible had happened to him. She looks past Grayson's sloping shoulders to the 'For Sale' sign that faces the sea. She is selling the house, there is no question of her keeping it, no thought of ever coming back here, far less to sleep in the villa in which her husband was murdered.

'Who drinks at this time of morning anyway?' she asks him. She is still in her pyjamas, the same ones she's worn for the past week, layered with a silk robe Peter had bought her from Hong Kong, hand-painted water lilies or something similar. Rosa has not tried to force it off of her and scold her into a tub of hot water. Rosa is concerned with a reference now that she will be leaving.

Grayson shrugs and mumbles something grumpy. The six o'clock woman runs past, making little explosions with the balls of her feet as she jogs, ponytail bobbing. Mira hugs her robe close, closes her eyes and tries to imagine that the backs of her eyelids do not burn – from the sun, from the lack of sleep, from the images that are stuck there whenever she drifts off. This man will not move from the step.

'Normally I'd be walking with Betsy at this time,' the man explains after a while. 'I've been coming awake anyway – although she's dead.'

'I'm sorry,' Mira replies. 'She was lovely.'

He looks like he is just preparing to walk away when she says, 'I suppose one drink couldn't hurt – a hot drink.'

They chat on his patio, she still in her pyjamas, he in his bathing shorts. He says he has a gun, she should get one, he offers to show it to her but Mira Whalen shakes her head. She is leaving in two days, selling the house, she tells him, there is no reason for her to get a gun now. Mira Whalen hears the beep of the buzzer as Rosa punches in the code and lets herself in. Today is her last day.

Mira Whalen is just beginning to enjoy her coffee, to feel the gentle heat of the early sun on her hands and face, when a woman rushes on to the patio. The woman is bloody, an incisor seems half gone, and the half that remains is partially obliterated by a pulsing purple lip.

'I'm calling the police this time,' Grayson says, disgusted, and the slapping of his feet on the floor follows a derisory snort, as if he is annoyed by the sight of her, dripping blood on his sand-coloured porcelain tile. She isn't crying. She sort of trembles through some sort of half holler before she collapses on the tile and stays there. Mira takes this to mean that she feels she is safe from what she is seeking to escape and sets about seeing that, as much as is possible, this is so.

It is Mira who leads this woman inside, Mira who slides shut the glass doors that lead to Grayson's patio and secures them, Mira who finds and pulls a string that drops a sisal blind to cover the door so that the outside is no longer visible. Grayson disappears for a moment and comes quietly back with a cordless phone, but when he speaks into it that he wants to report an assault, it is Mira who almost jumps out of her skin.

The woman whimpers. It sounds like 'No.'

'Don't be silly,' he says. 'I'm calling it in.'

The woman starts to cry, to try to walk away. She pleads with Mira, silently, to stop him, but Mira is also helpless while Grayson talks into the receiver.

'Yes, an assault. A man, I think, keeps beating the beje-sus out of his . . .' he looks at her finger, 'wife.'

The woman is looking at the door, willing herself to get up.

'I all right,' she says when Mira rises to help her, 'I good.' It sounds like *thwud* and the woman touches her lip, as if she cannot believe that it has been so badly battered that she now sounds like Elmer Fudd. When she stands up, Mira notes that her skirt is torn and you can see her panties through it.

'You're not!' Grayson barks, and then he is back to the receiver again, giving the address of his big house on Baxter's Beach. Mira Whalen knows that the giving of this address ensures that the police will come, that they will come quickly.

The woman is looking around the room, checking for noises, for points of entry that haven't been taken care of. Mira listens to Grayson describe this woman to the police.

'Was it someone you know?'

Grayson pauses. 'We've seen her before, one morning he chased her down here. I've seen the husband too – ran back when he saw me coming, he did. Betsy used to bark at her whenever she saw her along the beach.'

Mira watches the dark chocolate woman gather her skirt, like its flares are her wits, holding together the edges of the biggest rip in her fist, like this action will bring sense to her situation.

'Don't call the police,' says the woman. 'I all right. I going.'

He stands in her way, in front of the blinds hiding the doors back to the beach, and keeps talking into the phone. He moves from side to side, maintaining his position each time she tries to go towards the door.

'I have a daughter,' he says to Mira, post-description, 'I have a daughter, and I'd be damned if I let a man treat her like this.'

'No, not you,' he says into the receiver, rolling his eyes.

Mira Whalen waves to Grayson, makes it clear that he should cancel the report, tell the police not to worry. The police here are useless, she says to Grayson, she knows they are useless. Up to now they cannot find who killed Peter; what makes him think they can help this woman?

The woman starts crying, tears that run down her sullen expression in steady streams, without sound. Mira believes that she should hug her, so she goes close, stretches out her arms, lays them on her thick flesh and pulls her close. She tells her that she should stay. Here, where she's safe. She tells her that everything is going to be all right.

Although she is unimpressed by the way the police have handled the investigation into her husband's murder, Mira Whalen blames herself for it stalling. Despite repeatedly being shown binders thick with the plastic-protected mugshots of every robber the island has ever known, everyone who has served time for murder or grievous bodily harm, Mira Whalen has come up empty, has kept shaking her head 'no' when English and local detectives alike asked her if she recognised any of these men from the night they were robbed and her husband killed. No other witnesses have come forward with information about anyone seen in the vicinity of Mira's house, no gun has been found, there are no useful fingerprints, and DNA testing in criminal investigations has not been implemented yet. Peter's killer remains a mystery.

It had not made sense to the detectives that Mira Whalen would not remember the robber who had killed her husband. It had not made sense at all. Her statement said she had pulled a stocking off his face, so she should have been able to have a good look at him. But Mira Whalen does not remember the face behind the stocking, she remembers the hand that held the gun and there is no registry of criminal hands they can offer her. They suggest counselling, tell her to call them if anything comes back to her, anything at all, but at this point Mira Whalen just wants to leave the island, just wants to take Peter's ashes away with her and never come back. It is because she blames herself, however, that she agrees to look through the binder one more time, to stare into the face of every convicted robber, murderer and violent offender that Baxter's Beach has even known.

'You sure you ain't recognise nobody?' pleads Sergeant Beckles. 'Here, let me show you again.'

She'd rung them to say she was leaving, to say thanks

for all their help, just to be polite, and he'd asked her to come back, to take one more look. This is not protocol. Protocol would dictate that he wait for one of the detectives from Scotland Yard or the local CID before showing her the same binder they had borrowed from the Baxter's police station, but Beckles is not concerned with protocol. Beckles is concerned with showing the big-ups that a sergeant from a poor background with twenty years in policing can solve, with nothing more than his belly, a case that confounds them, with all of the fancy equipment and techniques they have brought with them from England.

So Mira looks through the stack of photographs one more time before pushing away the weathered brown binder Sergeant Beckles has brought in. She shudders, although the room they are in at the police station is sweltering hot. Mira Whalen is seated on a little folding metal chair on which she cannot get comfortable. She looks around a large room with walls that reveal their many incarnations of colour in patches of peeling paint. Uniformed policemen and officers in civilian clothing sit at a number of wooden desks, on the phone, rummaging in drawers, recording statements from victims and witnesses. Files and papers are everywhere and flutter soundlessly in the buzz of the station. Catalogues of crimes litter the surfaces of the desks, are stacked high on the mismatched motley crew of chairs, gather dust on the tops of rusty filing cabinets. Mira Whalen tries not to look too hard at the civilians like her, the people whose obvious discomfort demonstrates that they did not expect to be here, but she cannot help it. She wonders whether these people have also suffered at the hands of the robber who killed Peter.

It is her fault, thinks Mira, that Peter is dead, that he has sacrificed his life to save hers. Peter was a man with everything who hadn't given a thought to giving it all up for her, even though they had been quarrelling about the affair, even though he had been sleeping in the spare room when she had screamed. He had still come running. And now she was a woman with everything she'd ever wanted, but she did not have Peter, or Beth, or Sam, or a child of her own, or a true friend she could call or a mother she could curl into and cry. And she could not even do him the honour of remembering the face of his killer.

She didn't expect to see the face of this robber in these photographs, she did not expect to see a mugshot that would trigger her memory, that was not why she came here. But Mira Whalen still leaves the police station in a stupor. She does not hear the policeman ask her whether she would like him to drop her home, whether she would like him to call someone to collect her, or a drink of water before going. Mira Whalen cries as she walks, stumbling along the street towards Baxter's Beach.

CHAPTER THIRTY

Tone
5 September 1984

Tone wakes up to a new face. It is one of those faces that make him want to scream Jesus Christ, Joseph and Mary. Anybody who thinks this hustle is easy, that men like him are lazy, has never had a day of getting up to a face like this. He peeps at the woman again, starts trying to figure out how to get out without having to see that face come alive. It looks to Tone like one of those silicone Reagan masks Adan sometimes wears to look like the fucking President when he is robbing. No matter who you are, what you really look like, you put on that mask and you look like the President of the United States of America. But when you take the mask off, it melts and wrinkles like jelly, sits in the corner of the room like a spirit that has shed its skin and left it to await reinhabitation next time it might be ready to do something sinister. Adan had told him that Lala hated that mask and what it represented. Adan had told him that recently, when he needed it for a job, he suddenly couldn't find it any more, he had been forced to use one of his wife's cheap pairs of stockings instead. These women, Adan had groused before spitting, they think they know how to fix everything that want fixing.

Tone realises now that they are in a nice room, a penthouse suite, from the looks of it, all chrome and marble and discreetly tinted blue glass from floor to ceiling. He hadn't paid too much attention the night before when he had stumbled back here with his client. The place is beautiful, but with the AC on it is also very cold, it makes him feel like he could have died.

He considers turning his back on the woman and staying a little longer under the covers without having to see her face, but he is afraid that any small movement will wake her. He knows this kind of woman. The cocaine has become so much a part of her that she has already assumed some of its superhuman powers – the ability to hear a pin drop from a mile away, to feel the slightest movement during deep sleep, to stay awake for thirty-six hours straight or to sleep without dying for a week. Should he move a muscle, this woman will awaken, because in her sleep she can hear the *tick-tock* of his mind, and the moment he thinks to sit up, before he actually moves an arm or leg, an alarm will go off inside her head and she will swing bolt upright, see him there, remember last night, look around to make sure she has not been murdered and is coming awake outside of her own dead body, look around for her purse to make sure she has not been robbed, look over to the bedside table for evidence of even a smidgen of powder left over from last night and, not trusting her eyes, lean over to test the surface of the table with her tongue instead.

Tone decides that stealth would be silly. It is possibly the boldness of this decision that causes the woman to keep sleeping as he dresses, makes himself a cup of hot water for breakfast, counts the three crisp hundred-dollar bills the woman placed in his pocket last night. Ugly or no, this is one of those women who knows how to pay him so that it never feels like he is taking her money in exchange for sex. In unspoken deference to this story, he has refrained from counting the money until the morning after, when she is still sleeping, when the after-sex talk about taking him to meet her children and grandchildren becomes as absurd as the thought of doing anything but getting as far away from her as possible.

He lets himself out by the service entrance, thinks about checking in on Lala and Adan and thinks better of it. He swallows the sour spell of fury he feels when he thinks of Adan, the bitter spit of guilt that sometimes keeps him away. He will see him tonight for the job; he needs to stay level, unbothered, like the Tone Adan remembers from before he married Lala.

It's his own fault, thinks Tone. He knew about Jacinthe, what he knew was why he'd brought her. And now look.

Tone climbs on to his jet ski, revs up and into the blue, skirting the early bathers for deeper water. A white man is waving at him, an old white man in black shorts. This white man does not want a ride on the jet ski, this white man wants to give him a note he says is from Lala. The note says she wants to meet him in the tunnels at the entrance he knows about. Now.

When he sees her busted lips, her eyes swollen so far shut that she has to throw her head back to look at him prop-erly, he understands for the first time that he will never be

271

rid of the Thing. That it will never leave him. The moment a tear squeezes past that eye swollen shut, and glitters across the blue and purple bruises on her face, the Thing is there with him, threatening to make him forget himself entirely.

She tells him everything, about Adan asking if he was behaving strangely, about his intention to return to the big house, about Sergeant Beckles' questions, about her leaving. She talks with the dust dancing on the shards of light coming through the limestone ceiling, like the fairy dust Cinderella dances in before she disappears.

In the tight space they stand in, they are side by side, he and Lala; it feels wrong to squeeze in front of her the way he did so very long ago, it feels wrong to face her, to look into her face while she is relaying what Adan said. What he did.

'He say he going back,' she confirms, 'he say he going back and kill the lady that see him. He shoot the man, Tone, he say he shoot the man.'

Tone is worried. He knows Adan is a robber, but as far as he knows, Adan has never killed anybody. Adan asked him to hide him in the tunnels because a job had gone sour, but he'd never mentioned a murder. Tone is pounding the side of the tunnel with a piece of twig he pulled from above ground on his way in. He is thinking that he has shared the existence of these tunnels with Adan, suggested them as a possible route to transport weed brought in from St Vincent on fishing boats, to get to town. He is asking himself whether, based on his reluctance to show him the shortest route from shore to city, Adan will decide to explore the caves himself, whether he could be doing that now. He is not speaking but his brows are furrowed, like he is focusing his eyes on the same problem his mind is puzzling over.

'I think he really going kill me this time,' sobs Lala. 'I can't stay here no more, Tone, I can't stay in truth.'

The twig hits the side of the tunnel a little harder, its bark starts to shed to expose the yellow fibre underneath. The floor is seasoned with bits of stem, dying in the dust.

'He not going kill you,' Tone declares, 'not in truth.'

Lala does not reply. She reaches her hands to the neckline of a dress with fine filigree collar tips, and tears it until her neck and chest are exposed, then she turns sideways, into a few slivers of light. She is deep plum where the pointed tip of the umbrella has bruised her.

'Why you choose that man, Lala?' Tone accuses. 'Why up to now you ain't left he?'

'He is my husband,' says Lala. 'He ain't just a man to leave him so.'

'Ohhhh.' Tone feigns understanding. 'Well let your husband kill you, then.'

'I was saving to leave him . . . He take my money, Tone, he thief it, I was going to run, I was going to catch a plane, I—'

'You is a child that he could just take you money so?'

Lala understands this, what Tone is saying. She understands that he must question her in this way about Adan because it saves him the hard questions he would otherwise be forced to ask himself.

She cries as he scolds her, and when the sun changes position and the dust can no longer be seen, they are silent.

Tone says he will fix it. He will get her the money for a ticket. He gives her the money he has made from the German and promises more in a few days. She can take a plane, go somewhere big; if she doesn't know somewhere, he has a brother in the Big Apple, she can get lost somewhere where Adan will never find her, and maybe one day Tone will come, he will come to the Big Apple and find her. But it will all take time. A ticket is nothing much, but a place to stay, enough to keep her until she can get a job, try to sort her status, these things will take time. She will need as much money as they can gather. He will need a few days. Can she survive a few days so he can get her some money? Maybe she can stay somewhere else, other than the house, she can stay somewhere else and wait for him. It can't be by his mother because Adan comes around sometimes, looking for him, but if she can only find somewhere . . .

She says it is OK. The people in one of the big houses on the beach have told her to stay there, in a white man's basement, until things cool down and she can do whatever she needs to do next.

Or they could go to the police.

She shakes her head. No. If she does, the police might ask more questions about Baby and she cannot answer any more questions about Baby. Tone nods. What happened to Baby is another one of the secrets that bind them.

CHAPTER THIRTY-ONE

Lala

5 September 1984

The incident with the orange starts with thanks.

'Thanks,' Lala tells Grayson through a pulsing purple lip, after she has left Tone in the tunnel, after she has walked the beach and burrowed into bushes at the sound of a voice like Adan's, after she has returned to Grayson's door in the same strange dress she left it in and has told him she will stay with him until she works out what will happen next. Grayson beams his approval, he tells her he was afraid she would not have come back, he tells her to come in, sit down.

'Thanks,' she tells him, when he makes her a cup of warm peppermint tea and holds an ice pack to her face when she is finished.

'Thanks,' she says when he repeats his promise that she can stay in his grand house as long as she needs to. She needs to get away from that man, Grayson tells her, his kind do not get any better. And Lala repeats her thanks.

Grayson shows her a beautiful blue-grey room in his basement where a white wooden single bed with a soft comforter printed with waves beckons. She sits on this bed, runs her hands over the comforter, touches the pristine white pillowcases on top of it. When she turns to say thanks, again, Grayson is gone.

Lala is sitting in that room, looking out through a shuttered window onto a sheltered patio and the crashing waves below it. She is marvelling at the fact that the very sea that splashes the concrete foundations of his grand guard walls, that licks and lashes the delicate wrought-iron railings with the points like spears, this very sea is the one that, from the window in her husband's house, once threatened to swallow her. This water that stays behind Grayson's porch and patio and writhes against its own restraint, that applauds each encroachment on the stone tiles before dragging itself back and into the beyond, this is the very same water from which she runs daily.

She goes up to the window and lifts the sash and stares at the sea. And into that rectangular patch of vision Grayson steps with a bag of oranges. Like maybe he thought it best to keep watch outside her bedroom, just in case someone had seen her come here, just in case something in her tempted her to go back.

He does not eat his oranges the way normal people do. He does not peel the dimpled skin until it is all gone and break the exposed flesh into segments he can put neatly into his mouth and swallow. Instead, he eats the entire orange at once when the skin has been roughly removed with his bare hands so that patches of bitter white rind still cling to the sweet citrus below it. Grayson sucks and swallows his oranges whole, pausing only to spit an offending piece of white rind or a hard grey seed into his palm. He does not treat oranges like a luxury costing too many dollars per bag, like something to be savoured; he eats them like they are made to be devoured, without thought to where the next one is coming from.

When he sees her, he stares, like he is surprised she is there, peering through the window, like his worst fears have been confirmed and she is in fact planning an escape. And this, perhaps, more than anything, is why Lala reaches out a thick black hand and takes an orange from him, an orange newly peeled and bitten and placed into his palm. This is why she sinks her teeth into pulp still smarting from his fingers, and swallows juice his lips have already touched. He stands and watches her eat it and reaches up a bristled hand to brush away a swollen piece of citrus that sits beside her nose, and when his hand lingers on her face, she notices that his fingers have already cooled with the exit of the sun, that his skin is already sand-dusted by the billowing air, and she holds them there because her own face feels hot in comparison.

'Feels like a fever,' he tells her. He's retired, but he knows a fever when he feels one. He puts down his orange and leaves to fetch a pan of cold water and a soft cloth and a bottle of something with a pharmacist's label on it, a prescription written for someone else. Grayson bathes not just her breast, but her entire body, wiping her softly so that he does not offend the throbbing tooth, the oozing wounds, the scarring lip. When he is done, he bandages her breast and strokes her brow and helps her into a smaller woman's blousy nightgown and tucks her into bed.

'Thanks . . .'

Lala is soothed into sleep so strong she is unable to hear him say 'You're welcome.'

Lala used to tell her friends at school that her mother had named her for a song, one she insisted her father sang to her mother regularly when they were courting. The way Esme told it, Lala's father was not just the random sailor Esme insisted he was; theirs was the type of love that lived in poetry. Lala used to tell her school friends that her father owned many ships and someday he would send for her.

By the time Lala was old enough to question this story, to test the weight of it, her mother was dead and Wilma would not help her. She had never met her father, said Wilma, he was probably one of the street rabs her mother had taken up with. Lala grew to understand that she must not ask Wilma about her father. This father therefore haunted her by his absence for the rest of her life.

In Lala's imagination, it was her father who had named her. She surmised this because the only other thing that incensed Wilma more than her granddaughter asking her who her father was was her asking her how she had come to get her name. Lala told Wilma how she remembered her mother singing this name to her when she was little, holding her close and singing the two notes, over and over, so that Lala understood that the way to sing her name was important, it was something she should not forget.

Wilma withered under the weight of this name. Lala did not know then, but her name was Wilma's reminder of the insolent humming of her daughter when she told her that she was expecting and Wilma tried her best to convince her to drink as much okra and parsley and red radish as she could stand in an effort to get rid of the baby. Esme refused. She had not just refused, she had hummed as she did so, those same two notes under her breath all day while Wilma tried to talk her out of motherhood.

This is why Wilma refuses to call Lala by this name, why the child and then the woman eventually forgot how it was meant to be sung. Instead, Wilma calls her granddaughter Stella, her middle name, or she does not address her by name at all.

How could Wilma not expect this child to look for her mother's humming, to be drawn like a moth to a flame to anyone who wished not only to retrieve this name, but to dust it off, shake it out, try it on with her? From the moment they met, Adan had called her no other name but Lala, had sung her name in every tone he could think of to see if she would recognise it, would remember exactly the notes her mother intended her to.

It was one of the reasons she had loved him.

CHAPTER THIRTY-TWO

Tone
5 September 1984

The first hint of federation is the boat – Adan doesn't think it is big enough. The vessel that has brought the cargo sits waiting five miles off the shoreline for the little fishing boat Adan has hired to go out to meet it. The plan is that this little fishing boat will then bring three hundred pounds of marijuana Adan has not yet paid for on to the beach near the mouth of a cave, and Tone and Adan will lift and drag the huge bales of tightly pressed weed into the tunnels. There they will separate them into their constituent parts – heavy square bricks the size of concrete blocks – and sequester them in one of the dusty dead-end chambers that is difficult to get to. They will wrap these bricks tightly in several layers of plastic and put them high up on a ledge that Tone has already pointed out to Adan, and then Tone will deliver the blocks to Adan's customers in ones and twos and threes and bring the money back to Adan for onsend to the source of the supply.

But things do not go according to plan.

When the fisherman turns up, the boat he is using is too small, Adan thinks, to carry all the cargo, and two trips are likely to arouse suspicion. So says Adan. He has had to pay the coastguard captain to look the other way, but the captain can only do so for so long. One trip is all they have.

The fisherman is an elderly man whose callused bare feet traverse the sand without hurt or hurry as he readies the little vessel to launch. He is a big man himself, with weather-beaten skin the colour of charcoal, and he doesn't seem to be unduly affected by Adan's bluster about how he has tricked him by bringing a boat too small to carry the cargo, how he is jukking out his eye by demanding more money if it will be two trips instead of one. The fisherman does not seem to see the need for much conversation at all. Adan quarrels and the fisherman merely readies his boat.

Tone stands waiting at the mouth of the cave, smoking a cigarette and thinking. Although it is a calm, clear night, one of the ones where stars twinkle like diamonds in a velvety sky and the milky quarter-moon looks like one painted in a story book, there is an undercurrent of chaos. Ma Tone would tell him that the lead in the bottom of his belly means that he should abandon the plans and walk away, he thinks, but Ma Tone is not here and Tone therefore tries to deny that he should. Ma Tone would not approve, he knows, of him applying her wisdom to a matter such as this.

The second sign of federation happens a few hours later when the fisherman comes back with a boat laden with tightly wrapped plastic bales and Tone is shoulder to shoulder with Adan, heaving these bales off the fishing boat and struggling under the weight of bales much heavier than he had imagined they would be.

281

'How come these so heavy?' he begins as they watch the fisherman leave for the second trip, his pocket bulging with money Adan has gathered from the series of investors whose identity he hasn't thought to share. Tone is brushing the grit from his calves, removing a new pair of Bally sneakers one of his clients bought him, shaking them free of sand, rubbing a smudge of wet leaf from a lace and replacing them. He wipes the sweat from his forehead with a washcloth, runs his elegant fingers over those fine facial bones and waits for them both to recover their breath sufficiently to drag the first set of bales back to the cave.

Adan is sitting on a nearby rock and smiling, his lips stretched so high and wide that his one gold cap catches the moon and flashes Tone a reminder of the time they ventured together to Chinky's little shop to have it fashioned from the melted necklace of one or other of Adan's unfortunate victims. When the grill had been fitted Adan had smiled at Tone, just like he is smiling now, and Chinky had clapped Tone on the back as if to beckon his agreement when he said *as man, gold grill suit Adan good good in truth*. Those were the days before Adan had met and married Lala, Tone remembers, those were the days before Tone had started spending nights with tourist women.

'It cold, eh?' observes Adan, and Tone realises that he is shivering. He pulls a slim black hoodie closer about his face and neck, holds on to his shark tooth and keeps his hand there.

'It bitching,' he agrees, and Adan flashes his gold cap again.

'You want a pull?'

Tone shakes his head – no.

'Suit yourself.'

Adan reaches into the pocket of his tight black joggers and pulls out a small spliff and a lighter, which is soon crowned by an erratic orange flame. He cups his big hands around the lighter and brings it up to his lips, where the roach sits waiting.

Tone does not warn him that a spliff can draw attention to them if there are police patrolling the beach looking for errant lovers or lawless men. He does not remind Adan that they could be discovered by adventurous tourists who might be drawn by the sickly-sweet smell of the weed and think that Adan and Tone are out there selling it. Tone looks around instead, to see if there is anyone about who could cause them worry. There isn't, but his chest is still heavy somehow, he still shivers from time to time when he is more than accustomed to the chilly night-time breeze.

When the fisherman returns with the second half of the shipment, Adan flicks open a switchblade, slits one of the bales, withdraws the tip of the knife and tastes it, and Tone knows then that Adan has duped him. The cargo isn't marijuana. The fisherman takes his money and goes. Four huge bales sit ominously on the sand like the shaped and sanded brothers of the boulders that climb the perimeter of the beach.

'As man, you ain't tell me nuttin' 'bout this,' Tone begins. 'You say you was bringing in green, big man.'

Adan shrugs, flicks the knife shut and brushes his arms off distractedly, as if Tone is a bug alighting on his skin on

283

a humid afternoon. Something he can swipe away if he cares to, but only if he cares to.

'You know how much money this is in these bags?' Adan starts to drag one towards the tunnel.' Hurry up, ain't got time for the coastguard tonight.'

Tone hesitates, because he knows that he has plans to give the money from this job to Lala. But he didn't agree to no coke, so he takes a last, deliberate drag from his cigarette and drops it on the sand, crushing the orange embers with the heel of his brand-new sneakers.

'As man,' he starts slowly, 'I don't deal with no coke, Adan. I don't smoke it, I don't touch it. I don't sell it. I ain't no coke man.'

For a minute the crickets sing loudly and the waves splat against the shore and the two men stare at each other.

'I know,' Adan says slowly, 'I know you ain't no coke man, Tone.'

Tone doesn't move.

'So why you ain't tell me about the coke, then?'

'We ain't got time for this now,' Adan says dismissively. 'We could settle this later, I could pay you some more for the trouble.'

Tone rocks back and forth on his heels, shakes his head, squeezes his eyes tightly shut.

'It ain't about the money, Adan, as man,' he protests.

And in truth, it isn't. It is about the fact that since they were boys in the half-ruin of Ma Tone's house, Adan has been the bigger one and therefore, the boss merely by pre-ordination of his size. It is about the fact that fate has concluded that Adan's primacy in everything should also result in his right to love Lala, who still inhabits Tone's dreams at night. It is about the fact that Adan knows that his superordinance is the natural order of things, so that it does not even occur to him that there is something wrong with asking for Tone's help in hiding a few hundred pounds of ganja when he knows full well that ganja isn't what they will be hiding. And all the things that it is about converge in one statement of principle that Tone cannot deviate from.

'I ain't helping hide no coke,' he says. 'I tell you I ain't no coke man.'

Adan puffs up with sudden rage, flails his arms, sucks his teeth.

'Don't talk no rasshole foolishness, Tone!' he begins. 'You say you was gonna help me and now you backing down? What happen to you, bwoy?'

For Tone, his relegation to a mere 'bwoy' is the proof of the very insult that has made him refuse to help hide the cocaine in the first place, and the small openings in his mind, the doors propped apart by the happy times of a shared childhood, by the common threads of the adult struggle to survive, slam firmly and finally shut. He starts to walk away, thinking about Lala, about how, perhaps, he will try to leave with her, start over somewhere where he does not have to prowl the beaches looking for women who look for dick, where he does not have to close his mind to the woman beneath him and focus on the one in his head in order to give wealthy tourist women the good time they hire him for, where he does not hustle tourists for jet skis in the quasi-American accent his kind uses to ensure that they are understood, where he does not have to deal weed for Adan, or sell stolen goods, where he is not relegated to the life of a soldier for a thief. Tone is thinking he will buy two tickets and not one, he will queue in the long line at the embassy and suffer the sun and the sweat and the risk of the shame of a refusal to get a US visa, and then, when he does, he and Lala will leave for the United States of America and they will stay there.

'Bwoy? Bwoy? I is way more man than you, Adan,' Tone affirms, 'from long time now.'

There is something in his voice when he says it that unlocks a drawer in Adan's mind. It is the mental drawer in which, unbeknownst to himself, he has filed away the stricken expressions on Tone's face any time Adan has returned home to find him there a moment or more too early, it is the drawer in which he has filed his mental notes about how Tone took to knocking on the Pepsi door once Lala became pregnant, how he never seemed to want to stick around once Adan arrived at home, although he seemed to have been so comfortable a moment or two before in Lala's presence alone. The drawer unlocks and Adan fumbles around inside of it, disbelieving what has only now been made clear to him.

'What the rasshole you mean by that, Tone, eh? What you really mean by that?'

But there is no need to ask the question.

'Pussy like you, Adan,' Tone continues, because it is time, because he has been holding his tongue for almost two years. 'Play you bad, you feel I going let you bad me up like Lala, pussy? Cause only a pussy does beat he wife so. You want to see who is bwoy?'

And there, before their very eyes, Tone grows tall, turns terrible.

'As man,' he threatens, 'call me "bwoy" again, Adan, and see what I do wid you.'

There is silence. The sea stops its roar, the crickets do not whistle, the branches of the coconut palms cease their sway and tremble. Adan is stunned. He is staring at his friend, grown into a giant before him, he is listening to a confession released in a roar. He understands that Tone is not sorry, Tone is scornful. And his scorn is the worst insult of all.

So Adan laughs. A long laugh that resonates with the nervous trees and reassures them until they stop trembling. A wide, down-from-the-belly laugh that would make someone think the worst was now over, if anyone else was there. This laugh would make such a person anticipate the back-clapping, knee-slapping good humour of reconciliation, of the realisation that *we is we* at the end of the day, that bad man don't fight over gal, that this is just a little thing, a thing to be surmounted.

'So that is what happening, eh?' says Adan. 'That is what happening.'

He shrugs in the manner of a man resigned and Tone feels himself exhale. The friendship is over, Tone realises; most important now is getting Lala away. Adan will not suffer this knowledge silently.

Tone is walking away when he hears the thud of the heavy bag Adan was holding hit the sand, feels the rush of wind that tells him that Adan is in pursuit, that this will not end peaceably. And just like that he perceives the Thing

He Cannot Name, realises that it has been with him even tonight, hiding in the murk of his shadow. Tone grabs a rock he did not know was sitting on the beach, he turns, he swings, catches Adan below the chin and snaps his head backwards and is spattered by the blood of his best friend.

Adan growls like he is more beast than man, like the bringing of blood means that he will now have to fight to the death. It is a terrible sound, but it is mixed with another, equally feral, that Tone realises is coming from his own throat. This Thing He Cannot Name is not a thinking thing, it takes him over until he is a flurry of arms holding the rock and Adan is a big, solid boulder from the beach that he cannot leave without breaking. They are on the ground and Adan is butting him with the blunt handle of a gun that Tone did not realise he had and his mind is on the knife that Adan used to test the coke. But Adan does not draw the knife. A knife is something you use on a worthy enemy, one who has wronged you enough to deserve a savaging. The handle of a gun is something you use because it happens to be in your hand when you have to bring a boy to heel – it is the equivalent of a bad man's bitch-slap – and the choice is not lost on Tone. He does not feel any pain because of this choice, this gun, but the blood slicking his face and staining his shirt is an inconvenience, it makes it hard for him to see and he can tell that he is spilling the source of the vital energy that he needs to surmount this challenge and escape alive. He can tell that he needs shelter, a moment or two away from the onslaught of Adan's big gun, to catch himself, to recover enough to retaliate, or to run.

He stumbles towards the cave that marks the entrance to the Baxter's tunnels. These are the tunnels that he knows like he knows his mother's house; they will provide him a place to catch his breath, to lick his wounds. He might not be as large or as strong as Adan, but if he must run then his size and build will benefit him, decides Tone, and Adan cannot match him in there.

Tone is making for the tunnels and Adan is in pursuit behind him when a thin white woman appears on the beach and almost bumps into them. He cannot wait, he runs into the tunnel, just as Adan's gun, tired of butting, begins to bark.

CHAPTER THIRTY-THREE

Mrs Whalen
5 September 1984

The path to the beach is nearly obscured by cherry palms framing a tiny shaving of navy blue. This is the path to the beach seen in travel magazines, dimly lit by a coconut-milk quarter-moon and fringed on each side by the spiky fronds of lush tropical foliage. It is the path the magazines suggest you take barefooted, led by a lover whose feet are similarly unshod and who knows that, just past those fronds, is a starlit beachscape waiting for you to make memories. This is not the type of path that makes anyone think of security, so when she decides to take this path, to clear her thoughts on her last night before leaving Paradise for good, Mira Whalen does not wonder whether a big black man with a scar will jump out of the shadows on her left just as she reaches the end of this path. She does not wonder whether he will raise a gun towards her. And when he does, she wonders why she did not anticipate that he would.

She looks to her right and wonders why she did not con-template for a second that an ectomorphic Rasta would be running for his life towards the yawning throat of a cluster of boulders to her right, a black hoodie falling away from his head and neck as he flies. The big black man is

290

sprinting after this Rasta who is running towards the rocks, pursuing his escape from the bad man, who is holding a gun. And when the cloud parts to reveal the full face of the moon, the path is lit from above and she sees the hand holding that gun, she knows it, and she starts to scream because, while the face might have escaped her, while she might not have been able to recall the hulking build or the broadness of the back or the menace in the manner or that curly recessed scar, she would be able to tell this hand anywhere.

And after all the fruitless worrying, the theorising, the time spent staying away from harmless civilians and being frustrated with the police, after all that – here he is.

Before her very eyes. The murderer.

And the man stops his running and looks at her and lifts his gun, and he is no longer interested in the smaller man running into the boulders, not just now. She tells her feet to run but her feet will not listen. And her eyes, mesmerised by the hands that have haunted her, watch those hands lift the gun until it is level with the robber's face, and squeeze the trigger.

CHAPTER THIRTY-FOUR

Mrs Whalen
5 September 1984

There is more than one shot, and Mira Whalen is unsure of which one has hit her, but she is sure that she has been hit when she feels a sudden struggle to take a breath she took for granted only a moment before. She only starts to run after the gun is silent, her feet only obey her after the big black man runs on, towards the Rasta and the boulders, but once she starts to run she runs as if her life depends on it, because she understands, at once, that it does. Mira Whalen makes for the big houses behind her, she does not try to reach her own gate, she makes for the gate beside hers, because she believes that Grayson will be there and she knows that Grayson is a doctor.

But Mira Whalen can only make the first few strides in the opposite direction, back up the path towards the big houses. On the third stride she sinks, eyes wide open in surprise, and her face lands with a thud in a soft mound of sand that fills her mouth and her eyes and her hair. She wants to look back, to see if the robber will come back to finish her. She wants to shout for Grayson, whose sand-dusted patio and sisal-shaded glass door are a few strides ahead. But Mira Whalen cannot speak. She cannot scream. She can hardly breathe.

She focuses on trying to lift and turn her head, to fight a calm that starts to descend upon her, but her head will not move and the calm is coming anyway. She thinks of swimming, and drags her knees up on each side of her body, trying to leapfrog her way forward, which works a charm, but it is so calm, so quiet, that she wonders why she is making the effort, whether on the other side of that calm is where she will find Peter.

Mira Whalen finds it is true what they say about life flashing before you – a parade of random moments marches behind her eyes, snatches of a life she never knew she had been recording. She confirms also that the order defies explanation: the marbled-chocolate tree bark she had fixed her eyes on the last time she'd lied to Martha; the brilliant blue sky behind the hug she got from Sam that day in Wimbledon when she'd fished his box car out of a grate; the custard-coloured spit-up on her favourite pants that first day that Peter had brought Sam to their flat and given him to her to hold and he'd spat back out every spoonful of mashed banana she'd tried to feed him.

Her very own life story . . . which she now knows has ended on the wrong side of a badman's gun.

In the manner of fairy tales, she is granted a last wish, and so she returns in her mind to the night Peter was murdered in an effort to do something, anything, differently. Something that will lead to him still being alive . . .

Suddenly she is there again, back in their bedroom, and

The robber is once again pointing a gun at her, once again squeezing the trigger.

Click.

She does not fall.

Click.

More nothing.

Her refocused senses search for proof she is indeed still alive. She is.

She is in her bedroom – hers and Peter's. It is again the night of his murder. She feels the sweat curling down the back of her neck, the panic constricting her throat, the tears soaking her cheeks, as if for the first time. She does not want to raise her hand to wipe her face dry for fear that the robber takes her movement as the precursor to some form of resistance he will not tolerate. She looks at his face.

There is the robber. Swearing. There is Peter. Pleading. There is another moment's breathless silence punctuated by the crash and hiss of water.

There is the gun.

Click.

Peter is screaming as the robber breaks his nose with the butt of the gun. He is shielding his eyes when the robber yells not to look at him. This is her voice. Sobbing. 'I love you, Peter.' There is Peter, curled up on the edge of the bed like a child, begging for her life. For *hers*.

She is looking at this stocking-covered face that made her husband cry. This is the stocking-covered face she tried so hard to remember. She stares at it now, this face, and she knows that beneath the stocking this face is beautiful, beautiful and deadly. She wants to see this face, wants to look into the eyes of the man who dares to terrorise the man she loves. She wants to claw at that stocking, that face, until she draws blood with her bare hands.

There is the buzzer sounding from the street just as it did that night Peter was shot. Peter had bought this house on the basis that the two of them would hear nothing but the water, but the sound of the buzzer is loud and she is not sure whether it is because the sound is really loud or whether it is because she knows this sound is the only hope of her getting out of their room alive.

There is the gun.

Click.

There is her husband. There is the robber. There is she. Running to grab the gun.

This is the gun. Its barrel is smooth in her fingers. Smooth and cold and heavy, the way she might have thought it would feel if she'd ever thought about it before. But she hadn't, and the hand behind it is stronger than hers, and in retrospect it was a stupid thing to do, to grab this gun, but she has grabbed it and she cannot stop staring at the hand that holds it, a big hand, with large velvet fingers that swallow the light and remain unmoved. There are ridges and furrows on the back of this hand and she believes she can see the blood beating through its veins.

'Monster!' she is screaming. 'Fucking brutish monster!' and before she knows it she has clawed off that stocking, she is seeing that face, that winding scar, those deeply recessed eyes and broad, flat nose, that square, strong skin. When he strikes her cheek with the hand that holds the gun, she knows that she will lose the memory of that face she is trying to etch so firmly in her mind. She feels her own face jerk and drop, her chin lands below her collarbones. The gun does not click now, it pops, it roars. And when she lifts her chin, Peter is already dead.

There is her husband's body, his head resting on an outstretched arm as if he is merely asleep. And the gun goes back to clicking.

Click.

Movie again: the time she had broken her ankle and Peter had lifted her to the toilet every time she had to go and had seated himself on the edge of the tub and laughed at her mortification that he planned to stay there until she was done, the nurse's sallow, stony-faced stare while she cried, the time they had been picking tomatoes in the garden and Sam had toddled into view sputtering a mouthful of mud and her stomach had ached through their laughter because the expression on Sam's face was funny but it was also a reminder that she was proving incapable of carrying a baby of their own.

She prays silently because the robber is pointing the gun at her and she knows she will be killed next. Psalm 23. Which she bungles because she cannot remember it. Or any psalm. She should've gone to church more. The gun cracks.

She screams when she is shot, just to let the man know that she is protesting her murder, that she will not go quietly. Just to let the person ringing the buzzer know that they should not wait to be answered, that they should come quickly.

Moments are measured in heartbeats, which progressively lengthen.

In this version of the night her husband died, Mira Whalen dies with him.

In the murder in Mira's mind, the kids do not come running when she starts screaming that Peter is dead. There is no white-knuckled Beth calling the police, no wild-eyed relief when Rosa reports for work and makes circles with the rotary phone to dial Mr Watson. No, in the murder Mira Whalen imagines, she feels the will to live leave her body when she realises that Peter is dead. It makes her think of the last of the dishwater draining down the sink-hole. It is not an unpleasant feeling. It is a feeling she is feeling again now.

CHAPTER THIRTY-FIVE

Tone
5 September 1984

Tone is running. He is running through a maze and his eyes are almost welded shut, stuck together with the blood that weeps from his head. He knows this maze, he knows it like he knows his own mother's house, so it does not really matter that he cannot see properly. *Here* is where his feet must slow because there is a sharp turn to the left, where the tunnel thins and it is harder to move in the dank and the dark, *here* is where he must get ready for an incline, where the floor of the tunnel will be slippery with mud because earlier today there was a heavy shower and there is a leak in the roof of the tunnels just above this spot where the water seeps through and makes the floor soggy. *Here* is where Tone has an idea. He can still hear Adan behind him, Tone can, he can hear him breathing a sort of breathless pant in the dark that is more about anger than oxygen. He can hear stones bustle and break when Adan's broadness hits parts of the tunnel that Tone's small frame has never had cause to touch. He can hear Adan call out to him, tell him to stop, this is foolishness, stop and let we talk. *As man.*

Here is where Tone has the idea that will save his life. At the end of another fifty yards, Tone does not turn right and through the tunnel that will lead to the exit near where he and Lala sheltered almost two years before. Instead, he turns left, he goes deeper into the labyrinth, towards places where the moon does not penetrate and the black you see when your eyes are closed is the same as the black you see when they are open and you cannot run unless you know exactly where you are running, exactly what part of the tunnel is coming next. Tone slows to a walk, squeezes his eyelids shut, trusts his head, his hands to guide him. *Here* is where the tunnel opens into an antechamber with a rash of slippery stalagmites underfoot, like the bald heads of rising dead, frozen in the rising. *Here* is where the chamber narrows, where someone who doesn't know this cave might see a glimmer of light, might think that they are about to go into a tunnel again, one that will lead, ultimately, to sunshine.

'You right,' says Tone, at the right time, 'you right, Adan, this is foolishness, let we talk, man. *As man.*'

His voice echoes and amplifies. *Here* is where he crouches as he speaks. *Here* is the tall stalagmite he nicknamed 'Pastor' because it reminded him of the head of his mother's church congregation, the way it loomed above the other rock formations, leaning into them as if imparting a wisdom it could not afford for them to miss. Tone ducks behind Pastor and is silent, becomes part of the congregation, listens for the truth that will give him life.

'I tell you so,' says Adan, 'we ain't friends from since we was little? Can't let a little something come between we so.'

Adan draws closer, listening for Tone's voice to tell him where to turn in the deep dark.

'OK, let we talk.'

When Adan enters the antechamber, when he follows the echo, he sees a lightening of the dark ahead. It is a lightening that suggests that somewhere ahead there is an exit, that with a few steps he will be standing with Tone in a larger room from which they could leave the tunnel as friends.

But Adan does not want to be friends.

'I tell you this ain't make no sense,' he assures, drawing the knife and flicking open its blade. 'I tell you—'

When Adan steps through the opening from which gleams the promise of light, his foot is perplexed at its failure to find solid ground beneath it on the other side. Tone understands this, because he hears, from behind Pastor's skirt, the sharp inhalation that marks Adan's surprise. He hears also the quick scuffle as Adan's hands seek the security of the stones beside and beneath him. Many, many years ago, when Tone used to retreat to these tunnels and think about the man who had held him down and raped him, he had come across this very chamber, had almost stepped through this very opening, next to which Pastor perpetually spoke a silent warning. Your hands cannot find the edge of Pastor's skirt, the stone pleat of which can save you, if you are brandishing a knife. Or a gun. Like the story of any good gospel, you must approach this opening empty-handed. Your eyes cannot see that this is not the light of a promised exit on the other side. *There* is where, three hundred years ago, ten soldiers went tumbling as they dug out these tunnels, where a terrified lieutenant screamed for the others to stop while Pastor stood and watched him. This opening is the mouth of a yawn, where the floor of the cave falls away a hundred feet into its throat. Adan is swallowed by this throat, against the stone side of which he bounces and breaks on his way down.

When it is quiet, Tone releases Pastor, stumbles to his feet and makes his way back out again before collapsing on his face in the sand, as if forced into prostration by an undeserved grace.

CHAPTER THIRTY-SIX .

Lala
5 September 1984

Lala cannot sleep in the sterile silence of Grayson's grand house, so her eyes are already open when she hears the scream. Grayson had gone back to his room when she had first dozed off, but she had awoken only a few hours after – the house was too still and the air conditioning much too cold for her to settle down in, the abundance of blankets on the bed insufficient to keep her warm. She is lying in the dark, staring at the stark white roof and the moulding that borders it, when she again hears the scream that has haunted her worst nightmares since Baby was born.

She listens. There are noises, but the scream doesn't come again. It is probably just a skinny-dipper shocked by the crippling cold of the water, she reasons, but she cannot settle, her stomach is queasy with unease.

She spends what seems like a long time looking for more blankets in the unfamiliar closets of the room. She spends longer looking for the remote to turn off the AC so sleep can be possible, and eventually she accepts that she won't be able to go back to sleep. She wanders into the kitchen for a wine glass of water, which she fills from a faucet in the dark. The kitchen gleams in the glare of the moon

302

from the skylight – the surface of the stove and the front of the fridge look like silver, the countertops like slabs of semi-precious stone. For a moment, Lala thinks she should take something to remind her she was here, because she is sure that somehow she will wake up and this will be a dream – she will be back in Adan's house by the beach, trying her best to remember his name. Instead she wanders into the dining room with her water, and then into the lounge, where she takes a seat, nervously, not wanting to wake Grayson if nothing is wrong, having the awful feeling that something is very terribly wrong indeed. She dozes fitfully because, despite her discomfort, she is tired. She is very, very tired.

When she starts awake, it is because she hears the scream again, from just outside the house, screaming so familiar that it pulls her from her dreams. She first heard this scream the night she birthed Baby and she understands what it must mean. She is surprisingly calm, is Lala. It is as if she has been waiting for this moment her entire life. She pulls on a pair of sneakers Grayson said belonged to his daughter, pats her passport in the back of her underwear. Lala is ready to run.

Grayson bursts out of his room as she is trying to solve the mystery of the locked door to the patio. He is wearing a pair of white briefs and an unbelted white robe and his ginger chest hair is climbing out of the rectangle the open robe makes.

'Stay indoors!' barks Grayson. 'Call the police!'

He is grumbling as he checks his gun. When he opens the door and runs on to the patio, the open robe flaps behind him like the cape of some great white superhero. Lala starts to run behind him, but Grayson locks the door from outside by punching some numbers into a box at the side of the door. This is when Lala feels the first swell of panic. She shouts at him but he is running towards the screaming, which has started afresh, and he does not seem to hear her. She bangs on the door but it remains closed.

From the lounge Lala sees the woman on the steps of the patio, writhing. The furrowed sand behind her shows that she has crawled there. It is the woman who held her, who told her everything would be OK, who lives in the house with the guard wall she recognised. It was the guard wall of the house at which she had found Adan that morning Baby was born. This woman, Lala recognises, is the one who had screamed that night, whose scream had haunted her. The woman is bleeding and the blood is pooling beneath the beautiful wrought-iron railings. Lala weighs the possibilities for just a second before she understands what is happening, who has done this. She does not feel safe, even though she is inside. She finds a wooden block on the countertop in the kitchen, in which six knives sit sleeping. She unsheathes one and uses the block to break the glass of the door to the patio.

The woman is gurgling. It is an involuntary gurgling, like she is not aware she is doing it. Blood leaks from the side of her chest and has soaked her pyjamas just there. Grayson is stooped next to her, trying to stem the bleeding with his balled-up white robe. She can stop, thinks Lala, she can make sure this woman is all right, not on the doorstep of death, not bleeding her last within sight of Baxter's Beach. Or she can run, because running is the only way she will herself escape.

'Go inside, Lala!' barks Grayson, pressing the robe harder into Mira's side. 'Call the police.'

Lala is frozen to the spot, watching the bleeding woman with her own right hand welded to the handle of a sharp chef's knife.

'Inside, Lala!' Grayson insists. 'Press the red button on the keypad by the door, press it three times, and then go inside and call the police and the ambulance.'

'I . . .' stammers Lala, 'I . . .'

Grayson leaves Mira's side, starts to push Lala back to the glass doors, runs back to Mira, strips back her robe and leans in against her bleeding chest. Lala stands by the doors and cannot move.

'Call them, Lala!' orders Grayson. 'Call them now!'

Lala turns towards the house, runs inside, picks up one of the cordless receivers, dials zero and tells the operator that she needs the police and an ambulance. Right now, at the back of one of the big houses on Baxter's Beach, the one with the white wrought-iron railings. And then she stands there, helpless, while Grayson beseeches Mira Whalen to stay with him, while he presses and pumps against her chest.

Lala wonders whether she should run. There is nothing she can do for Mira Whalen now, she thinks, Grayson is the best person to be with her, and if she stays she risks running into Adan, who she knows is the reason that Mira is now fighting for her life. There is no telling what Adan will do if he finds her here. In the distance, she hears the first howl of a siren and the decision is made for her.

She runs past Mira Whalen on the patio steps, past Grayson trying to save her, and she keeps running. Past the little gutter where, years ago, she'd met Tone. She rounds the corner of Baxter's Beach and sees the slate-grey tarmac of the street at the other end of which is Wilma's immaculate little stone house, its cold and calculated neatness. She stays low, crouches by dunks trees, lays flat on the ground at first sight of the misty light of oncoming vehicles. She decides she must get to the airport. It is the only solution, it dawns on her suddenly. She has the clump of money she has recently taken to wearing in her bra, she is dressed in one of Grayson's shirts, pants he no longer wears, a pair of stretchy leggings and sneakers belonging to a woman she doesn't know and a headscarf that hides her missing clumps of hair. She does not have much money, she does not have a memento of her baby, a little bag of Baby's clothes, perhaps, to dress a future sibling in, a little bangle to save in a box and give to a grandchild a generation ahead, she does not have a blanket in which the scent of her baby still blossoms, a scent she can get lost in when she needs to have her near, to talk to, to apologise. But she has herself, she has her hands, she has the money to buy a ticket.

She has enough.

EPILOGUE

6 September 1984

Tone wakes up the following morning in Baxter's General. As soon as he wakes, he realises that he is handcuffed to his bed, that two armed policemen are seated near him on the ward. Sergeant Beckles comes to tell him that he is under arrest for the kidnapping and murder of Baby Primus. The doctors expect to discharge him this morning, says the sergeant, and they will take him to the police station after that and book him in.

Tone's head is hurting him, his mouth feels full of cotton he cannot expel by opening it, by swirling his tongue around to touch his teeth. His back is sore and his belly is bandaged. Tone says that he is not a murderer. The one man he might have killed is a Mexican man whom he met when he was fifteen years old and never saw again. He could have killed that man, says Tone, he dreamt about killing him, about breaking his neck or strangling him until he begged for mercy, but not another soul, he swears it.

It does not matter. Sergeant Beckles considers the case closed – he recites Tone's rap sheet of violent assaults occasioning actual bodily harm, his previous stints in prison. He will take Tone's statement as soon as he can get a doctor's confirmation that he is lucid, says Sergeant Beckles,

307

and don't waste his time with anything but the truth. He already knows about Lala, says Sergeant Beckles, he already knows about the two of them. Just tell the truth. Many a man has killed for a woman, Sergeant Beckles tells him, he wouldn't be the first and he won't be the last. And Sergeant Beckles thinks of Sheba, the one woman he thinks he might kill for.

At the mention of 'woman', Tone thinks of Lala, wonders where she is, if she has heard of his arrest. He smiles ruefully at the thought that he is back to dreaming of her again, dreaming of her humming while he is not free, but he is comforted by the knowledge that Adan cannot hurt her, he cannot hurt her ever again.

Within hours he is hustled from the hospital and into a waiting police car. It is while he is inside this car, with policemen to his right and his left, before and behind him, and his head is throbbing wildly at the sound of screeching sirens, that he catches sight of a BWIA jet just lifting into the sky.

Tone raises his hands to touch the image of that plane in the window of the police car. He touches his fingers to his lips. He sits back in the seat of the patrol car.

He smiles.

ACKNOWLEDGEMENTS

There comes a point in the production of anything when you realise how many shoulders you have been afforded to stand on, how many collective experiences have been brought to bear on the development and enrichment of your own. I could not have written *How the One-Armed Sister Sweeps Her House* or finally witnessed its publication without:

Ivy, Elise, Violet and Pearl, and all the ancestors who remain with me and guide me (still).

My parents and my children, for whom the publication of Mommy's book still ranks a distant second to what she will be cooking for dinner, so that my return to the kitchen is the real delight.

Wendy, Belinda, Chris, Kei, Professor Jane Rogers, John Milne, George Jackman, Joyce Stewart, Samuel Soyer, Christopher Chung-Wee, Cecile Gittens and every other English Literature or Creative Writing teacher who has taken the time to help me learn about this particular type of alchemy.

My (always willing) readers – Lornie, Heather, Lisa, and Andrew Armstrong – and supporters, especially Wale, Tracie, Robert, Jeremy, Ayesha, Pet and Hazel.

The Vermont Studio Centre (and, in particular, my 2015 cohort), the Writers' Colony at Dairy Hollow, and my very special group of Bajan bards: the Writers' Ink posse, especially Esther, Linda and Sharma, who are always ready with community and critique.

Clare, who first believed, and whose strength and acumen keep me in awe, and all the team at Aitken Alexander.

Imogen, Amy, Yeti, Antonia and the wonderful team at Tinder Press, who've been so patient and welcoming. Iris, Julia, Judy, Miya and the rest of the teams at Harper-Collins Canada and Little, Brown USA, who ensured I felt at home and at ease. And those who started the journey with me and with Lala, and who still cheer from new paths and places, including Geffen and Leah, who shared my passion for Lala's story, a love for anything vintage, and the possession of a pop-down cellphone (miss you!).

Housecat, for more than I can ever express in words.

Thanks, all.